Talk with Your Child

Also by Harvey S. Wiener

ANY CHILD CAN WRITE
TOTAL SWIMMING

372.6   Wiener, Harvey
WIENER   Talk with your
Child

DATE DUE

HARVEY S. WIENER

Talk with Your Child

VIKING

VIKING
Published by the Penguin Group
Viking Penguin Inc., 40 West 23rd Street,
New York, New York 10010, U.S.A.
Penguin Books Ltd, 27 Wrights Lane,
London W8 5TZ, England
Penguin Books Australia Ltd, Ringwood,
Victoria, Australia
Penguin Books Canada Ltd, 2801 John Street,
Markham, Ontario, Canada L3R 1B4
Penguin Books (N.Z.) Ltd, 182–190 Wairau Road,
Auckland 10, New Zealand

Penguin Books Ltd, Registered Offices:
Harmondsworth, Middlesex, England

First published in 1988 by Viking Penguin Inc.
Published simultaneously in Canada

The following page constitutes an extension of this copyright page.

LIBRARY OF CONGRESS CATALOGING IN PUBLICATION DATA
Wiener, Harvey S.
Talk with your child.
Bibliography: p.
Includes index.
1. Children–Language.   2. Education, Preschool–
Parent participation.   I. Title.
LB1139.L3W474   1988   372.6   87-40302
ISBN 0-670-81411-3

Printed in the United States of America by
Haddon Craftsmen, Scranton, Pennsylvania
Set in Garamond No. 3
Designed by Victoria Hartman

Grateful acknowledgment is made for permission to reproduce the following illustrations:

From *Parents & Kids Together* by Lisa Lyons Durkin. By permission of Warner Books.

From *The Berenstain Bears' New Baby* by Stan and Jan Berenstain. Copyright © 1974 by Stanley and Janice Berenstain. By permission of Random House, Inc.

From *Commander Toad and the Intergalactic Spy* by Jane Yolen, illustrated by Bruce Degen. Illustrations copyright © 1986 by Bruce Degen. By permission of Coward-McCann, Inc.

From the cover of *Highlights for Children*, issue of June 1987. By permission of Highlights for Children.

Dennis the Menace cartoon. Dennis the Menace® used by permission of Hank Ketcham and © by North America Syndicate.

From *Grandfather Twilight* by Barbara Helen Berger. Copyright © 1984 by Barbara Helen Berger. By permission of Philomel Books.

From *Annie and the Wild Animals* by Jan Brett. Copyright © 1985 by Jan Brett. By permission of Houghton Mifflin Company.

From *Piggybook* by Anthony Browne. Copyright © 1986 by Anthony Browne. By permission of Alfred A. Knopf, Inc.

From *The Purse* by Kathy Caple. Copyright © 1986 by Kathy Caple. By permission of Houghton Mifflin Company.

From *Harry and the Terrible Whatzik* by Dick Gackenbach. Copyright © 1977 by Dick Gackenbach. By permission of Clarion Books/Ticknor & Fields, a Houghton Mifflin Company.

From *George Shrinks* by William Joyce. Copyright © 1985 by William Joyce. By permission of Harper & Row, Publishers, Inc.

From *Imogene's Antlers* by David Small. Copyright © 1985 by David Small. By permission of Crown Publishers, Inc.

From *Oh, Were They Ever Happy* by Peter Spier. Copyright © 1978 by Peter Spier. By permission of Doubleday, a division of Bantam, Doubleday, Dell Publishing Group, Inc.

From *Sophie's Bucket* by Catherine Stock. Copyright © 1985 by Catherine Stock. By permission of Lothrop, Lee & Shepard Books, a division of William Morrow & Company, Inc.

The poem "Incident" is from *On These I Stand* by Countee Cullen. Copyright 1925 by Harper & Row, Publishers, Inc., renewed 1953 by Ida M. Cullen. Reprinted by permission of Harper & Row, Publishers, Inc.

For Melissa, Joseph, and Saul
word lovers
word crafters . . .

"Expecting the main things from you."

Acknowledgments

This book has occupied my thoughts for a long time, but it grew and took shape in innumerable conversations with parents, children, teachers, colleagues, and students. I want to acknowledge publicly all the help and support I received on the project. First I want to thank my wife, Barbara, who first had the idea for this book. Her despair over the impoverished language resources of preschoolers she regularly faced commanded our attention over many years and compelled us both to offer help for modern parents who want to prepare their children for the demands of literacy at school. Our own children are nonstop talkers, and we wanted to share our strategies for engaging kids in dialogue. To my colleagues and friends Nora Eisenberg, JoAnne Anderson, Karen Greenberg, Janet Lieberman, and Don McQuade I offer thanks for listening, advising, and encouraging me through the ups and downs of research and writing. My friend Judith Zipkin, a talented children's librarian, helped me immeasurably in preparing book recommendations for youngsters and in developing appropriate questions to stimulate conversation. John Wright, my friend and agent, saw the value of the project immediately and nurtured it like an only child. I'd never have managed without his help. Dee Shedd, my loyal assistant for many years, slaved over the manuscript, typing and retyping, cutting and pasting, making deadlines manageable. Tracy Brown, my editor at Viking Penguin and a new father himself, gave me unswerving support, and I have benefited enormously from his faith in me. Many of my students at Columbia Teachers College offered valuable insights about talking with young children, as did the countless mothers and fathers around the country whom I begged for ideas and insights. Finally, to my own children, whose delightful conversation lights my days, I say thank you for talking with me. Don't ever stop.

Contents

Talk with Your Child

1

Talking Is Teaching

Who talks with your child?

If you're the mother or father of a preschooler or a young school-age child and you haven't yet directed this question to yourself, you're going to be unhappy about the answers you get once you take stock.

Your child's nursery school or kindergarten teacher? Don't count on it. Even with the best of intentions, your child's teacher is a group leader, initiating experiences for clusters of children to share, and rarely free enough or organized enough to engage your youngster in one-on-one dialogue for language and social development. Many teachers still cling to what strikes me as an outdated model for learning: the teacher center-stage in a roomful of children, all eyes riveted on the performer up front, who talks, questions, cajoles, entertains, prods, encourages, approves, or disapproves.

But you remember that scene from your own elementary school days, don't you? How many chances did you get to talk in that setting on any day? How many times did you get to answer—or to ask—a question or to provide a sustained utterance that made a convincing point or that developed a full explanation? How many times did you exercise the basic human impulse for conversation where someone said something to you,

you said something in return, the other person built on what you said, and so you went, talking and listening and learning? If you're like me, you probably can't recall too many times that you actively engaged in using oral language for learning.

Unfortunately, things have changed little since we went to school. Sure, kids are asked to learn more today—there's so much more that we know now! And kids' parents are sending them for more and more formal instruction at younger and younger ages. All-day kindergartens; children's weekend college; Suzuki violin; day-care programs; nursery schools; foreign-language classes; afternoon gymnastics and karate and swimming lessons; sculpting, painting, paleontology, science labs on Saturday mornings at the museum or at the local high school—these, for three-, four-, and five-year-olds, are rules, not exceptions, for many American families. But the activities add little to a child's conversational opportunities. In fact, if he tries to talk with his friend during floor exercises or at the lab table, some adult is probably telling him to keep quiet and pay attention. In almost every structured learning situation I've witnessed, informal conversation among kids is viewed as a great evil that must be wiped out immediately because it prevents learning. As if learning can proceed without it!

Social scientists, psychologists, and researchers call our frenetic efforts at formal instruction for young children "hothousing," and they don't like it much at all. Hothousing forces early structured learning environments on youngsters to develop them quickly; it forces their rapid growth like seeds in the moist sultry air of a greenhouse. Drawing upon structured, often authoritarian, usually high-pressured programs (like many of those I've mentioned above) at the expense of relaxed, informal discourse, hothousing sacrifices the potential for home teaching in simple and regular conversation with children.

Yale psychologist Dr. Edward Zigler, former head of the federal Office of Child Development, decries the push toward universal preschool education. "We are driving children too hard," he says. Our current policies "needlessly deprive parents and children of valuable time they could spend together."

In a similar vein, perhaps you read the crackling response

written by Valerie Singer to a proposal by William D. Wheeler in *The New York Times*. Wheeler advocates formal schooling for youngsters starting at age three and Singer fulminates against it, speaking, I believe, for many concerned parents who have thought at length about their children's needs. She says that separating mothers and children too early can destroy a vital bond and that this separation can cause havoc in both lives. She reminds us that preschoolers must learn both mentally and socially and that such learning is best achieved beyond class-room doors. Don't throw your child into another person's care at a tender age. "Spend the money and the energy," she asserts, "strengthening the bonds at the child's home, and the rewards will be felt far beyond those four walls."

We're not talking simply about day-care for children now at home or at nursery schools, both realities of modern American life as parents return to the work force out of desire, necessity, or both. It's the rigid school environment imposed in any setting for really young children that Singer and Zigler bemoan. Certainly they are not alone in condemning highly structured learning for young children. Dr. Patricia Minuchin, research professor of psychiatry at the New York University Medical Center, is another one of many who oppose inappropriate formal instruction. If a child is to learn best, she insists, the child needs play as well as interaction with the environment and the people in it.

But who are those people? As I've said, it's not the child's teacher, either in nursery school or elementary school or in one of the formal learning centers to which many of us turn to supplement what we see as an inadequate classroom program, or to give our kids all the extra dividends we feel will help them succeed as adults. Unfortunately, a few innovative models aside, teaching-learning delivery systems in any "school" setting are about as conversationally static today, no matter what the level of education or the nature of the subject matter, as they were when we grew up.

School programs aside, you've probably tried to arrange for informal interactions with your child and other children in the neighborhood on weekends or after school. Certainly kids talk to each other. Even parallel play, each child at his or her own activity, may be accompanied by talking: monologues, play songs, object identifications, sociodramas, or real and imagined stories. Other children pick up strands, laugh at utterances, make their own contributions. The talk that accompanies play is very important, for it helps children reflect their sense of adults' rules for children's oral behaviors, including word games, verbal play, accurate narrative retellings, embellished and exaggerated entertainments, and social interactions. Yet as important as these desultory verbal connections are, they don't go far enough. They don't help the child stretch linguistic resources beyond a basic level. They don't generate ongoing discourse. They don't stimulate thought through the kinds of questions and answers that mark many elements of conversation for learning.

Maybe your child is lucky enough to have grandparents living close by and is interacting with them on some regular basis. Or maybe it's another relative, your sister or brother or a cousin down the street, some older sibling, or some friend of the family, "Aunt" Katie, who lives nearby and who took a shine to your youngster and likes having him or her around. Maybe you drop your child off at the home of some mature babysitter who watches Johnny or Jane while you're at work. Perhaps a babysitter-housekeeper-governess comes to your home and looks after your child there. These can be wonderful opportunities for your little boy or girl, and you want to continue stimulating them to grow and flower.

Still, in terms of minutes and hours—just compare them with the time your youngster sits by the pulsating light of a television screen—these social moments with adults and their important talk-time dimension can play a relatively minor role in a child's social and linguistic development. And the quality of the talk— listen to the conversation (if any) between your youngster and these adults. There's lots of talking *to* and *at* but little talking *with*. Do you note the engagement of ideas and their expansion through discussion, explanation, and application? Do you hear more than isolated chatter, Aunt Katie at her chores talking aloud to the pots and pans or typewriter or on the telephone to a neighbor, your child at the junk drawer in the kitchen or at a special toy in the front hall, both people engaging in separate, unrelated talk? Are there verbal interactions, questions and answers, assertions and judgments, requests and related actions? I am not hinting that the passive social conditions many adults arrange when young children are present are harmful or even not valuable. What I am suggesting is that your child needs more. To share the fabric of language and, later, the reading and writing skills inextricably woven into its development, your child needs a conversational partner—gentle, loving, open-minded, inquiring, respectful, patient, relaxed, intelligent.

Who's left for this partnership?

You.

The parent.

You have to motivate conversation for regular language experience between your youngster and adults. Conversation is vital both for language building and for helping kids face and deal with life's problems.

If this last point seems too obvious—conversation helps children deal with the problems and fears of daily living—it doesn't seem as if we've incorporated it extensively enough in our dealings with the kids in our lives. Among the many interesting tips reported to working mothers and fathers from their children in *The Working Parent Dilemma,* Earl A. Grollman and Gerri L. Sweder highlight the importance of conversation in a child's-eye view of successful parenting. One of their subjects, Linda, an intelligent seventeen-year-old, teaches a lesson to us all: "If parents want to have a good relationship with their kids, they've got to be prepared to talk with them." The authors drive the point home. They say that children want to discuss feelings, especially fears. However, "many children and parents brush aside all sensitive subjects. Listening to your child and answering questions can make an enormous difference in his emotional security and will strengthen your relationship with him."

In regard to critical thinking and decision making, a parent who takes time to talk with children is a parent building essential skills for life. Dr. John Clabby and Dr. Maurice Elias, two psychologists who have studied problem solving among children, underscore the important role for parents here. Routinely starting with three- and four-year-olds, the authors of *Teach Your Child Decision Making* praise the creativity and flexibility in a preschool child's thinking. "Teaching a child to make decisions and solve social problems," they say, "develops his or her capacity to think independently." Parents, they believe, need to promote problem solving at home by building "decision-making observations into everyday family routines" and by "generating alternative solutions to problems out loud, such as how to prepare dinner or what to do during the course of the day." You can see, of course, how the conversational household can nurture the seeds of creative thought and make them grow.

Building emotional support systems aside, my main interest here is in language and in the dramatic effect a conversational household can have in advancing a child's vocabulary, comprehension, and critical thought skills. Don't underestimate your power to seed a love for words, a passion for reading, a delight in writing. Educators look more and more for the parents' help in these early years and with very satisfying results. One program, based on the work of psychologist Phyllis Levenstein and sponsored by the Family Service Association in Hempstead, New York, teaches mothers how to engage in educational play with their children and how to encourage linguistic development. Designed essentially for underprivileged children, the Mother-Child Home Care Program boasts extraordinary outcomes for many of the poverty-level toddlers who join. IQs soar more than eighteen points. Inattentive, uncooperative kids talk more, concentrate better, ask questions. How? "Mothers are taught to speak to their children at every opportunity to develop language skills," says program director Edith Wasserman, who believes that every child can benefit from such interactions. "I'm not just talking about deprived children," she insists.

The community of researchers and scholars out there tells us unequivocally that parents have a powerful influence on their children's learning.

Talking and learning depend on each other.

Are you satisfied that you're talking enough with your child now? In general, family statistics in this regard are pretty grim. American mothers, says the Department of Education, spend less than thirty minutes a day talking with their children. Fathers spend even less than that—about fifteen minutes a day.

When they do talk, parents usually talk *at* kids, not with them. They rarely view children as valid conversational partners. Research by Dr. Paula Menyuk, director of the Language Behavior Program at Boston University's School of Education, suggests that even from a child's infancy parents who talk with babies stimulate early language growth. Examining fifty-six families, all with new babies, Dr. Menyuk saw that children who developed strong communication skills had parents who gave their infants time to talk and who responded to their infants' language signals. Even with the best of intentions, mothers and fathers who talked steadily at their babies, providing extensive language input without opportunity for some kind of output, were of no noticeable help in developing children's language. By making comments to or raising questions for babies, and then pausing even if you know your child is too young to respond verbally, you establish important conversational patterns. Your pauses tell your baby that you expect her to answer somehow; and they also give you a chance to acknowledge what your baby "says" and to interpret it. Here's Dr. Menyuk's advice (you'll hear me echo it dozens of times by the time you finish this book): "Get your babies involved in discourse with you by asking lots of questions. Then listen to the responses and provide further feedback."

Do you talk regularly with your child or are you one of the only-a-half-hour-a-day culprits? Do you know how to provide optimal conversation opportunities for your youngster? If you're like most mothers (and many fathers), you probably knew, without even having to think about it, how to use language often around your child at the infant stage. Morton Hunt, in his fascinating book on cognitive science, *The Universe Within,* reminds us of how skillful many mothers are in using special language with infants, what psycholinguists call Motherese. We have within us an instinctive sense of our role as language builders. We often use that special high-pitched voice that helps us expand on words so that children learn to say them better or more clearly. We try to make educational toys available and try to make time to show our young children how to play with them; we read books and play naming games and engage in question-asking and -answering activities.

But do we use our native talents as language givers optimally?

Researchers like Shirley Brice Heath in her extraordinary study *Ways with Words,* a book about how children learn language in two North Carolina communities, chronicle the declining interest of many parents in their children's growth as language learners after a flurry of attention in the child's very early years. For some reason or other some parents stop paying attention to word and sentence building and conversation as their child grows older. Maybe we feel that we've done all we needed to do until that point and that our child must learn the rest himself. Maybe we feel that the schools—nursery school, day school, church or temple school, special learning centers—should become the language and conversational core in our child's life. Maybe we're focusing our attention on other things—a newly arrived child in the family, a career moved to the front burner now that our child is growing older, a return to college to finish a degree, a renewed attention to long-range projects we'd put off to start a family (volunteer work; a new, time-consuming job; fund raising or other charity efforts; a stint on the local school board)—and just don't set time aside to talk with our children as much as we should.

Or, maybe we just don't know how to help. A 1987 study of 239 Baltimore students by Joyce Epstein at Johns Hopkins University found, unsurprisingly, that kids had higher reading scores if their parents involved themselves actively in learning. Yet—and here's the unexpected news—Epstein says that although mothers and fathers *want* desperately to help their children succeed at school, most parents just don't have a clue about where to begin. Only twenty percent of the parents reported that they knew how to help their youngsters. Eighty percent didn't know what to do, but, according to Epstein, they sure wished they did.

Talk with Your Child will help you help your youngster succeed at school when he finds his way into the formal education classroom. The book is designed for children and parents to enjoy language for the thrill of sharing ideas as well as for the necessary experience with words that is so essential in learning how to read. I don't care how busy you are with your career or your social, professional, or economic life: you have enough time to talk with your youngster, and I'm going to show you how.

I'm not going to add to your burdens by making you more of a formal reading teacher—I don't believe in asking parents to teach phonics or to drill in vocabulary—and I'll bet you're providing too many structured learning situations for your child already. However, I am going to help you enjoy your children more as you learn to use *talking* as a means to encourage social and intellectual development as well as to stimulate growth of language awareness. I want to point out some simple activities in which you can exchange ideas comfortably with your kids. As parent, you must help your child use language actively. You must encourage conversation about the child's version of life experiences.

So, let us begin. How does your home setting shape up as an oral language household?

A CONVERSATIONAL INVENTORY

I've created this twenty-five-question test to help you evaluate your use of and attitudes toward talking with young children. In the blank space beside each question write either 1, 2, or 3 according to this scale:

3 = Most of the time
2 = Some of the time
1 = None of the time

1. Do you have meals with your children and do you engage in conversation at the table? _____

2. Do you question your child about his daily experiences? _____

3. Do you share *your* daily experiences in conversation with your child? _____

4. Does your child have the chance to hear you often engage in discussions about events in your day, your impressions of politics or world events, movies you have seen, books you have read, and so on? _____

5. Do you avoid telling your child to stop talking so much or to mind his or her own business when he or she tries to take part in a "grown-up" conversation? _____

6. Do you read aloud to your child? _____

7. Do you ask your child to "read" to you, even if he makes up the words (because he can't read yet) from pictures on the page? _____

8. If you read aloud to your child, do you engage him or her in conversation about the words and pictures on pages in the book and about the ideas in the book itself when you're finished with it? _____

9. Do you invite your child's opinions about objects and ideas—clothing, a new food, a television program—and do you encourage truthful answers? _____

10. When your child asks a question, do you respond to it thoughtfully and invite further questions until you clear up any problem or misunderstanding? _____

11. Do you encourage your child to expand one- or two-word statements that he or she makes in response to questions? _____

12. When children argue do you try to get them to articulate the problem and to seek a satisfactory resolution by talking instead of by solving it quickly yourself or by meting out appropriate punishment? _____

13. Do you provide choices for children when a decision has to be made, and do you encourage them to explain the reasons for their choices? _____

14. Do you mediate disputes in the home—between siblings, between you and the children—by encouraging the free airing of ideas, opinions, feelings, and thoughts instead of by issuing a ruling to bring about peace quickly? _____

15. In planning vacations or other family events, do you invite children's participation in choosing sites or in determining activities relevant to the occasion? _____

16. Do you encourage your child to answer the telephone, and do you establish general guidelines for the manner and format of telephone conversations? _____

17. Do you try to find alternatives for frequent silent play when your child is at home alone without other children for companionship? _____

18. Do you encourage your preschooler to play near you as you're working around the house, and do you carry on a running dialogue about the objects around you, the day's events, and so on? _____

19. When you are invited to, do you generally accept a role for playacting a character in an imaginary scene that your child has invented? _____

20. Do you see your role as "home teacher," as guider or talking partner, rather than as a teacher of content and skills; that is, do you use time with your child mostly for conversation rather than for instruction, such as how to write the alphabet or how to sound out letter combinations? _____

21. Do you disagree with the statement that little children should be seen and not heard? _____

22. Do you ask your child to explain the pictures she draws or the designs she constructs? _____

23. Do you invite your child to explain some particularly negative behavior that you have noted before you address the wrongdoing? _____

24. Do you play verbal word games with your child—riddles, nonsense words, rhymes, and so on? _____

25. Do you find yourself naming and identifying objects or concepts that are unfamiliar to your child even though he or she might not ask you to? _____

If you get 66–75 you have a conversational household, and you'll find that the suggestions I'm trying to make here will enhance the approach to child rearing that you've already tried to establish, one that builds upon talking with children. I've got lots of ideas for helping you expand your influence over your youngster's opportunities for language advancement.

If you get 56–65, you're probably aware of the importance of talking with your child but have not adequately integrated conversation for language building into your family routines. If that's you, you're going to find a number of useful suggestions here. I've tried to anticipate most of the questions you might raise as you shift your conversational engine into higher gear: where to find time, how to engage kids actively in dialogue, how to keep conversation off a one-way street, and many others.

If you get below 56, you've got some serious rethinking to do. Part of your job as parent is to help shape and develop language growth, especially if you want your child to succeed at school. Some simple, pleasurable activities you can add to your regular contact with children—at the dinner table, in the supermarket, at the park—will quickly improve your score on the Conversational Inventory! I think you'll find a large enough menu here in this book so that you can choose activities that suit your children's needs and your own style of child rearing.

A great sense of urgency about children's literacy pervades the media and the governmental agencies concerned with education. A 1985 report of the Commission on Reading of the National Academy of Education exhorted parents to participate in a child's language development. In summarizing that report— "Becoming a Nation of Readers," which was sponsored by the National Institute of Education—one of the writers, renowned Columbia University educator Diana Ravitch, makes these points: Parents should support the school's mission by helping children learn at home; a parent's instruction "powerfully contributes to children's interest in reading and to reading achievement in school"; and, perhaps most important, "As children grow, *parents should talk with them,* discuss their children's experiences, daily activities, favorite stories or movies or television programs, and urge them to tell stories about trips to the zoo, museum, store, library, park. *Children must learn the importance of words as conveyors of meaning and must develop background knowledge."* [Emphases mine.]

If children are to learn the importance of words to convey meaning, parents must learn how to stimulate that learning. Unfortunately, most "how to" books for literacy focus on formal home teaching and start too far up on the language continuum.

Researchers agree that literacy progresses along an interactive continuum as the child develops. I call that continuum the *language line:* speaking, listening, writing, reading. As parents, you have to help your child make that progression by drawing upon the basic elements of oral conversation. Talking is a precursor of reading and writing, which do not replace, but instead supplement, oral communication as a means of language learning. In a sense, the image of a "line" is imperfect because it implies a consistent step-by-step progression. That's why I use the word *interactive.* In fact, after children learn to speak, they advance their language knowledge through all those dimensions of verbal experience, and there is no exact movement from one to the other. The four proceed together. Reading advances a comprehensive awareness of words and their possibilities, which the child reflects in conversation; conversation builds language awareness that makes it easier to understand the printed page; the developing storehouse of verbal skills enables a child to approach an empty white sheet, pen or pencil or crayon poised above it, ready to put words on paper.

I'm advocating here an active, yet basically unstructured, home program for influencing your child's literacy. I join the U.S. Department of Education in sounding the clarion for interested parents. The department's report on teaching and learning calls for mothers and fathers to create a "Curriculum of the Home" that teaches children what matters. This effort requires little extra time from parents, who can achieve this curriculum simply through their daily interest in their children's progress. I call your attention particularly to the stress that this report places on talking with kids. "Conversation is important," says its author, Chester E. Finn, emphatically. "Children learn to read, reason, and understand things better when parents:

- read, talk, and listen to them
- tell them stories, play games, share hobbies
- discuss news, TV programs, and special events."

If you're ready to start your home-talking program, let's take a quick look at some current theories about how children learn thought and language and how you can influence that learning.

2

The Language Line:
Speaking, Listening,
Writing, Reading

How does a youngster learn language? What are the conditions that prompt a child to learn how to read?

These enormously provocative questions challenge anyone interested in children and learning, yet they defy description even by the host of scholars—linguists, psychologists, psychiatrists, psycholinguists, sociolinguists, reading researchers, rhetoricians, grammarians, semanticists, philosophers—who have turned their passionate interests to the puzzle. One of the leading research reporters in this field, Jerome Bruner, addressing the prestigious audience of academics from various disciplines in the Max-Planck Project Group in Psycholinguistics, puts it aptly and succinctly: "The acquisition of language has always been a puzzling phenomenon. How can human beings learn so complex a system of rules for producing and comprehending messages so quickly, so well, with such subtle flexibility of use, a system of rules so complex that we who concern ourselves with language can scarcely decide how to describe it?"

With such a diversity of scholars examining such a dynamic and exciting problem, any layman wading through the research is soon shooting the rapids, flooded with theories and countertheories. For us the pertinent question about language learning here is, how does a person outside the child's own self have influence over the child's acquisition of language skills, especially as they bear on print-related learning?

I do not mean in this chapter to give you a lesson on everything you wanted to know about language theory but were smart enough not to ask. But I have tried to extract some general agreements reached by good thinkers in the field of language learning and teaching so that you can see how important your role is as conversation-maker with young children in giving them the start they need at home.

FIRST, THE BASICS

In the first place, you should know that most theorists now agree that children have concepts before they have language, not the other way around. Language development, then, though it reflects conceptual development, lags behind it. That means that researchers no longer view children as blank slates, passive learners waiting to be led through a maze of vocabulary, grammar, and syntax by adults who understand all the rules. The old behaviorist theory is a water bag shot through with holes. We do not believe now that all the knowledge of language a person gathers is a direct, absolute, one-to-one result of what he or she observes in the surrounding world.

So you can relax. You can lay aside one of the many rocks that you carry about in your sack of burdens about child rearing. You are not the word and rule giver, though, as you will see later on, you do have a primary role in enhancing a child's language development and expression.

Your child is essentially an active, dynamic language learner even before he or she knows any language. Think of your youngster as a miniature linguist, constantly making assumptions about language and trying them out. Through the work of the great theorist Noam Chomsky and his followers we believe that infants are predisposed to learn language systems by some intrinsic feature of the brain's structure.

This built-in tendency is an extraordinary quality if you think about it because it incorporates all the general properties of diverse languages. Although we may speak different languages, these languages share many common qualities. A child born into this culture or that must accommodate the particular linguistic system surrounding him, and unless our ability to learn reflected all the general principles of language, we'd be lost to it forever. Into whose communication system we're born is a throw of the dice; we've got to be ready to learn no matter where we take our first breath. Those who support the idea of an innate tendency toward acquiring language point to the universals as evidence of a child's predisposition to learn. Thus, despite the various tongues of the world, children pick up the rules of their immediate language environment simply and quickly without formal instruction.

Even more interesting and to the point, children who live in communities that rely on a common language are all bombarded with different spoken-language stimuli in early stages of development. Despite this fact, they develop fundamentally identical language rules. You and your neighbor down the street, both with toddlers, provide different speech environments for your children, yet both children will understand from a sentence someone speaks just who is performing some action and what the action is. By means of an innate learning program deep in the brain's structure, in no time your little boy or girl figures out how to command spoken English.

You want to remember that children seek out words to express a notion or an idea existing in their minds. They do not need words before they have the idea or in order to generate it. Here, it's not the old chicken-or-egg puzzle. We're pretty sure that the notion is first and then the word comes to name it. We believe, too, that children can perform many advanced mental operations such as sorting things into groups and making determinations about objects, actions, and people who carry out the actions. Children can do all this well in advance of having the language for those operations.

Psycholinguists use the following diagram to show the interrelated features of how children learn language:

PRIMARY	LANGUAGE	
LINGUISTIC $\longrightarrow$	ACQUISITION $\longrightarrow$	GRAMMAR
DATA	DEVICE	

The terms are a bit cumbersome, so let's restate them:

HOME	THE	LANGUAGE
SPEECH $\longrightarrow$	CHILD $\longrightarrow$	RULES
ENVIRONMENT		

Do you see the pieces here? The early home setting provides the auditory basis of language for the child, who is a remarkable acquiring system by nature of his physical, mental, and genetic makeup. Because of the child's native abilities, he develops rules and guidelines for using the language he hears. In words that the philosopher Michael Polanyi might use, the child knows more than he can say—a trait Polanyi believes stays with us throughout our lives.

Children are remarkably aware of their own language development. Psycholinguist Eve V. Clark is quite sure that kids practice language and that they know what they're doing when they practice: What are they practicing? "They repeat sentence frames," Professor Clark says, "substituting one word for another; they try out different sentence types; they practice newly acquired sounds and words, saying them over and over again." If you listen to your child talking, you may not be able to distinguish language practice from actual language use. But you may be able to overhear a bit of extraordinary language self-awareness, like this practice recorded by a researcher way back in 1914 as he listened to a twenty-one-month-old talking to himself:

Daddy walk on grass   R [child's name] walk on grass— no   Daddy walk on grass—yes   Daddy walk on snow   deep snow   know that word

According to Clark, in their language-practice monologues youngsters also work on trying to get sounds and pronunciations right, on changing from one type of sentence to another (for example, from negatives to questions to statements), on generating question-and-answer sequences, and on substituting pronouns, nouns, adjectives, and verbs in correct sentence positions. And kids do all this as they recap the events of their day. Your son or daughter is pretty smart, don't you think?

Need more information to convince you that your young child is a language-making genius? Many researchers also believe that children not only have information before they have the language to identify it, but they also know what they are trying to achieve through language even before they start using it to carry out their efforts. First attempts are with gestures, with voice sounds, and with intonations.

If you've watched a toddler at the edge of a crib who is trying to signal that she wants to get out, you know the combination of strategies that she uses beyond language to communicate her point. She smacks the bars and shakes her head; she moans and gurgles and coos, sometimes varying the pitch of her voice. Thus, she has resources other than words to let you know what she wants although, ultimately, language will be the strongest means at her disposal once she learns that it can fulfill so many of her needs at once. Bruner summarizes this point neatly. Language, he says, helps "to deal with events that the child already understands conceptually and to achieve communicative objectives that the child, at least partially, can already realize by other means."

I want to make another point or two about language learning before we look more closely at the parent's role in all this. You've no doubt assumed, and correctly so, that children don't come to complete understanding and knowledge simply in a sudden flash of insight. Most people believe that children progress through a series of overlapping stages as they learn, and I thought you'd be interested in viewing (or reviewing, for those of you who can recall some introductory psychology course you've taken) some of the more interesting theories of what those progressions look like.

Of course we start with Jean Piaget, the great philosopher-psychologist who defined what he saw as four stages of mental processing, or what he calls "cognitive development," through which children pass. Although Piaget himself did not write about how children learn to read or write, many people interested in those areas of development draw upon his theories because they provide a backdrop for understanding the process of how knowledge, in general, is acquired.

Piaget's Four Stages of Development

Stage 1. the sensory motor stage
    (from birth to approximately two years old)
Stage 2. the preoperational stage
    (from about two years to about six or seven years)
Stage 3. the concrete-operations stage
    (roughly, from seven years to eleven years)
Stage 4. the formal-operations stage
    (adolescence).

Only the first two concern us here.

In the *sensory motor* stage the child slowly learns to distinguish himself from other objects and to distinguish other objects from each other. He learns not to see the surrounding world simply as an extension of himself. When your one-year-old empties out your bread basket or knocks all the soup and vegetable cans from the bottom shelf of the pantry, she's merely stretching her mental operations as she continues to relate the idea of herself to the objects she touches. What children cannot do at this stage, Piaget believes, is to see actions or thoughts symbolically. When they start absorbing internally the actions (or motor patterns, as psychologists call them) that they've learned in order to cope with their surroundings, they begin developing symbolic thought. In other words, we can characterize the child's performance at this stage as rooted in direct actions.

In the *preoperational* stage, the child develops internal symbols. Piaget believes that the first symbols are not verbal and that they probably involve images and physical sensations. The ability to think symbolically is what enhances the learning of language and not the other way around. Words themselves are symbols—you can see how important an element symbolic thought is. All children learn how to think symbolically. It's nothing you have to teach.

Why the word *preoperation?* Piaget believed that a key element of mental action (what he called an *operation*) was reversibility. Children at this stage cannot reverse thought. In a now famous experiment, he showed short, squat glasses of water to children in the two- to six-year age group. When he poured the water from the short glasses into tall, thin glasses, the children invariably said there was more water in the new glasses— even after frequent repetitions. Similarly, if you showed a child a wad of dough and then rolled it out in an elongated snakelike shape, the child would say that there is more dough in the new figure. A child at this stage cannot carry out an operation because he or she cannot reverse actions, cannot see, for example, that by pouring the water back it would fill the squat glasses exactly, and that by reversing the snake of dough it would lead back to the wad.

Without the ability to reverse thought, a child cannot see that the same object can exist in two different physical states. At the preoperational stage, children also cannot avoid centering their thoughts on a single aspect of a situation. They do not understand both similarities and differences between objects or that objects may belong to two or three different categories at the same time.

(In case you're interested, Stage 3, the stage of concrete operations, identifies children who have well-defined mental operations that are reversible, though their cognitive activities are anchored in the present world of specific objects and events. At Stage 4, youngsters enter the world of possibilities, hypotheses, and future events; their mental activities are not limited to the actual here-and-now world.)

As you take up some of the suggestions I'll be making throughout this book, pay some attention to your child's cognitive stage of development in the Piagetian scheme. It might free you of some frustrations in trying to advance conversation to a level beyond your youngster's ability.

Some more information about stages. I thought you'd like

to consider the steps that psycholinguists believe children climb as they learn language. I want to caution you here, though, that the stages overlap—don't think that your child will go from one to the other, rejecting every part of the former stage in order to participate in the next one. Also, realize that age groups are only approximations; and from Stage 3 onward, language development is not much related to age. For example, normal children vary dramatically in how soon they begin one-word utterances and in how long those utterances endure. Bear in mind, too, that very little relation exists between intelligence and speed of language learning in normal children. Some learn fast; some learn slowly; but neither rate tells you anything whatsoever about intelligence.

I'm summarizing much of the information below from the work of Helen S. Cairns and Charles E. Cairns, a team of first-rate linguists at Queens College of the City University of New York.

Stages of Language Development Characteristics

Stage 1. babbling (early months)	babbling, cooing, squealing, gurgling; not speech sounds but "acoustic signals"; baby is flexing speech organs, not using language.
Stage 2. nonsense words (6–12 months)	sounds organized into syllable patterns, but no recognizable words; sounds seem more like speech than at babbling stage; also sounds have intonations, as if child is speaking sentences. ("Auditory feedback" essential here: child must hear words and sentences in return; deaf children, proceeding normally through the babbling stage, babble less and less at this stage and grow silent.)

Stage 3. one-word utterances (approx. 1 yr. onward)	single words used to elaborate meanings—e.g., *Toy* can mean "Look at the toy" or "Give me the toy" or "I broke the toy."
Stage 4. two-word utterances (approx. 2 yrs. onward)	two one-word utterances put together; e.g., *Baby toy* to indicate possession.
Stage 5. beginning grammar (2–3 yrs. onward)	longer sentences used; increasingly, verbs show tense, nouns have plural or possessive endings; words often omitted in sentences ("Take Johnny park," "Cassie toy there"); growth in kinds and number of words used.
Stage 6. advancing grammar (3 yrs. onward)	complex grammatical sentences; still many spoken "errors."
Stage 7. adult competence (approx. by puberty)	command of sentence devices and patterns.

Michael Halliday, whose *Learning How to Mean* is one of the seminal scholarly books on language development in children, compresses these into three phases:

Phase 1:	the child's initial language system: what he uses to function in the world.
Phase 2:	the transition period from the initial language system to the adult language system.
Phase 3:	the learning of adult language.

With scientific care Halliday studied the language development of his infant son, Nigel, throughout these phases. You'll be meeting Nigel and his mother and father from time to time in this book.

Recent researchers at the Kennedy Institute for Handicapped Children in Baltimore now say that language-acquisition patterns in the early stages of life provide insights into normal or abnormal child development. The ages at which children learn to babble and say "dada" and "mama," for example, may signal a range of problems from psychiatric disorders to sensory disorders to learning disorders. You can see how critical it is for mothers and fathers to stay attuned to their children's language development. By identifying language problems early and arranging for special assistance, parents can help block pathways to failure later on—learning difficulties, behavioral problems at school, social ostracism, family tensions, and so on.

In a recent issue of *Contemporary Pediatrics,* Drs. Arnold J. Capute, Bruce K. Shapiro, and Frederick B. Palmer, associate professors of pediatrics at the Johns Hopkins University School of Medicine, report on a language test they developed that allows physicians to detect a wide range of child development problems. The Clinical Linguistic and Auditory Milestone Scale (CLAMS) provides systematic evaluation of language development in children. Essentially a standardized and validated comparative measure, CLAMS allows pediatricians to gather information both from you and your baby and to compare your child's prelanguage and language development with that of other children in the same age group. The two tables below give you a general sense of what the milestone scale measures.

By examining the tables, you can get a rough idea of how a child stacks up. Your pediatrician can give you a more accurate reading, and you should consult a pediatrician if you have any doubts about how your child's language is advancing. Once again, remember that children vary in their speed of language acquisition. Boys, for example, always mature linguistically at a slower rate than girls. You don't want to fly into panic if your youngster varies from the standards. A good physician will help you address any problems you may perceive in your child's language skills.

Let's see how a concerned parent can use some of the general approaches to language that we've been considering. Our goal is to enhance essential home learning and to move a child toward

AGE IN MONTHS*	MILESTONE
0.25	Makes some response to sound
1.25	Smiles in response to stimulation
1.6	Coos; makes long vowel sounds
4	Turns toward speaker Says "ah-goo" Makes razzling sound
5	Turns toward ringing bell
6	Babbles
7	Looks up sideways toward ringing bell
8	Says "dada" and "mama" indiscriminately
9	Plays gesture games like peek-a-boo Looks directly at ringing bell Understands word "no"
11	Uses "dada" and "mama" as names Responds to one-step command and gesture indicating activity Says first word
12	Says gibberish "sentences" without using real words Says second word

*After age 2 months, ages have been rounded off to nearest month. Source: Clinical Linguistic and Auditory Milestone Scale, developed by Arnold J. Capute, Bruce K. Shapiro and Frederick B. Palmer

linguistic competence as demanded by the school, the community, and the larger culture.

THE SOCIAL NATURE OF LANGUAGE

The purpose of language is to communicate. Whether we speak or write or read, our objective is to give or to receive

AGE IN MONTHS*	MILESTONE
13	Says third word
14	Responds to one-step command without gesture
15	Says 4 to 6 words
17	Says gibberish sentence with some real words Can point to five body parts Says 7 to 20 words
19	Forms 2-word combinations
21	Forms 2-word sentences
24	Uses pronouns (I, me, you) indiscriminately
30	Uses pronouns (I, me, you) discriminately
36	Uses all pronouns discriminately Has 250-word vocabulary Uses plurals Forms 3-word sentences

Source: Drs. Arnold J. Capute, Bruce K. Shapiro, and Frederick B. Palmer

information. Jerome Bruner reminds us of the obvious: "Communicative competence has to do with dialogue."

So important is dialogue in growth to adult language that Michael Halliday identifies it as the essential means by which a child can achieve the skill. To Halliday *informing* is our most important linguistic function. Think of the degree of sophistication it takes to realize that language can communicate information to someone who doesn't have that information. Young children—up to about two—do not seem to possess this notion. Yet to adults, this informative function—the "I have information to give you" activity—is the major element in adult thought about language. As they move to higher levels of facility, children learn that language is interaction, and they initiate and participate in dialogues. Only at this point does language take on its informative context.

As you surmised from our discussion of developmental stages of language growth, not only the practice but also the learning of language is essentially a social phenomenon. This also holds true for acquiring knowledge in general. Thus, although a child may have the tendency toward and equipment for learning, without a social context—a setting that supplies interaction—little learning takes place.

What does this mean? Lev Semenovich Vygotsky, the brilliant Russian linguist and psychologist who died tragically of tuberculosis in 1934 at the young age of thirty-eight, studied the interrelations between language and thought. His experiments and conclusions are pertinent here because he so clearly ties language and thought to social interaction. My friend Kenneth Bruffee, professor of English at Brooklyn College and one of the leading authorities on collaborative learning, has explained clearly how Vygotsky emphasizes the social dimension of learning. I will draw upon Bruffee's work in sharing Vygotsky's premises with you.

Vygotsky traces the inherently social feature of learning from some of the child's earliest acts. When an infant reaches out to grasp a spoon that is out of reach, for example, the child is trying to connect himself with that object in some way in order to know it. But the object does not cooperate. It remains in place, refusing the child's efforts at acquaintanceship, as objects always do. So for a moment, shiny silver spoon immobile, child's hand stretched outward and groping, no contact takes place.

That is, until Mother or Father steps in and moves the spoon closer. The child picks it up, smiles at it, hits the floor with it, puts it in his mouth. When the infant reaches for an object, he learns that he is sending a message, that his reaching invariably can arouse some adult to respond. Reaching for an object is really the first step in learning how to point. An effort to grasp, the child determines, is not merely an effort to reach an object; it is instead an effort aimed at another person. Vygotsky's idea is that learning is not simply a direct relation between an object and a subject, here the spoon and the child. Instead, learning involves other people. Even in so uncomplicated an act, in which a child is trying to get acquainted with something, the mediation of a third party is essential.

When the child learns to speak, all he has to do is name the object, and some cooperating adult will see that he gets it. At its most basic level, therefore, language is another form of pointing. The fundamental quality of knowledge to the infant is that the path that stretches from him to an object and back again always passes through another person. "After infancy," Bruffee says, "the vehicle we use to traverse this path is language."

Can you see how essential the parent's role is in establishing the child's view of language and learning? If language and learning are intrinsically social, collaborative activities, parents play a much more active and dynamic role in child development than many people have assumed. Educators now believe that learning throughout much of life—and this includes classroom learning from the elementary school straight through to postsecondary institutions—depends upon social support systems and must involve other people as agents. We don't learn by sitting and listening to smart people talk; we do learn by engaging in conversation in which we make choices rooted in the give and take of human exchange. As children grow, Vygotsky points out, they must use spoken language to master their surroundings. "The more complex the action demanded by the situation . . . the greater the importance played by speech in the operation as a whole."

When parents do not actively establish conversational households—when, say, they find little time to converse regularly with their kids or they let televisions, radios, and stereos assume central auditory roles in the home or they shoo children off to be alone in their rooms—they discard opportunities for helping the child practice learning in its most essential form. Conversation is the pathway to knowledge.

So essential is the social, conversational dimension of learning that even a child alone will resort to speech to advance knowledge. Vygotsky describes another fascinating experiment in which a four- or five-year-old girl tries to reach a piece of candy high up on a shelf. She learns how to use a stick and a stool by herself, while a researcher sits nearby and takes notes about what she says as she talks through the situation alone. It's interesting that the child talks. But she's not talking to the object, the desired piece of candy, or the tools at her disposal. Sometimes she'll address somebody else, like the researcher sitting in the room with her. But mostly she is talking to herself. She addresses herself *as if she were another person.*

Do you see the point here? The youngster in this case is changing a solitary task into a collaborative one. Vygotsky's conclusion is that, as development continues, the child for whom language has appropriately progressed learns to turn socialized speech inward; instead of appealing to the adult, she appeals to herself. We can gather from this once more a sense of the central role of the parent in the child's ability to learn. By having an available adult to appeal to as the child develops, she practices that very important skill of inwardly directed socialized speech. Structuring conversational situations—informal, spontaneous, loving, and attentive—parents provide a model for the kind of thinking that we now believe is essential to effective learning.

THE PROBLEM UNDER GLASS

Communicative competence has to do with dialogue. How are we doing as a nation of modern families in regard to home communication?

"My father works all the time," Kathy told the authors of *The Working Parent Dilemma.* "He leaves around 7:00 A.M. and doesn't come home until 7:00 P.M. By then we've eaten, and he eats by himself, mostly in front of the TV. Even on weekends he goes in to the office." Another youngster said, "Everyone thinks my mom is terrific because she's smart and works hard and is famous. She has time to travel all over giving talks. The only person she has no time for is me."

Even our kids are telling us that we're not engaging in home conversation. Unfortunately, we disregard socialized speech both at home and in our educational programs.

Here are a couple of interesting cases in point.

Troy, an eleven-year-old child left back twice at the Hempstead public schools for low reading scores, takes a reading workshop on Thursdays and Saturdays at Hofstra University's clinic. His mother is a single parent with a secure blue-collar job. Although Troy admits that they don't talk much together, she worries about her son's progress and strains a tight budget to pay for weekly sessions with a psychologist and for the twice-weekly tutoring at Hofstra. Troy's tutor had noted the child's interest in plants, flowers, and vegetables and used the word *radish* in a reading lesson as an example of a word with a short *a* sound. Troy's face was blank. He had never heard of a radish, had no idea of what one looked like, how one grew, what one tasted like. Not bok choy or *hakone,* radishes are relatively unexotic vegetables, and an eleven-year-old should have known about them, if only vaguely, the tutor felt. Hadn't he seen them in a supermarket? Hadn't his mother or older brother ever pointed out the bunches of small red globes with green tops piled high in the produce section?

The next week the tutor brought Troy a radish from her garden, and he tasted it for the first time, savoring the flavor, but gasping at the unexpected bite on his tongue. After a detailed talk about planting, Troy sowed radish seeds in an oversized flower pot, reading with rapt attention the difficult instructions on the packet. At the following session, he wrote (and then read) a paragraph about his experience. When the seedlings broke the soil a month later, Troy was ecstatic.

A teacher in a more affluent middle-class community works with a group of three-year-olds at the Temple Judea Nursery School in Massapequa, New York. On a Tuesday morning in early December each child made a winter scene with glue, construction paper, and Ivory Snow. "What's the white stuff?" one little boy asked. No one could identify the contents of the detergent box. All the children knew that they had washing machines at home, knew their parents used them, but not a one in the class acknowledged standing beside mother or father and talking about the stream of white powder, the instant-frothing of suds, the rattle and hum of the motor. No one had language to identify this decidedly commonplace item and experience. Even if the children had seen washing-machine detergent at work in the past, not one parent had talked to them about it. As a result, a moment fraught with linguistic potential had made little impression on the boys and girls in the class.

On Wednesday the teacher took them on a visit to a local Laundromat and the class talked all about its mysteries, writing a story together the next time they met.

The issue here is not the importance of radishes or soap powder, certainly, but the problems these anecdotes reveal about children in our time and about our roles as parents and teachers in helping them learn about the world. Troy and the nursery school toddlers are part of a growing number of linguistically inpoverished youngsters throughout the country. Modern-day parents may write with their children, may read with their children, may read *to* their children, but outside these highly structured and often anxious learning situations, parents leave children pretty much on their own to confront experience and to develop language that makes meaning from it. This is unfortunate: experience and the spoken words to identify it are much more basic to literacy than formal instruction in reading and writing at home.

The youngsters I have identified lack steady and regular conversation with adults. In the day-to-day moments of a child's life, parents and teachers must be the guiders, the shapers, the language givers. The more language experience a child has before learning to read, the easier for the child to understand the meaning of words when they appear on a printed page.

Conversation, experience-sharing, active interchange of thought and idea: if not through adult guidance, how and where are children to work through their impressions of the world, to experience a rich linguistic environment, to develop the necessary vocabulary and thinking skills of a literate citizenry? Facing simple, everyday events, how many parents seize the opportunities for dialogue that encourages practice with language, that stimulates critical thought, that eases a child's personal fears and problems? In short, how many parents, how many teachers, take time to talk with children? Families do not have discussions together, complains Clarissa F. Dillon, a first-grade teacher in Bryn Mawr, Pennsylvania. As a result, "the children's oral language has declined markedly. . . . Families are smaller and often do not spend a lot of time together. Thus children are not learning from adults. . . ."

Educators note even for the most well-meaning adults a surprising lack of experience in conversation with children. Equally important, we note, too, a lack of awareness about the value of talk in preparing a child to read, to write, and to think.

Our appliances direct language at our children—a modern GE refrigerator salutes the family with a flashing LED HELLO; user-friendly computers engage them in print-based conversation—"Good work, Tommy! Are you ready for the next question?"; but we do very little talking with each other. Numerous interviews convince me that many of today's mothers and fathers know neither how to talk to their children nor how to use conversation as a means for teaching words and helping children to develop concepts. Parents invariably ask, "What can you say to a _____-year-old? What do you talk about?" Few establish conditions for the regular talking through of experience.

The kinds of recent theories I've introduced in this chapter assert quite clearly that *talking* is a key element in a child's social and intellectual growth, as well as in the child's growth to language awareness. My basic premise is that adults must help children use language actively by talking about everything they possibly can—unstructured play, daily events, television programs, dreams, books, radishes, and laundry detergent. By encouraging conversation about the child's view of experience, the parent lays the foundations for literacy. Not only does the child shape and give permanence to experience with language, but through talking the child also *learns* a range of language and syntax that books will help solidify later on in more precise form.

And, as children grow older, not only books but also regular conversations with peers, parents, and other adults serve as a pressure-valve for the pains and anxieties of growing up. "I can't talk to them!"—that frequently heard lament from parents as well as their children, each moaning about the other, is a cry that starts in the conversation vacuums of the modern family's living room. First-grade-teacher Dillon gives grim voice to an unpleasant reality. "For many families today, a good child is a quiet child somewhere else."

As parents, we need to honor the value of home discussions. The gold of family conversation still has to be mined in most of today's households.

WHAT CAN PARENTS DO?
"GIVE THE CHILD HIS CHANCE"

Judith M. Newman, editor of a collection of essays called *Whole Language Theory in Use,* paints a rosy picture of the quality of parent-child interchange, a picture not at all consistent with my observations. She believes that parents regularly and spontaneously invite children to be partners in conversation. She sketches this enchanting family scene: "Parents respond meaningfully to their children's language efforts. They sustain their children's involvement and participation in ongoing conversation. Intuitively aware that children learn to listen and talk by listening and talking, parents track children's meaning, interpreting and filling in as required by the situation."

Many parents, it is true, do achieve some of what Newman asserts *some of the time,* and we can learn considerably from them. Later on I'm going to quote one or two of the parent-child interchanges she and others record, just to give you some models for your own home dialogues. However, the press of complex life in the twentieth century generally has limited our linguistic involvement with children, especially as they grow beyond three and four years old. What we do by instinct at the crib or beside the high chair, many of us abandon as our child gets older. Newman has mistaken worthwhile goals for absolute achievement. The erupting stream of complaints about children's poor communication skills, more and more a volcano as our assessment efforts progress, bury her assertions.

If we're avoiding conversation because we feel that kids really want to discover things by themselves and don't want to hear adults' opinions or that we want to avoid emotionally sensitive topics, we're making a big mistake. Child psychologist Dr. Charles E. Schaefer believes that what a child doesn't know *can* hurt him. If we avoid sensitive topics, we give the signal that we're uncomfortable talking about them and hence we close off lines of communication. As a result, Dr. Schaefer points out, "children become anxious, confused, and ill-prepared to cope with life's stresses and pitfalls."

What can a parent do? If you're ready to help your child advance language skills so that he or she can read and write better, you want to consider some of these simple recommendations for establishing conversational families.

Eleven Cardinal Rules
for Establishing Conversational Families

1. Engage actively in play with children.
2. Ask questions often; invite question asking.
3. Listen thoughtfully to responses; ask more questions.
4. Tell stories; read stories; act out stories; discuss stories.
5. Discuss the day's best and worst moments.
6. In facing decisions with your child, review options; then ask your child why she chose what she did.
7. Whenever possible eat meals together; talk to each other at meals.
8. Shut off the car radio on a family drive.
9. Shut off the television frequently when the whole family is all together.
10. No headphones allowed at home if someone else is present.
11. If it can be avoided, don't talk on the telephone if someone else is present in the room.

Do these seem too obvious? Let me assure you that they are not. Too many homes I've observed structure their household quite opposite to these principles. Especially in regard to telephones, radios and tape recorders, televisions, and other wonders of our modern age. I'm no reactionary—in fact, as you will see in Chapter 8, I recognize the value of today's media in helping children learn and apply language. However, television programs, rock music, and long phone talks have their place, and that place is in a limited part of the day when we're trying to establish tight conversational bonds early in our child's development.

And, as you might have guessed from my suggestions about "hothousing" in the last chapter, I don't think that pushing a young child off to school or some other structured activity beyond the home or the extended family environment is the way to essential bonding. Don't confuse your needs—the need to return to work or to school, the need to be free of care burdens during long stretches in the day, the need to attend to personal goals—with children's needs. A working parent who sends a three- or four-year-old for reading or foreign language or science or karate classes should consider whether the child both wants and needs to learn those skills as much as the parent needs to be free of the child for the length of time he sits in a classroom, gym, or laboratory.

No matter how much formal early schooling we provide for really young kids, we cannot overlook the important role we ourselves play in readying our youngsters for school's demands. As Valerie H. Singer writes to *The New York Times* from Rocky Hill, New Jersey, sending a child off for formal schooling at a tender age "assumes there are no ill effects for parent or child in daily, lengthy separation at such an early age." Mrs. Singer complains bitterly that "when teachers desire 'readiness' to be instilled in 3-year-olds, what they really are looking for is passivity and suppression of initiative and spontaneity. Both reasons ignore and even mock the vital needs of the developing child."

What can a parent do? I know that the pace of life in our towns and cities, the pressing financial burdens on many families, the need for personal fulfillment all impel parents to selfless careers, to advanced schooling, to community service. All these demands on the family insist that child care and diversions beyond the immediate household are essential and unavoidable.

But we must address the really important questions here. Must we use the formal teaching-learning setting as much as we are using it for our children? How can busy parents provide home settings that prepare a child for important learning experiences awaiting them in school—yet how can we achieve this without pushing our children into tense, highly structured preschool environments? How do we on our own stimulate children to learn language?

The remaining chapters in this book will give you suggestions for launching your own home programs to encourage active, spontaneous conversation with children. Bear in mind what Professor Roger Brown, specialist in child language development, writes: "Believe that your child can understand more than he or she can say"—it is Michael Polanyi's idea again. Brown continues, making a point that is absolutely essential to the purpose of this book: "Seek, above all, to communicate. To understand and to be understood. To keep your minds fixed on the same target. . . . If you concentrate on communicating, everything else will follow." To this excellent advice, Jerome Bruner adds: "The best practice for mastering dialogue is to enter into it. Give the child his chance."

3

Chatting at Cribside and Other Tales in the Nursery

Conversation is language's two-way street. In this chapter I want to consider both drivers easing down the road, parent and child. We want to look at the ways of moving toward dialogue, the essential skill in learning how to use words and sentences as information givers. Of course, the little conversations you hold with your infant and toddler are not dialogue in any exact sense. However, the way you talk with your baby can help establish patterns that advance learning of vocabulary, language rules, and dialogue. Also, you need to pay attention to the ways that your child uses—in fact the ways we all use— language, so that you can bring your youngster closer to being a communicative partner.

Professor Jean Berko Gleason of the Department of Psychology at Boston University says that learning language demands interaction. A normal child ready to learn is simply not enough; he also needs "an older person who engages in communicative interchanges with him, and some objects out there in the world as well." We're going to examine how best to involve the very young child and the world in those interchanges of communication.

BABY TALK: PARENT TO CHILD

Mothers, did you realize that researchers throughout the world have scrutinized, dissected, analyzed, labeled, graphed, and tabulated the talk you use with your children? The results of these studies help us to identify characteristics of successful talk with infants and to understand the reasons for our using baby talk and for sustaining it as long as we and the child choose. Advice given in influential books like *The Parenting Advisor,* edited by Frank Kaplan and bearing the approval of the Princeton Center for Infancy, only can hoist your anxiety level and snatch joy from parent-child relations: "Do not use baby talk," Kaplan says. "Inasmuch as babyish first words are so appealing, you will be tempted to repeat them to your child. Don't! It definitely will not help your baby learn to talk. She thinks she is imitating the way you talk."

In all fairness, I don't think the Princeton folks are talking about those special qualities of early parent-child communication that I'll explain in greater detail below—specially modulated voices, simple sentences, repetitions, expansions, and so on. I think they're talking more about the funny little words we make up with our child's complicity to replace standard vocabulary: *choo-choo* for "train," *boo-boo* for hurt or injury, *wee-wee* or *ka-ka* for excretory functions. Still, no such words or exaggerated syntax that you might use with them—"Baby see choo-choo?"; "Jimmy want play ball-lee?"—will impede your child's learning to talk. All kids give up baby talk before long. I've never heard an eight-year-old talk about making a *wee-wee,* except as a big joke or in conversation with an infant.

So I'm going to suggest that you not take a word of this advice from the Princeton Center. Besides the pleasure baby talk gives parent and child, it plays a very important function in bridging the dialogue gap from infant talk to more adult talk. The point that Kaplan and his staff are missing is that we really don't use baby talk to teach children language, although we may think that's what we're doing. Yes, we probably are trying to teach when we say words again and again in such statements as "Top. Top. See top?" or when we use very simple sentences to communicate with speech-ready children. Still, more practical ways surely exist for teaching how to communicate for the adult world than by giving children unadvanced verbal and syntactical forms. Just on the basis of simple logic, then, you must acknowledge that baby talk is not primarily and exclusively directed at teaching babies how to talk. You saw in the last chapter that children have the innate tendency to learn language on their own. Lucky for them: If they had to count on baby talk to learn how to speak, they'd be in trouble!

If baby talk that adults use on children is not essentially a language-teaching tool, what is it then?

Baby talk is a social tool that we use to improve communication and understanding between talking partners. Parents use baby talk, Harvard psychologist Roger Brown points out with particular insight, in order "to keep two minds focused on the same topic." In this important level of communication the parent attempts to plug into the child's mental and linguistic abilities.

In baby talk, Mother's (and Father's) speech is guided by how the child performs. Mother adjusts her talk as the child shows a need for the adjustment. A mother in one of the studies puts it very well as she explains communicating with her son:

> There are plenty of times I don't stop to think that he's two, and I'll just mumble something at him and don't really think about whether or not he can understand it. And that's when he's most likely not to respond at all.

I believe this shows the mother's awareness that she needs special kinds of language to speak with her youngster, given her particular goals in communicating. Parents who use baby talk appropriately want only to assure communication. They watch the child thoughtfully for signs of confusion or lack of responsiveness and seize the moment should such signs appear, adjusting the level of input.

Observations of mothers and children together show, for example, that a child holding a ball and grunting would elicit a repeated one-word label from mother, "Ball. Ball." This is an

example of a type of baby talk, a one-word utterance designed
to connect an object with its name. But if the child showed
attention to the object by then grabbing it or reaching for it—
or even by repeating the word *ball*—the mother would probably
expand the word to a whole sentence like, "See the ball?" or
"That's a ball." Neither of those sentences qualifies as baby
talk.

How did the mother know to switch? When she realized that
the child understood, she moved the level of conversation up
a rung. "And that," says Professor Brown, "is always the case.
Parents seek to communicate, I am sure, but they are not content to communicate always the same set of messages." Here
is the essential point about talking with very young children,
and I'm going to let Professor Brown make it: "A study of
detailed mother-child interaction shows that successful communication on one level is always the launching platform for
attempts at communication on a more adult level."

A good image, that, a launching platform. When you talk
baby talk, you're attempting to assure that you both understand
each other so that you can then travel upward into another
sphere of communication. One interesting report on this subject, by a researcher at the University of Connecticut, claims
that first among the early talking skills children master when
they start using language themselves are those we observe in
the baby talk used by their parents.

Below is a list of noticeable elements of baby talk that parents
can use with their children. I include them here not because
you don't know them—you must be practicing so many of these
techniques already simply on your good instincts as a parent.
Peter A. and Jill G. de Villiers are right to highlight the ab-
surdity of "scholars teaching parents how to teach children to
talk—the fact is that parents don't need it and children don't
need it either." I do want to confirm some of those practices,
however, just in case you doubt them and need some support.
Also, I thought you might be interested in some of the effects
of parents' practices on the communication process. Many
of them rear up again in the child's own speech productions
later on.

Baby Talk, Parent to Child: What to Aim For

1. *A higher than usual pitch.* Very young infants can tell the differences among and do respond to varied frequency ranges. We note increased heartbeats, fluttering eyelids, closing eyes, and turning heads. In experiments we can determine the range that yields the most positive responses to pitch tones. The most successful baby talk operates in that range of tones. When we talk to other adults, we use pitch in a much lower range, a range infants would not hear. What's especially interesting is that their own vocal noises adjust when we stimulate children with sounds at different pitches. Our use of higher-pitched voices is probably to get and hold the child's attention. In this way we model the social features of communication. To talk with people you have to listen and pay attention.

2. *Patterns of rhythm.* You want to be sure to use songs, rhymes, and language play among your strategies for making communicative contact with babies. Studies show that even newborn infants move their bodies simultaneously with rhythmical adult voices. There's an enormously soothing quality to sound patterns and to songs, and their use in the nursery enhances interaction in any language. Just listen to children at ease in the playground and you'll hear how much they obviously have drawn upon language songs, rhythms, and games for their own speech production.

3. *Simplicity and repetition.* The structure of sentences used to speak with children should reflect our sense of the child's readiness to use language. For example, with a seven- or eight-month-old we can use complex speech because the child at that age is not yet poised for learning. Talk to children in the eighteen- to twenty-eight-month-old range, on the other hand, should be much simpler. Thus, you want to use brief, simple sentences for your child when he or she shows signs of language readiness. The use of one-word tags as object identifiers is essential in giving the child words that help her identify categories of objects in her surroundings and that relate those objects to her experiences.

Your hints about when to draw upon simplicity and repetition should come from the child's own word play, her attention to your efforts at labeling, her requests for names of familiar objects with body language or grunts and other noises, and her efforts to say words.

4. *Direct verbal stimulation.* By "direct" I mean words and sounds targeted at the child specifically. We know that, in itself, the quantity of talk surrounding the child has little noticeable effect on him. But the quantity of direct mother-child exchange has an extraordinary effect.

A dramatic experiment in 1973 with children from nine to eighteen months old showed that when the mother provided direct verbal stimulation, linguists could actually measure improved language competence. (If you're interested, research jargon would put it this way: Direct verbal stimulation from the mother correlated highly with a child's measurable language skills.) The amount of Mother's speech not targeted directly at the youngster did *not* correlate with language development.

What does all this mean? Simply using language in the child's presence earns no points in linguistic advancement. But talk directly with your child and he becomes a more competent user of language. What other evidence do you need for the importance of talking with young kids!

Also, we know that with four-month-olds, the behavior that, more than any other, most followed a mother's vocal sounds after ten seconds was a sound made by the infant, followed by a smile. So, sounds directed at your really young child can stimulate not only replication, but also that glorious gift to Mother and Father, the simple turning upward of an infant's lips.

5. *Whispering.* Like high-pitched vocal sounds, whispering serves a social function in that it attempts to draw and hold the young child's attention. By whispering we expand the range of possibilities for human speech and model it for the child.

6. *Patterns of intonation.* When you make your voice rise and fall in definite patterns, you direct communication specifically at the child. Normally we do not use a rising intonation in speech with adults except when we ask questions. With children in the two-year-old range, on the other hand, simple statements

as well as mild commands often end with a rising voice. Some experts believe that these special intonations serve as cues to the child for when he should respond. He can tell by your use of intonation exactly which words and sentences are intended for his ears. Other researchers believe that a child learns intonation patterns of the language before he learns anything else about language. Listen to an infant's babbling from far off and you'll be amazed at how much like natural speech it sounds, even though you can't distinguish any real words.

Following these tips about talking with infants, you can pretty much guarantee communication. You'll be able to hold your infant's attention. He will grow quiet and will invariably turn his face toward you. You'll be able to establish eye contact. All these are critical features of conversation that adults practice throughout their lives, and early interchanges with infants help to establish patterns for later use.

THE PURPOSES OF CHILDREN'S LANGUAGE

British linguist Michael Halliday discovered in his son Nigel's early speech development that the child's sounds, noises, and expressions in the earliest phase of development owed nothing to adult language. Of what importance then is it for us to talk with children in their early years?

Adults influence the child's language right from the start because the adult translates the child's coos and grunts and other noises in terms of the adult's own language system. Do you realize that what the infant really means is never actually known in fact? The message received is the message *as it's interpreted by the parent,* a message that can be produced in adult language. And therein lie the essential roles of Mother and Father: translators, interpreters, message straighteners.

All speech, children's or adults', has a number of functions— that is, ends or purposes that we're trying to achieve when we're talking. Halliday has explained them imaginatively, roughly in their order of complexity, and I have adapted them to pass on to you. Knowing these will help you make sense of your child's expressions as he grows to language.

The Ends of Language Use by Young Children

1. *The "I want that object" end.* Here the child wants something, but he doesn't care who supplies it.

2. *The "Do what I'm telling you to do" end.* Here, the child directs language at a particular person to influence that person. It's behavior domination at an early age! Kids watch us use language to control them, and they learn the trick real fast. (It's one they don't ever forget, unfortunately. Wait until they become teenagers and you'll see what I mean!) For the "Do what I'm telling you to do" end you typically can identify two kinds of communications. Your child will suggest his own specific demands, like "Let's play," "Let's go upstairs," or the like, as well as more general ones, such as "Keep doing that" or "Do that another time."

3. *The "We're in this together" end.* Working toward this end, the child intends interaction with the people and objects around him. He can communicate greetings; he can communicate knowledge of people's names, Mommy and Daddy especially; he can communicate responses to calls like "Yes?"

4. *The "This is me" end.* With this function of language your child reflects personality development. He demonstrates his own specialness, showing preferences, interest or lack of it, emotional responses, and so on. What emerges here is a differentiation between your child and his or her surroundings.

5. *The "I want to know why" end.* Using language for this purpose, your child is trying to learn about the world around her. At its most basic level, this end reflects her insistence on names for objects. Names are essential in the child's developmental scheme; with them she can classify objects in the environment, a vital thinking skill. You can see here the blueprint for all the later questions in the child's repertoire.

6. *The "Let's make believe" end.* Here we note language to reflect worlds designed by the child's own mind. Thus, communication in this function reflects imaginative stories and tales,

pretending, and make-believe. As this end advances, your child assumes different personalities and creates unique environments for play.

7. *The "I've got some news for you" end.* Here is language in its most sophisticated use. Don't expect to see it until well after you see the other linguistic ends reflected in your child's communication growth. Children are simply unable to develop the advanced notion that words and sentences can give information to those who don't have it but might want it. Yet this function is what adults usually have in mind when they consider what language is and does: Language gives information. The schools, too, see this as the most essential goal of communication.

You can see the problems here. A child, especially in a formal preschool setting, may be unable to use language in this way, though it may be demanded of him. It's also a problem in that children, lacking the skill at using words informatively, have a completely different view of language from adults. "This in fact," Halliday points out, "is one of the reasons why the adult finds it so difficult to interpret the image of language that a very young child has internalized."

Let's again consider some by now familiar cautions. Remember, we're talking about communication, so you can expect lots of body language and noises well before words and sentences. Your child will not move through an awareness and application of these language functions in any regular, predictable way. Some utterances, reflecting a particular end, will appear before others; some will recede before they swell, only to return on another day's tide. For some children the ends will flow in an order different from the one I presented. You should never expect a linear movement when it comes to child development. Each child is so special, so different, that genetic makeup and environmental stimulus working together give no assurances of clear-cut patterns. Besides, those functions I've listed are hypothetical and are still awaiting more comprehensive observation and assessment.

That said, I think that these postulated language ends for children really can help you understand and respond to your youngster's communication signals, whether they are verbal or not. Aware of the possibilities, you can focus your attention carefully on what your child is trying to mean.

For instance, pointing to or grunting at an object may mean more than just an effort to possess it. Your daughter may be signaling the "Do what I tell you to do" function. "Play with me!" her actions and sounds may be commanding, though you might not have considered that possibility. So, if you deliver the ball to the playpen, thinking you've met your child's needs, and she shows unhappiness still, you might have to go a step further.

Additionally, no matter how frustrating it is to an adult when a child loses interest in a toy or game, or when she shows utter displeasure at something you believe is pleasurable, stop for a moment before you throw up your hands or react with annoyance or anger. Your child is using communication in these cases to define the limits of her personality, and she needs room to honor that need. Don't turn linguistic muscle-flexing into an unnecessary skirmish of temperament. Maybe later on she'll take up that expensive new doll that she refused with disgust or she'll wave good-bye or say her new word for grandma, though she utterly rejected those acts before. Seemingly contrary actions are not necessarily a reflection on you nor are they deliberate efforts to embarrass you or get your goat. See them instead as a personal use of language and communication to assert the self.

Children know their own linguistic capabilities, but sometimes we fail children because we don't know how to interpret their functions of language. For example, consider that a child using communication to pretend may have no intention of communicating realistically. This does not signify any necessary lack of connection to reality. When my daughter Melissa was a preschooler, one of her friends had a delightful imagination, always constructing scenes and events that my wife and I acknowledged as flights into fantasy. The child's parents, however, never saw them in that spirit. When we would repeat a particularly lovely bit of her conversation about imagined people, places, and events, her mother's response invariably was: "Jennifer lies."

What I'm saying is that you can learn to tune in better to your child's communication signals if you keep in mind the various language ends that she stores in her linguistic and psychological play chest.

"THE LANGUAGE SPONGE"

I spoke with Dr. Richard Culatta, director of the well-known Speech and Communication Disorder Program at the University of Kentucky in Lexington. Watching what goes wrong in the communication processes of young children gives him extraordinary insights into what it takes to raise kids who can communicate normally. "The child is like a language sponge," he says. "Even though this sponge has incredible linguistic potential, we don't build skills by trying to squeeze things out. We build skills by getting things to soak in."

To Dr. Culatta, the parent's main job is as a data base. Parents have to pump up their children's language systems by supplying words for the multitude of experiences in a child's life.

Where do you begin? Simple, says Dr. Culatta. "Start with self-talk and parallel talk."

They're good suggestions.

1. *Self-talk.* Self-talk is your ongoing stream of language to describe for a child what you're doing as you perform some action—at home, on the street, in the supermarket:

> "See what Mommy's doing? Mommy's standing at the pot of water. Here's the pot on the stove. See it? Mommy's putting in the beans. String beans. See the string beans? Billy likes string beans, doesn't he? Come watch the water bubbling. See the water? Very hot! Water is very hot! Now, Billy make string beans. Use your toy pot. Show me your pot. Good. That's Billy's pot! Yes. Billy's pot."

2. *Parallel talk.* With parallel talk, you describe for the child what's she's doing, not what you're doing:

> "You're playing with Papa's hat, aren't you? That's Grandpa's old felt hat. It has a big brim and a little red feather. You're

putting Grandpa's hat on your head. Where's Janie? There she is! I see you! That hat's too big on you, isn't it? It's a big hat! Now you're putting it on your dolly. Doesn't dolly look silly with that big hat? What a silly looking dolly! Why don't you put Janie's wool hat on dolly's head?"

Let's use the first conversational stream—the "self-talk" model—as our example for discussion. More than just string beans are cooking here. The mother's steady output of words provides invaluable data for the child.

First, it supplies language, even though the child may not understand it all. Notice the embedded object identifications: in very few words the mother has identified three items—pot, beans, and water. Her simple sentences and expansions, along with her special intonations, announce to the child that this is communication directed exclusively at him.

Second, and perhaps this one is less obvious but certainly no less important, Mother, in using "self-talk," clearly connects words and sentences with the child's environment and experiences. She identifies string beans in the child's own world of tastes and pleasures. She calls attention to the water's motion in the pot. She provides a caution about boiling water. She sets the child to duplicating action with his own toys, thereby striving for integration between words and activity. Making those connections between experience and vocabulary is, again, a critical role for the parent, one I will return to frequently in trying to get you to build conversation into your family life.

In both self-talk and parallel talk, all the questions mother asks indicate that although she's doing all the talking, she's engaging in conversation. "See it? . . . See the string beans? . . . See the water?": These are all invitations to responses through body language, grunting, head shaking, or words. Billy doesn't talk, but he's surely participating in the dialogue. Mother provides opportunities for him to respond in any way he chooses. She's talking *with* her son, not at him.

Every day, your youngster is bombarded with sensory experiences. How does she make sense of it all? In part, her own genetic, physical, and mental equipment will help determine the impact of the surrounding world on her personal being. And, linguistically, she has a built-in filtering system. Psychologist Elissa Newport at the University of California, San Diego, and her colleagues, insist that "the child has means for restricting, as well as organizing, the flow of incoming linguistic data." The child "filters out some kinds of input and selectively listens for others."

Still, without an adult to focus attention on the varieties of experience, your child can miss many opportunities for learning and language development. Innumerable moments can slip by— a shivering sparrow in the rain, a white gull swooping down on the water, a fire truck screaming down the street, beans bubbling in a pot—unless the parent focuses them, pulls them into the language and experience spotlight. Even in the poorest homes, where parents cannot afford to expand the quantity and quality of experiences for a child, mothers and fathers can still draw attention to mundane events and can raise them to glory.

That's what was missing in the lives of the children I described in the last chapter—Troy, the youngster who didn't know what a radish was, and the nursery school toddlers who were thoroughly mystified by laundry detergent and washing machines. Those children needed an adult to help them focus on and explore segments of daily experience.

What every parent must develop is, simply, an eye to the world. For some, such an eye is a special gift. Some parents— my wife is one of them—know how to see bits of gold and silver everywhere in the child's immediate landscape. Every experience is glittering with linguistic potential, is rich in possibilities for conversation and teaching. Other parents must train themselves to keep that eye open amid the various distractions of our complex lives. But this is nothing that cannot be learned.

The parent who wants to help her child develop language skills must regularly ask herself important questions. Which experiences can I move to center stage in my child's life today? Which events, even the patently ordinary, can I invigorate with language and attitude to open a curtain on a new vision for my child? Enthusiasm, attention, interest: these will transform a seemingly ordinary moment into an extraordinary one.

In later chapters I'll look at some of your daily experiences in more detail to try to help you see them as appropriate conversation pieces. But what I'm trying to say here is that you must be open to everyday events that invite language; and that you can use language to help your child make sense of those events and to see them shine. It's a double-headed coin.

Dr. Culatta provides some useful guidelines for building language skills in young children:

1. *Try to get across a concept.* Help your youngster appreciate words and ideas rather than simply lexical definitions. Notice how the mother I've cited above to demonstrate parallel talk deals with two concepts at once, the idea of hats going on heads and the idea of small versus large.

2. *Name and describe attributes.* Note how Janie's mother draws upon features of the hat to build a concept of meaning. A hat may have a brim. A hat may have a feather. A hat may be made of wool.

3. *Identify differences.* This is one of the key elements in critical thinking, an ability to see how related things are different. Differences are fairly explicit in the mother's conversation about hats with her little girl. One hat is big, the other small; one hat is felt, the other wool; one hat is Grandpa's, the other Janie's.

4. *Generalize.* Here is another major dimension of critical thought. You have to extend meanings beyond specific examples at hand. You have to apply information in a broad sense, almost as if you're developing a principle or rule based on instances that you've noted. In the parallel talk about hats we see the mother prodding her child to see that hats go on heads and that, based on size, some fit and some don't. With her conversation, the mother moves the child to such an awareness. Researchers might argue about whether the child has the concept before she has the language; however, without the language, the concept remains chaotic.

BUILDING THE SCAFFOLD

As your child grows and uses language in more advanced stages, you need some strategies for helping your sons and daughters practice saying what they mean. Look at this wonderful interchange recorded by Halliday between his son Nigel, at twenty months old, and the child's parents. Earlier in the day, Nigel visited a zoo, where he had watched a goat who tried to eat a plastic lid Nigel was holding. The keeper explained that the goat should not eat the lid because it was not good for it.

    Nigel: try eat lid
    Father: What tried to eat the lid?
    Nigel: try eat lid
    Father: What tried to eat the lid?
    Nigel: goat . . . man said no . . . goat try eat lid . . . man said no

Then, after a further interval, while being put to bed:

    Nigel: goat try eat lid . . . man said no
    Mother: Why did the man say no?
    Nigel: goat shouldn't eat lid . . . [*shaking head*] goodfor it
    Mother: The goat shouldn't eat the lid; it's not good for it.
    Nigel: goat try eat lid . . . man said no . . . goat shouldn't eat lid . . . [*shaking head*] good for it

You can see how skillfully Nigel's parents stimulated the toddler to expand his utterances. Jerome Bruner calls the technique *scaffolding*. It's a wonderful word, really. You've seen scaffolds, haven't you, those temporary structures used for holding workmen and materials during the erection, repair, or decoration of buildings? The scaffolding used with Nigel is also for building—language building, of course. It too is temporary; it provides the props for word and concept growth as the parent helps construct a larger edifice of meaning from the child's experience and language awareness.

You should notice in this exchange between Nigel and his mother and father that the parents' efforts concentrate on drawing language out as well as to providing feedback for Nigel's observations. The feedback pours water back into the language sponge. Nigel's parents let him know whether or not they understand him. They get him to repeat in order to clarify his notions. They expand his incomplete statements once they recognize what he means. Through conversation—and scaffolding is just a form of structured conversation—Nigel's parents demonstrate language and thought in joint action.

As you see, one of the key elements in scaffolding is asking questions. Of the four remarks made by the Hallidays, three are questions, questions that compel the child to delve into his recollections and to draw upon his own language. Yet the questions are based upon the child's language, too: they use pretty much the words that the child has started with. The father's questions are purely informational: he's trying to get the facts straight. The mother's question taps deeper critical skills. Can the child explain why the man said no? This demands more than simple recall. Nigel is being asked to demonstrate whether or not he has understood and assimilated information.

Scaffolding is a skill you can learn with practice, a very useful strategy for early conversations with your youngsters about events in their day. Let's see if we can generalize about this technique so that you can apply it easily to everyday situations in your child's life.

A Parent's Guide to Scaffolding with Young Children

1. *Ask questions.* Construct questions to help give language to the experiences your child has. I'll talk about the demands made by different kinds of questions later on, but here you should be aware that your questions can request more information, repetition, clarification, critical thought, or expansion. They might even signal contraction. If you say, for example, "Now you cook some string beans in your little red pot. Do you understand?" your child might very well contract the whole statement. He might say only, "Beans in pot." That will show

quite clearly that he understands you even though he did not duplicate your remarks exactly.

2. *Repeat questions.* If the response to your initial question does not shed light on your inquiry, after an appropriate interval ask the same question again. However, avoid rephrasing the question entirely. In rephrasing, we sometimes change around the whole question, and a child thinking about a response to the first now has to switch gears to think about a second.

3. *Observe and draw upon nonverbal communications to help make meaning.* Use your child's gestures, body language, vocal sounds, and noises as aids to determine what he or she is trying to say and what further information you might want to draw out. As I've mentioned before, Nigel's head-shaking is an important clue for his parents. He does not, or cannot, say the words *It's not.* Instead he shakes his head from side to side to indicate the negative dimension he's after. Nigel's mother uses his body language as a signal to supply meaning with words. "*It's not* good for it," she says.

4. *Interpret your child's intentions and communicate with meaning in return.* One important purpose of scaffolding is to help your child see what he is communicating. Asking questions, requesting repetitions, repeating phrases yourself are all means to that end. What you say to your child as you're scaffolding should build upon the communicative context he has established. You've got to work at understanding what your child is saying; and you have to contribute meaningful responses to keep the conversation on track. There's no place here for a series of distracted responses like "Uh-huh"!

Much of your response in this area will be in expanding into full sentences a few words your child may have strung together. Thus, Nigel's mother says, "The goat shouldn't eat the lid; it's not good for it" when Nigel says "goat shouldn't eat lid . . . good for it." Your child might say, "Birdie fly"; you would probably expand it: "Yes, the birdie is flying away to her nest." Researchers are not sure about the exact results of expansions. Do they expand grammatical knowledge by modeling correct sentence form? Do they advance a child's knowledge and use of details in conversation?

One interesting study showed that children made large language gains when adults did not directly expand sentences but instead offered a further comment about the situation. Thus, a child who said "Birdie fly" might hear, "Yes, the birdie is cold and wants to go home." Early-language specialists Peter A. and Jill G. de Villiers believe that "the richness and variety of the language input to the child may be more important than frequent expansions."

5. *Do not correct errors.* At this phase of language development it makes no sense to correct your child's errors. Nigel's father restates the verb in the right tense and supplies a subject to the child's utterance "try eat lid." Father's sentence is, "What tried to eat the lid?" Our sense, though, is that when Halliday asks this question, he is more concerned with articulating a question to get more information than he is in providing correct grammar. (See Chapter 6 for more about error.)

Here's another instance of scaffolding, this one reported by Judith M. Newman. Note here how the parent plays an even more active role as conversational partner than Nigel's parents did. In this example, two-and-a-half-year-old Christopher plays with some puzzles on the kitchen floor as Mother washes the evening's dishes:

Mother: You practice over there. (1)
Christopher: You practice right here. (2)
Mother: All right. Well, I have to finish clearing up the supper right now. So practice by yourself. (3)
Christopher: Practice myself? (4)
Mother: Mmmmm . . . (5)
Christopher: Look, the basket, the basket is, the basket is broke these things. Me want help. You want help. I give you help. You want . . . (6)
Mother: I don't need any help. (7)
Christopher: Well, I better . . . (8)
Mother: Looks to me like you're the one who needs the help, not me. (9)
Christopher: [*grunt*] (10)

Mother: Do you need help? (11)
Christopher: YES! I DO HELP! (12)
Mother: What do you need help doing? (13)
Christopher: These, these, these won't let me pick them up. (14)
Mother: I'll let you pick them up. (15)
Christopher: No. Oh, don't know. Got pick one. No! (16)
Mother: If you're finished with them you can pick them up, but if you want to play with them, don't. (17)
Christopher: DON'T! [*pause*] Don't dare let you any. Oh forget the block. Got all my . . . and yours. Them, they're mine. That way that one. (18)
Mother: That one's kind of hard. Are you going to use that puzzle or another one? (19)
Christopher: Unh. Unh. Watch me. Both one. Think . . . Want any help? Don't want any help. It's to me puzzle. Got one puzzle, got two puzzle. (20)

It's easy to see the invaluable role that mother plays here in establishing conversation with the child. Scaffolding tracks the child's exchanges and keeps the communication moving in the right direction, given both the child's and the mother's goals.

Notice first how Christopher must reconstruct the terms of meaning for the situation once Mother rejects his initial request that she practice beside him. His question "Practice by myself?" shows that he has understood this piece of the conversation; Mother confirms it with her vocalization, "Mmmmm . . ." This simple interaction establishes essential conditions: both partners understand each other.

Next, notice how Mother builds upon Christopher's language clues. In 6, the child obviously is repeating a snatch of dialogue that he heard earlier, "You want help, I give you help." His offer of help to Mother may simply be an effort to get help for himself, yet his language does not say that directly. At first he says, "Me want help"; then he seems to move off the track somewhat as he volunteers to be Mother's assistant. What is so important here is that Christopher's mother takes his offer seriously to show that she understands what the child is volunteering. "I don't need any help" confirms that she understands what her son is saying. That feedback is a very important check on the child's efforts to make meaning.

Christopher's sense acknowledged, his mother returns to his earlier clue about needing help and makes the observation you see in 9. The child's grunt indicates his response clearly. "Yes," that grunt is saying, "you're right. I need help." But his mother wants him to translate that request into language. Therefore, she asks the question in 11. It achieves its desired end: Christopher speaks his need. "Yes! I do help!" he shouts.

Undoubtedly, the child's mother knows what he needs help with—the situation is so clear—but she goes further, asking the child to tap more of his own linguistic resources. The question in 13 gets the child to connect language with personal need and insists on expansion of ideas. As the conversation continues, note how Christopher's mother continues to interpret meaning, to comment on the child's observations, to draw out further responses to questions. Notice, too, how the child selects words and phrases from Mother's utterances to help him construct his own statements. Mother has built the scaffold, and the child climbs up at his own pace and according to his needs.

QUESTIONS, QUESTIONS, ALL AROUND

We're going to return to scaffolding and questioning in a bit, so that you can follow some guided practice. Earlier, you may remember, I highlighted the importance of questions in the process of scaffolding, and now I want to take some time to examine the demands questions make simply by the words we use to phrase them. As your child grows older, you'll expand your use of questions to stimulate thought and to gain information. Very young children, obviously, will not respond to many questions because of their complexity. Still, I think it best to look at questioning formats so that you have them all in one place and so that you can refer to them more easily as your little one matures.

Educators often classify questions as either *open* or *closed*. Open questions are broad, allowing a wide range of answers. "What did you do at the park today?" or "Why do you want to go for a walk?" are open because the child herself defines the terms of her responses. Nigel's mother used an open question when she asked, "Why did the man say no?" Given the events, the child could have answered correctly that the goat was bad or that the man was mean or that the man yelled at Nigel or that Nigel was careless. The point is that open questions allow for many possibilities. If you don't have a very exact response in mind, use open questions.

Closed questions narrow your child's range of answers because they demand a precise focus. Closed questions generally limit responses in their request for exact information. When Nigel's father asks, "What tried to eat the lid?" or when Christopher's mother asks, "Do you need help?" they are using closed questions. For exact, this-is-the-answer responses, use closed questions.

Neither an open nor a closed question is intrinsically better than the other. Each serves its purpose. In structuring questions, whether open or closed, you should be aware of the meaning of words most often used to frame them—*who, which, when, where, how, why,* and *what.*

Question Words: A Checklist of Meanings

Who asks	"What person do you mean?"
Which asks	"What one of many people or things?"
When asks	"At what time?"
Where asks	"In what place?"
How asks	"In what way did this happen? By what cause or process?"

Why asks . . . .   "For what cause, reason, or
                           purpose?"
What asks . . . . "Will you specify the name or
                           character or value of the ob-
                           ject? Will you repeat or ex-
                           plain what you said?"

As I said, although your young child undoubtedly will not
understand all the nuances of these question words, adults who
use them have certain expectations from responses the words
stimulate. As a child matures, we expect him to understand
what the questions seek.

Each question makes a particular demand. For the most part,
who, *which*, *when*, and *where* usually make clear-cut requests.
With *who* or *which* you expect a name; with *when*, some indi-
cation of time; with *where*, a location.

Why, *how*, and (sometimes) *what* are not quite so direct in
their requirements. If you expect a very particular response or
line of reasoning, the word *why*, for example, is a miscue for
your child, simply because it's impossible for him to know
exactly what you have in mind. Nigel's mother probably would
have accepted any one of the possible responses (there are
others certainly) that I suggested above to the question, "Why
did the man say no?" Hence, in that situation *why* was a bona
fide information probe. "Tell me," the word says, "from your
range of experience and opinions, just what you think is the
cause of this situation."

The *why*, *what*, and *how* questions are most useful in stimulating critical thinking because they allow a child to consider
options and to make choices based on individual judgment. A
why question is often a good question because it acknowledges
that numerous possibilities exist for valid responses. *Why* often
says, "There's no right answer to this. Say what you think, and
maybe together we can reach some agreement on what seems
right to us."

Although children learn the *wh-* questions (*who*, *what*, *where*,
when, *why*, and *which*) and the *how* question as early as their
third year, many of these questions persist as conundrums in

early language use. This is especially true of *why*. *Why* demands information about causes, purpose, and manner, difficult concepts for preschoolers. You can see, then, why children often answer *why* questions inaccurately ("Why are you touching that?" "It's a toy.") or why they propose so many unanswerable *why* questions themselves ("Oh, there goes the delivery truck." "Why the delivery truck?"). Young children often do not understand how to use *why* questions.

All the more reason for you to try to answer them (no matter how off the wall they seem) and also to ask them regularly. Only through conversational experience can children learn appropriate uses of the more complex question words. As linguists Peter A. and Jill G. de Villiers point out, children do not instinctively know when to ask a *why* question or how to provide a valid answer to such a question. "A child," they say, "must be witness to a large number of conversations that include *why* questions and answers" in order to understand the demands of *why*, for example.

Once again, you have your work cut out for you! Who better than a parent can offer children the language experience they need with question words? Later, when we look at asking questions about stories you read with your child, you'll see how penetrating questions can work in specific contexts. For now, you want to see that questions like "Why did the spider frighten Miss Muffett away?" or "What do you think we should tell Daddy about our afternoon in the park?" or "How are you going to make your pretend cookies?" invite the participation of a mind stimulated by challenge. Note how much more probing are such questions than questions like "Do you like Miss Muffett?" or "Did you like your afternoon in the park?" or "Do you have fun making cookies?" The first three demand a sustained response that the child must mold from his unique linguistic clay. The second three require only yes or no responses, often slamming a door on conversation. I'll caution you throughout to avoid seeking yes-no responses. They don't animate thought and, because they demand limited, one-word responses, they don't strengthen language.

Despite the value of the question words *why* and *how,* unfortunately, some parents tend to misuse them. Whether we are aware of it or not, the words don't always ask for information. They often make accusations and, as such, are really unanswerable. What information can we expect in return when we ask, "Why did you break your toy?" or "How did you make such a mess?" In fact, those questions impute a child for some unsatisfactory behavior, which she almost certainly cannot explain. A child who really tries to provide a response, especially an older child, invariably is seen as a smart aleck no matter what she says.

In such situations *why* and *how* are guaranteed to engender conflict. It's best when you're annoyed with what your son or daughter has done to do what Chaim Ginott, the brilliant child psychologist, recommends. Describe behavior. Don't judge it. "You've broken your toy. You won't be able to play with it any more," or "You've made a terrible mess, and I don't like it one bit!" are much more direct and appropriate utterances. The question words just don't get you to the same place.

It's obvious that we use questions for more than just requesting information. Something inheres in the nature of question-asking that allows us to circle an issue that, if stated directly, would be too difficult, unpleasant, strange, uncomfortable, or just too downright direct. The social conditions of language exchange often motivate the use of questions to achieve other ends.

Until this point, we've considered only questions asked by parents. Being a good conversational partner means paying careful attention to the questions your kids ask too. As they grow and quickly learn the extraordinary possibilities in language, their repertoire of question-asking skills expands like a flight balloon. One of the best and most whimsically presented categories of a child's galaxy of questions appears in Lisa Lyons Durkin's useful and delightful book, *Parents and Kids Together*. Consider these categories as you consider your child's questions:

How do you answer a child's questions? Honestly. Sincerely. Thoughtfully. And there's nothing wrong with saying you don't know an answer when you don't.

If your child asks you why the sky is blue, don't get flustered

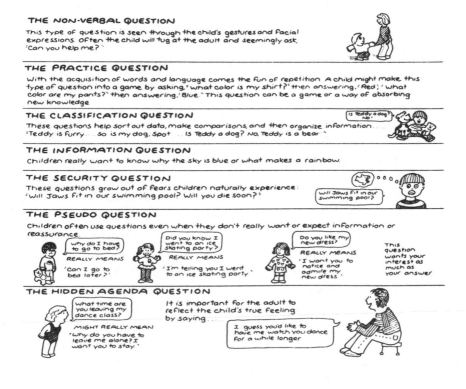

THE NON-VERBAL QUESTION

This type of question is seen through the child's gestures and facial expressions. Often the child will tug at the adult and seemingly ask, "Can you help me?"

THE PRACTICE QUESTION

With the acquisition of words and language comes the fun of repetition. A child might make this type of question into a game by asking, "What color is my shirt?" then answering, "Red", "What color are my pants?" then answering, "Blue." This question can be a game or a way of absorbing new knowledge.

THE CLASSIFICATION QUESTION

These questions help sort out data, make comparisons, and then organize information. "Teddy is furry... so is my dog, Spot... Is Teddy a dog? No, Teddy is a bear."

THE INFORMATION QUESTION

Children really want to know why the sky is blue or what makes a rainbow.

THE SECURITY QUESTION

These questions grow out of fears children naturally experience: "Will Jaws fit in our swimming pool? Will you die soon?"

THE PSEUDO QUESTION

Children often use questions even when they don't really want or expect information or reassurance.

"Why do I have to go to bed?" REALLY MEANS "Can I go to bed later?"

"Did you know I went to an ice skating party?" REALLY MEANS "I'm telling you I went to an ice skating party."

"Do you like my new dress?" REALLY MEANS "I want you to notice and admire my new dress."

This question wants your interest as much as your answer.

THE HIDDEN AGENDA QUESTION

"What time are you leaving my dance class?" MIGHT REALLY MEAN "Why do you have to leave me alone? I want you to stay."

It is important for the adult to reflect the child's true feeling by saying... "I guess you'd like to have me watch you dance for a while longer."

if you can't respond. Say, "You know, I don't know why the sky is blue. But I bet we could get a book out of the library that could tell us. Let's plan a trip there real soon."

If your child asks, "Will you die soon?" don't fudge. Say, "Everybody dies sooner or later, and we usually don't know when we're going to die. It's part of life. But I don't expect to die any time soon, that's for sure!"

If my child asked what Durkin calls a "pseudo question," I'd try to give information or assurance even though the child might not expect it. Nothing like the answer to a question says that you're paying attention to your child.

I'd answer "Why do I have to go to bed?" with something like, "Eight o'clock is a real good bedtime for you so you can get up nice and fresh tomorrow morning. Maybe you can stay up a little later on Saturday night when you've got nothing to do real early in the morning."

I'd answer "Did you know I went to an ice skating party?"

with something like, "I did know, but I forgot to ask you all about it! You come here right this minute and tell me what you liked best about that party!"

I'd answer "Do you like my new dress?" with something like, "I love it, especially that little mouse on the collar. What do you like best about that dress?"

As you can see from the "pseudo" and the "hidden agenda" questions Durkin calls attention to, parents don't have a monopoly on using questions for more than just drawing out information. Kids know this trick too, and the older they get, the more skillful they grow. You have to learn to listen for the real meanings behind some of the questions in order to communicate most effectively. I don't think that they're as easy to respond to as Durkin implies. In order to reflect the child's true meaning, you have to find out first what the true meaning is, and it's not always easy. Your child herself may not know what that true meaning is!

Simply heightening your sensitivity to the existence of "hidden agenda" questions, however, can help you avoid altercation and conflict in the household and can help sustain the conversational aspect of language. When your little girl says at dinner, for example, "Why do we have to eat now?" and you know she hasn't eaten for hours, what she may really mean (but has decided not to state directly) is, "My favorite program is on, and I want to watch television." Or, she may be getting back at you for refusing to let her play longer at Colette's house earlier that afternoon. She may also mean that she's not feeling well, and she just can't put any food into her mouth.

It's hard to predict the best way to deal with questions like this for two important reasons. First, the hidden agenda is not always clear, and the child may resist probing. Often the question will sound really strange and, though you may be aware that some other meaning lurks beneath the surface, quite unfathomable. Second, every situation makes its own special demands, given the purpose of the interchange, the moods of the participants, the surrounding environment, and other human factors.

I think the best strategy, then, is learning to listen to your child so that you develop a sixth sense about other-meaning questions. Mystifying conversations with young people are often rooted in miscues, the child saying one thing but meaning another and the adult taking everything at face value. Knowing about the "other meaning" factor helps you deal more creatively with a peculiar interchange.

In the situation I described above, I'd first determine whether my child were ill. Assured that he felt all right, I'd try to consider the possibility of other meanings. I certainly wouldn't lose my patience: "We always eat at this hour! Now you just behave yourself and stop being a pest and eat your dinner!" Such a response takes you nowhere.

Alternate responses? Again, depending on my child's age and how I'd read the situation, I might try one of these:

"Are you still upset with me because I took you away from Colette's house? Maybe we can make arrangements for you two to play again tomorrow for a longer time. But you know we usually get hungry around six o'clock. It's the most convenient time for us to eat at our house."

"I bet you'd rather be watching *Sesame Street* now, wouldn't you? But you have looked at quite a bit of TV today. You've really had enough. It's dinnertime now. You can watch *Sesame Street* tomorrow."

Not to say that these mightn't cause some more fussing, but at least I'd be laying my cards on the table openly. If my daughter insisted on not eating, I'd let her not eat until she got hungry later on. I would ask her to stay at the table, though, until we all finished. (My experience has been that the "I don't want to eat" strategy ends quickly when the child sits at the table while everyone else is eating.)

PRACTICE WITH SCAFFOLDING

Now that you've looked carefully at scaffolding and at questions, which contribute so importantly to its use, I thought you'd have some fun practicing.

I'm repeating below a conversation between a child and an experienced adult scaffolder. Except that I've left out the parent's contribution to the dialogue. What you'll read, then, is only the child's part of the conversation. What would *you* say to move the discussion along? What comments would you make, what questions would you ask, to keep the interchange going? Just fill in the blanks.

Below the dialogues with blanks you'll find the dialogues reproduced in their entirety so that you can check the remarks you would make against those made by the parent in the actual situation.

Scaffolding Practice

[Nineteen-month-old child]

Rachel: Fly. Big fly!
Mother: _____
Rachel: On door.
Mother: _____
Rachel: Fly on door. Over there!
Mother: _____
Rachel: Mommy open door.
       [Mother opens the screen door.]
Mother: _____
Rachel: Fly flew away. All gone fly!

Scaffolding 1: Actual Interchange

Rachel: Fly. Big fly!
Mother: WHERE'S THAT FLY?
Rachel: On door.
Mother: THE FLY IS ON THE DOOR?
Rachel: Fly on door. Over there!
Mother: WHAT SHOULD MOMMY DO?
Rachel: Mommy open door.
Mother: WHAT HAPPENED TO THE FLY?
Rachel: Fly flew away. All gone fly!

Do you notice the judicious use of questions here? All four of Mother's utterances are short, simple questions designed to engage her toddler in conversation and in thinking about the experience. The second question expands her child's two-word phrase "On door" to a full sentence, "The fly is on the door." It achieves its desired effect: Rachel expands her earlier statement so that it includes the subject "fly." The last two questions tap Rachel's thinking. First, Mother asks for a suggestion and Rachel makes one. (No possibilities for right-or-wrong answers here!) Next, Mother engages her child's sensory perceptions by requesting a report of the action, and Rachel responds accurately.

Let's try again. In this example, *pinano* is Joshua's word for piano; *Ja-Ja* is the name he uses for himself.

Scaffolding Practice 2

[Joshua at 18.5 months]

Joshua: [*pointing*] do pinano
Father: _____

Joshua: want do pinano
Father: _____

Joshua: I play pinano
Father: _____

Joshua: make music. play pinano music
      [*After banging on the piano*]

Joshua: pinano talk
Father: _____

Joshua: lamp talk
Father: _____

Joshua: floor can't talk
Father: _____

Joshua: da talk   Ja-Ja talk
Father: _____

Joshua: [*Loud voice*] NOT BANG PINANO
Father: _____

Joshua: fixing it
Father: _____

Joshua: [*Shaking head*] NOT BANG PINANO
Father: _____
Joshua: can't bang pinano   break it
Father: _____
Joshua: [*Shaking head*] Ja-Ja can't break it

Scaffolding 2: Actual Interchange

Joshua: [*Pointing*] do pinano
Father: YUP. THAT'S THE PIANO. DO YOU WANT TO PLAY THE PIANO?
Joshua: want do pinano
Father: WHY DO YOU WANT TO PLAY THE PIANO?
Joshua: I play pinano
Father: WHY? DO YOU WANT TO MAKE MUSIC?
Joshua: make music   play pinano music
[*After banging on the piano*]
Joshua: pinano talk
Father: NOT REALLY. THE PIANO MAKES MUSIC. IT CAN'T TALK.
Joshua: lamp talk
Father: NO, THE LAMP CAN'T TALK.
Joshua: floor can't talk
Father: THAT'S RIGHT, THE FLOOR CAN'T TALK EITHER.
Joshua: da talk   Ja-Ja talk
Father: YOU'RE A SMART LITTLE GUY. DADDY TALKS AND JOSHUA TALKS. PEOPLE TALK.
Joshua: [*Loud voice*] NOT BANG PINANO
Father: WHO TOLD YOU NOT TO BANG THE PIANO?
Joshua: fixing it
Father: THE MAN WHO WAS FIXING THE PIANO TODAY TOLD YOU NOT TO BANG IT?
Joshua: [*Shaking head*] NOT BANG PINANO
Father: WHY CAN'T YOU BANG THE PIANO?
Joshua: can't bang pinano   break it

Father: GOOD ADVICE. DON'T WORRY. YOU DON'T BANG
         IT TOO HARD. YOU CAN'T BREAK IT.
Joshua: [*Shaking head*] Ja-Ja can't break it

The father's probing in this delightful little interchange leads
the dialogue and invites the child as conversational partner with
questions, expansions, and repetitions. As a result, Joshua links
present reality with past events. He uses vocabulary to classify
objects in his surroundings. Note how he differentiates among
the piano, the lamp, the floor, and people like his father and
himself. Also, Joshua connects the objects with his personal
experience. The father's skillful use of questions and statements
builds the scaffold by which the child climbs to higher levels
of spoken language.

A FEW MORE THOUGHTS ON DIALOGUE

Michael Halliday, the linguist who provided us with our first
example of scaffolding (Nigel talking with his mother about the
goat at the zoo) explains that one of the most fundamental steps
a child takes in reaching adult language is learning to engage
in dialogue.

In Halliday's classification system this occurs in the transi-
tional phase, Phase 2, which you may remember from our discussion in the last chapter. In Phase 1, the child knows nothing
about the concept of sustained interaction through language.
In Phase 2, he starts to learn that language is a form of interaction, and he starts to engage in dialogue. Phase 3 marks the
child's entry into the adult system.

For the child, dialogue is a thoroughly new concept, one that
"involves the adoption of roles which are social roles of a new
and special kind, namely those which are defined by language
itself."

I don't want to belabor the obvious here, but it takes two to
have a dialogue. Because of the enormous learning that takes
place in conversation between young children and adults—I'm

not talking about learning words and sentences as much as I'm talking about learning to use them under appropriate social conditions—the parent's role as conversational partner is essential from the child's earliest years onward. Don't relegate that responsibility to teachers or their assistants in day-care centers, to home-care givers, grandparents, nurses, tutors, nannies, or the various other people who may play a role in your child's life. Sure, those people can help; but think of them only as adding bricks to the house that you have to design and frame out. Only the parent will put in the thought and care that good conversations with kids demand.

Find time in every day to engage your son or daughter in conversation. And use these tips for scaffolding to get the best out of language growth and development for your very young child.

4

Read to Me, Talk to Me

The avid attention that many enlightened parents are now giving to reading aloud at home is a welcome addition to Mom and Dad's important responsibilities as teachers and language givers. Few times in a day bring more delight than the intimate moments on an easy chair or on pillows propped against a headboard, favorite word and picture book in hand, a youngster's eyes glued to a page as Mother's voice brings magic to the room with the words she reads. You delight in the joy of a tiny, attentive body on your lap or beside you; your child delights in the melody of your voice, hypnotized by it, and the story it weaves, as well as by the drawings, photos, and print forms on the page. Jim Trelease's excellent *The Read-Aloud Handbook* has converted parents all over the country into regular read-aloud folks. (If you haven't read Trelease's book yet, you're missing some terrific advice about how to set up a home program and about which books to choose for reading to a variety of age groups.)

Yet there's more to sharing a wonderful book with your child than simply reading it aloud. To be sure, most of us love the read-aloud experience no matter which role we take, reader or listener, and I'm not trying to sell it short. If you think about it, however, for an active youngster bursting with curiosity and energy, a typical read-aloud session for a preschooler—the child sitting quietly (or not so quietly!), the parent reading so that the youngster can examine the pictures—can be a disappointingly passive activity for the child.

Like many other parents, we had tried to use reading aloud simply as a means of relaxing our children with delightful stories before bedtime. But our middle child, Joseph, much to our initial chagrin, simply would not follow the "rules." "You've got to stop asking questions so you can hear the story"; "Please, Joseph, stop talking and listen!"—I don't know how many times we said those words until we realized how inappropriate our rules were. Joseph's eyes would cover every inch of a page, darting back and forth from corner to corner, from top to bottom, from side to side. He was trying to wring information from the pictures and drawings, information that the sentence or two of prose beneath the illustration did not always supply. With his questions Joseph was groping for validation, support, social justification—in short, for everything that conversation supplies in our daily lives.

I think we made a great breakthrough in converting the read-aloud session into a dynamic exercise when we started welcoming Joseph's questions about a page and trying to help him answer them. We easily could read again the sentences he had interrupted, so our objections about losing continuity really made no sense. His questions showed us an engagement with ideas and vocabulary that we could never observe simply by reading aloud to him. We realized, too, that by *our* asking questions about a page and about the story after we read it, we could build word concepts, could make more substantial connections between pictures and sentences, and could help stretch our child's critical thinking skills. Most important, however, was that we found another natural, relaxed opportunity to talk with our child and to savor the delights of hearing his mind at work.

MOMS AND DADS AS READING TEACHERS

Before we look at how to explore a book with your son or daughter, let's consider the parents' most important jobs in helping children become better readers. Don't look here for advice on how to set up home reading classes. Your library shelves already are groaning with books designed to guide you on how to teach your infant to read, and you don't need me to add to the excesses. You can find out from other sources when to teach reading, why to teach reading, how to teach reading, and where to teach reading.

None of those is my intention, although I admit that I won't resist telling you what *not* to do about instructing your youngster in reading. You already know my attitudes toward parents as formal teachers of their children and my feelings about structured learning situations, so I hope you won't be surprised by my ideas. You'll find lots of people who disagree with me, especially those who produce the volumes that are already causing you insufferable guilt and strain!

Here's my recommendation. Don't teach your child how to read.

I'm going to say it again. Don't teach your child how to read.

Nothing will make you and your child more miserable than sitting with flash cards that identify words or than going over the sounds of letter combinations or than reviewing by rote the letters of the alphabet or than laboring over a simple text and listening to lifeless sound-outs without expression or sense of meaning. They'll hate reading. And you'll hate it too.

This is a teacher and a parent and a writer of books on reading improvement talking now. Don't teach your child to read.

Now, you can do many, many things to get your kids *ready* to read, and toward that end I'll try to keep you busy sharing fresh and joyful experiences with your children. But do you really see as one of your roles in life sitting at a table with your little boy or girl and sweating over words—words that should delight, but which are easily turned into monsters of frustration and anguish by zealous, well-meaning adults?

I know how eager you are for your child to succeed as a reader, and I know that you have doubts about how well your child's school, once he gets there, will give him all he needs for success. Maybe you've read the same grim news that I have. A 1984 study by the National Association of Educational Prog-

ress found that too many six-year-olds are unable to follow brief
directions or to describe simple pictures by picking out phrases
from a list and matching them to the illustrations. "Failure to
perform these rudimentary reading exercises," says Secretary
of Education William J. Bennett about those six-year-olds, "places
them in danger of future school failure." Forty percent of the
thirteen-year-olds in the NAEP study do not have middle-level
reading abilities such as searching pages for specific information
or relating ideas or making generalizations.

With such threatening statistics cropping up like dense un-
derbrush on the path to your child's future, you probably believe that doing something is better than doing nothing, given
the uncertainties your child faces as one learner among many
in today's crowded classrooms. With this I agree. But the issue
here is the *quality* of the something. Each of those popular
teach-your-baby-how-to-read books you may have thumbed
through invariably oversimplifies a complex learning task. The
one or two books you'll consult about how to teach reading
just won't give you enough information to do the job right. I'm
recommending that you give your children something that no
one else will give them: regular practice in conversational skills
so that your son or daughter comes to school ready to learn
reading in a flash. I hope you won't be impatient with me for
all the times that I repeat this point.

This is not to say that really young kids can't or don't learn
how to read before they get to school. You know that they can
and do. Yet research is quite inconclusive about whether or
not any abiding, long-range value accrues to preschool children
who are taught reading. Some studies show that in exactly the
same formal programs used with children in the same general
range of intelligence, younger kids made *less* progress than older
ones. Attention spans pose serious problems for many preschoolers. Forcing instruction can generate undesirable emotional responses.

In our family, only by their own will and determination did
two of my three children read before kindergarten, but through
absolutely no formal reading instruction that we provided in
our household. Of course we answered any questions about

reading as Melissa and Saul tried to learn. My third child, the middle boy, Joseph, with the same experiences as the others, learned to read only as part of a regular instructional program at Birch Lane School where we live. They're all solid readers now, so I don't feel that the ones who read at home first had any particular advantage.

What I do believe accounts for their current successes is our allegiance to the kind of language-rich environment I'm trying to model for you, a program anchored in the conversations we have made part of our daily lives. In an early study (1925) of more than five hundred gifted preschoolers who learned to read, most of the children received only what researchers called "incidental assistance." What they meant, of course, is that formal preschool reading programs did not figure significantly in the children's learning to read.

Many parents—and, unfortunately, many teachers too—believe that teaching reading is essentially teaching print words that stand for the objects they name. Hence, they use spiritless pronunciation drills and ubiquitous labels and flash cards to advance the skill. Richard C. Anderson, director of the Center for the Study of Reading at the University of Illinois, makes it very clear that children who can read a word right may still need assistance in integrating what the word means. Professor Anderson wants us to prepare children to apply their own knowledge to the words they read.

I groaned at the scene of Celie's reading epiphany in the otherwise delightful movie version of Alice Walker's *The Color Purple*, directed by Steven Spielberg. The heroine learns to read when her sister labels the world with little tags naming objects everywhere—windows, chairs, arms, legs, tables, clouds, rain, everything! I can't tell you how many parents I had seen perform this activity with their children long before Spielberg's film. I shudder at how many more will see Celie's experience as an object lesson for reading instruction.

What's wrong with the label-and-flash-card method? There's not any long-range damage done by it, I suppose. You can add somewhat to a child's sight vocabulary by labeling features of her room with the names of familiar objects. Nancy Larrick's

A Parent's Guide to Children's Reading, a book that more than a million parents have read, urges you to use labels and signs as a starting point for teaching your child how to read. I imagine that you can stimulate some vocabulary recognition by getting your daughter or son to read isolated words from a tagboard strip, in the manner shown on the cover of Glen Doman's long-popular paperback *How to Teach Your Baby to Read*.

It's not hard to understand the impulse that leads to such visual word-teaching plans for our children. We try to help our kids sort out ideas by incessantly naming things verbally for them as they grow. "Shoe," we say, or "toy" or "hat" as our child holds up or points to the object. Well, we reason, hearing the word is certainly an advantage in allying experience with language. Seeing the word must be equally important in connecting a graphic representation (letters in print) with the thing that the word stands for. With this kind of teaching we believe that we're emphasizing an important concept: Objects are represented symbolically by words.

But before committing to this strategy, you really have to weigh the issues that investigators seriously concerned with reading growth have highlighted for us. In the first place, sight vocabulary, though useful, is a minor part of reading skills. It's not worth spending any significant time on in your limited moments for talking with children during the day. Rudolph Flesch, author of the provocative *Why Johnny Can't Read*, believes that our shift toward the "look-say" method of reading instruction, which relies so heavily on a storehouse of sight vocabulary, is one of the major causes for our citizenry's decline in reading competence.

Second, and even more important, the assumption behind teaching children to equate a print representation of a word with the object it identifies is that recognizing a word is the essence of knowing how to read. And that assumption is wrong. The meaning of words on a printed page—that's essentially what we read most—resides in context. You just don't add up the individual meanings of words and thereby understand sentences and paragraphs. Reputable researchers like Nancy E.

Taylor at the Catholic University of America brand our traditional labeling activities as merely a vain hope that children will incorporate new words into sight vocabularies. Children have little reason to pay attention to what Taylor calls "these nonfunctional graphic representations." The written word *window* hanging above the object serves no purpose. It does not allow the child to get valued information from print, information to help the child do or know something.

An analogy here will help me expand the point. Think of the human organism. We may be made up of discrete entities— a heart, a liver, a brain, a pair of lungs—but our true beings are more than the various elements that make us up. No adding-machine calculus of parts and pieces provides much insight into our complex nature. It is the dynamic interplay of our cells and organs, along with innumerable other forces (many quite hard to grasp, such as soul, spirit, emotion, hope, ambition) that truly defines human beings.

Well, like human beings themselves, pages of print are much, much more than the sum of their parts. Words mean because they are surrounded by other words. Concepts and ideas reside in sentences and paragraphs that always say more than the individual words that make them up.

Current reading researchers suggest that in order to make meaning, children often substitute words of their own for words that appear before them. In a sense, they create their own texts from the starting points writers give them. The meaning a child extracts from a book has as much to do with his own experiences—physical, emotional, linguistic—as it does with the author's intentions.

Labeling windows and closets may show children words, but such actions don't do much to give print meaning. Besides, I believe that children, simply by existing in this complex visual world of ours, get enough instruction in connecting printed words with objects. If our goal is merely to teach the notion that print representations stand for objects, we're wasting our time, because kids learn this before we ever teach it to them. Your little boy knows that golden arches signal McDonald's, that white letters on a brown bag mean M&M's, that STOP on a hexagonal red-and-white sign means don't go on without pausing for a second.

Even with these nonbook page examples, where words seem to stand for things in isolation, context exerts its presence. If you write the letters *M&M* on a sheet of paper, don't be surprised if your prereader hasn't the slightest idea of what they mean, even though you know he can recognize them easily on a bag or box. That's the very point. The large white letters, the crinkly wrapping, the supermarket shelf with surrounding candy packages—all of those features provide the context of recognition for your child.

In a 1980 study, children incorrectly read words that were deliberately replaced in a familiar visual context. Thus, for example, if you printed the word STOP with the Burger King logo, your child would read STOP as "Burger King"! This situation surely supports the recommendation that parents must help their children direct attention at print. If you focus a child's eye on the graphic features of words, you start developing the notion that the words as well as the accompanying illustrations convey meaning. But you have to do all this with an eye to the new, nonpictorial representations of words that your child will meet in sentences.

One of the great contributions that you can make in helping your child learn reading is to show her that words have meanings. The mark of literacy is discovering meaning apart from visual contexts but within other contexts, the surrounding words of sentences and paragraphs. Thus, she has to be able to read the word *Coca-Cola*, for example, when it's surrounded by lots of other words, when it's written in letters other than the stylized white script of the company logo, and when it's unaccompanied by the red can. Researchers say that teaching a child the notion of print as a conveyer of meaning is teaching its *functional relevance*. This functional relevance is not automatically apparent to children. Adults have to show it to them. When you call attention to words and highlight their meanings, you make the essential connection for your boy or girl. When you talk about words and what they mean, you're the best kind of reading teacher your child needs.

Here's another issue to consider in case you want to ignore my advice and commit to a formal reading program at home for your preschooler. If you're going to attempt teaching phonics (which again is growing in popularity as a means of addressing word-attack skills) or any of the other important elements in reading, you're going to have to spend lots of time studying and learning how to translate what you yourself may do instinctively into a set of discrete skills that a very young child can learn. It's not easy to teach reading and do a good job of it, believe me.

To harvest a nation of readers, a laudable goal, unfortunately we have sown the seeds of hysteria at home. In many of what educators call "home-intervention programs," parents are specifically shown how to teach reading in order to instruct their preschoolers. One researcher identified a home-reading program that named thirty-seven separate activities for parents to inflict on their children! Just imagine trying to squeeze thirty-seven structured tasks into your busy days! Of particular interest is that the investigator, Nancy Taylor, found absolutely no evidence in her experimental sample that parents using these activities specifically achieved the goal of teaching their children to read. What did she conclude? It's a familiar point, one I've made many times before. Becoming literate is part of the social fabric of family life and, says Professor Taylor, "not some specific list of activities added to the family agenda to explicitly teach reading."

You know that your child's teachers are not perfect. But, let's face it, are you confident that you have the skills and talents to achieve what so many trained educators struggle toward all their lives, and to accomplish what they accomplish with varying degrees of success only after considerable experience and training? Can you rely upon an intervention program at home to teach so vital a skill as reading?

Don't get me wrong, now. Home-intervention programs by their nature are not inherently evil. *Talk with Your Child*, in fact, is recommending a home-intervention program designed to get you more involved with your youngsters by talking with them regularly. But unless you're aiming to make a career of teaching, you're wasting valuable time by using a "how to" approach to instruct your child in reading fundamentals. Even then, my advice would be to concentrate on other language-building exercises and let the classroom teacher do the job he's paid to do. You have much more important skills to hone with your son or daughter.

What are those skills? They are the rudimentary conversational skills, the human interaction skills, the daily talking and dialogue skills that no one else in your child's educational life will teach. You can bet that teachers throughout the grades are going to try to get your son or daughter to read. However, you can count on one hand the people who will talk with your child in order to help him or her develop the language competence that underlies powerful reading ability.

What can you do to help your child prepare to read prior to formal school instruction? Studies of early readers tell us that establishing a positive home environment is the single most important contribution to children's reading success. We can identify a number of significant features in such an environment. What's impressive under our microscope here is that skill with spoken language is an absolutely vital base for reading competency. "In all forms of language learning," writes Professor Taylor, "communicative interaction is a critical factor."

Esther Milner, who studied first-grade children for the relation between their readiness to read and the patterns of interaction between them and their parents, offers convincing evidence. The best-scoring readers, she says, came from an enriched verbal environment. The best-scoring readers, she says, engaged in conversations with their parents much more often than children who got low scores on reading measures.

I'm getting ahead of myself, though. Let's look at a wide range of environmental features pretty much guaranteed to enhance your child's ability to learn reading.

1. *A print-rich environment.* In the home environments of

early readers we can identify, unsurprisingly, easy access to a wide variety of print materials for children.

These include children's books, of course—Golden Books, alphabet books, cloth and paper storybooks—but also less obvious sources like TV guides, TV programs and commercials, cookbooks, newspapers, and telephone directories, as well as the standard cupboard and medicine-chest items, cans and bottles and boxes alive with print.

One of the key elements in becoming a reader is knowing about the uses of print and some of the mechanical features of reading, like handling books, turning pages from left to right, looking at letters in the same way, left to right, knowing that blank white spaces separate words, and identifying words in their surrounding environments. Also, knowledge of such concepts as "word," "sound," and "letter" is very important, and a print-rich environment can help to teach them. Despite their abstract nature—a word, after all, is not a kind of object like a chair or a toy—don't think that your youngster can't deal with such language abstractions. Although children vary markedly in their ability to grasp these concepts, research indicates that even some very young children can develop an awareness of what *word* and *letter* mean.

2. *A household where people do reading.* Saturating your child with print materials is not enough. You have to use the materials. Your child has to experience reading as a dynamic activity that people perform as part of their daily lives.

Certainly, reading aloud to a child plays an essential role, but it is by no means the only way of showing your child that print has meaning, nor is it the simplest. Those cereal boxes and soda cans and Band-Aid tins are invaluable informal-reading opportunities for youngsters. Talk about those labels; read them aloud; explain their message; watch your child identify products long before she's doing sustained book reading. Among the most crucial early connections you want to help your little one make is the connection between words and meaning. We use print to represent thoughts and ideas; we read print to get information.

I'm taking you back to an earlier point, the incredible value of informal as opposed to formal reading enterprises at home. Study after study emphasizes informal experience as the direct mechanism by which kids learn about the nature of print. Casual experiences do it, says M. M. Clark in a book called *Young Fluent Readers*, not systematic experiences. In an intensive doctoral study at Columbia Teachers College, Clark found that children who came to school knowing about print learned what they knew almost exclusively through informal activities. These activities developed naturally as specific tasks woven into the social fabric of the children's lives, such as reading signs and billboards and writing letters. What should impress you as much as anything else in this report is that the children resisted more formal instruction at home, such as lessons in naming letters.

Professor Frank Smith, one of this country's major figures in reading instruction, talks about "environmental print" as the essential way youngsters come to understand the function of written language. The only way for kids to develop the insight that print *means* something, he says, is to have someone read to them or to have them observe someone responding meaningfully to print. Smith doesn't mean the reading of books and stories here; he means "the occasions when a child is told or hears 'That sign says "Stop," ' 'That word is *Boys*,' 'This is the jar for candies,' or 'There's the bus for downtown.' Television commercials," he continues, "can do the same for a child—they not only announce the product's name, desirability, and uniqueness in spoken and written language but even demonstrate the product at work."

I don't mean to question short read-aloud sessions with your youngster. Careful investigations emphasize that parents read regularly to children facile with language as part of the child-rearing process. Reading to children helps them learn about the very nature of written language, its structural elements, its forms, rhythms, patterns, and conventions. But I did want you to consider the many other environmental contexts in which words leap out at you and your children.

Reading to kids from books and box tops is only one act in the "We do reading" script for home productions. Mothers and fathers themselves have to read too. Lucky for your little boy if you're one of those "I'd rather read than do anything else" people. You'll have no trouble conveying your joy and enthusiasm for the printed word. Please make sure that he *sees* you reading, though. It doesn't matter what you read—*Ms.*, *The Wall Street Journal*, *Cosmopolitan*, *Ebony*, *Popular Mechanics*, a letter, a paperback novel, a recipe. Instead of waiting for bedtime to sink your teeth into that juicy new selection, take even ten or fifteen minutes before lunch or dinner to let your youngster watch you read. Perhaps he'll join you with his own book. Talk about what you're reading. You want to set yourself up as a model for him to emulate. When you read, your message is that reading is a pleasure, that print words communicate ideas, and that books are to vital our existence.

3. *Parents who respond to children's adventures with print.* In a nutshell, here I'm talking about quality interaction between children and parents over a page of words and pictures. But I do need to elaborate because we know so much about this dimension in a young child's march to reading excellence. "Making print meaningful to children does not occur by chance," Nancy Taylor cautions us. "It is highly dependent upon adult interaction."

Two key elements are gripping hands here. First is your skill at providing the right kinds of experiences and information for your developing reader. Second is your skill at recognizing your child's interest and ability level. Both influence print-related learning. In fact, the better you are at figuring out your child's potential for literacy, the better your child will learn to read and write.

Figuring out that level—researchers like Vygotsky call it the "zone of proximal development," the difference between the child's real ability and actual achievement—requires attentiveness to what your child needs. If she shows no interest in print-related materials, her level of development may not yet be suitable to the kinds of experiences you're providing. Try something else, but don't force the issue. Here again, we're at a delicate place. Surveys of parents show that the way children behave in these "parent, book, and child" sessions often influences their parents' behavior toward the children. In other words, a mother or father may not pursue reading at home if the parent senses that the child may not be interested.

But how do we define "interest"? Don't let what seems like your child's indifference to a print-related activity turn you away from the interaction altogether. Perhaps your baby is not yet ready for what you're trying to show. Perhaps something else would better hold his attention. Perhaps a moment later in the day would serve up a better opportunity. Don't let unrealistic expectations interfere with mutual contact over words at home.

A parent who responds to a child's adventures with print is a parent who answers questions. Early readers are constantly demanding more and more information about print; and studies show that a parent's willingness to answer children's questions contributes markedly to early reading success. If you have a normal child, you don't need me to tell you that he'll overwhelm you with his persistence in asking about the pages in front of him. Your special challenge is to be available for and open to questions. They may exhaust you, but they're indispensable for good learning.

What's also interesting, though, is that researchers have linked children's performance on accurate prereading measures to the number of questions *parents* ask. Elfrieda H. Hiebert of the Department of Curriculum and Instruction at the University of Kentucky is convinced that "parents' question-raising influences children's print-related learning." We spent some time in the last chapter talking about questioning strategies, and I recommend that you look them over again as we move on to consider talking and reading as a dynamic partnership.

4. *Easy access to papers, crayons, and pencils.* Early readers are kids who scribble, draw, and write. They like to copy. In fact, some researchers see a causal relation here; preschoolers who show an interest in reading often develop it from their interest in copying and writing. Professor William Teale at La Trobe University in Victoria, Australia, calls it the "pencil and paper factor," and is pretty sure that experience with writing reinforces a child's learning how to read.

You want to make available, then, the young writer's tools of the trade. At our house we have a "Writer's Drawer" on the bottom left side of my desk where our children can go anytime they want to put something down for keeps. Our Writer's Drawer includes lots of paper of different sizes and textures—lined and unlined, white and yellow, index cards and tagboard strips, heavy colored paper, stationery and notepaper, envelopes and napkins. We make lots of writing implements available too: plain lead pencils, water-soluble felt-tip pens, skinny and fat crayons, colored pencils, ballpoint pens. A small chalkboard and chalk in each child's room invite note leaving. We print little messages at night and look eagerly for answers the next morning. Other items your youngster might enjoy for writing include a typewriter, a set of alphabet stamps and a stamp pad, and a cheap plastic-label maker.

And, of course, the more you talk about the scribbles and drawings and letters your children write, the more you advance reading skills.

As you look these features over, I hope you can see that they are within the reach of every concerned, interested parent. Home-care givers other than parents can supplement these conditions in your household—yes, you're going to have to teach your care giver—but mothers and fathers have to set the pace and tone. I'm not talking necessarily of having to squeeze more time into a day already crammed with too much to do. I'm talking about changing the quality of the time you already have set aside for your child's needs. I'd love it, of course, if you could find more minutes and hours to spend with your youngster, thus reducing the number of minutes and hours she has to spend in structured programs or under the care of a sitter or housekeeper. Your own heavy schedule may prevent more ideal conditions. Still, by paying more attention to stimulating a young reader, you should find that you can use reserved time more productively.

I hope I've made my point here about your essential role in helping your child learn to read. I'm going to let Margaret Meek, author of *Learning to Read* and a member of the English and

Media Studies faculty at the University of London Institute of Education, summarize it for me. "It is not the bookish home," she says, "nor necessarily the middle-class family . . . not high intelligence, good eye-movements, acute ears, right-handedness, nor even extensive vocabulary that makes the successful beginner. The supporting adult, who shows him what a book is and how print works, who helps him to discover reading and expects him to be successful, makes all the difference. Together, adult and child learn about reading."

THE READ-AND-TALK MOMENT: HOW TO DO IT

Whether you are reading a book aloud to your child or whether she's just looking through the pictures, build *talking* into your patterns of response.

What do you talk about when you talk about a book with a young child? I'm going to make some general recommendations here, which, of course, you should feel free to adapt according to your child's age, skill, and level of interest.

For our discussion I'll use *The Marvelous Mud Washing Machine* by Patty Wolcott. With simple repetitive phrases and delightfully silly but realistic drawings by Richard Brown, the book tells how a boy full of mud gets cleaned off happily in a fantastic machine very much like a car wash. He sits in a green chair that he himself guides along a track; water squirts at him; soap bubbles coat his skin; big brushes rub him clean; shampoo from a giant bottle soaps his hair; more water rinses him off; an electric body-drier finishes off the job. It's a child's dream fantasy. What could be more delightful than getting yourself scrubbed in a car wash?

In regard to general questions and dialogue springboards, the easiest way to approach read-and-talk time is to think about the three possible points of entry into conversation: before reading, during reading, and after reading. (In Chapter 9, "Fifty Talk-About Books for Young Children," you'll find summaries of some other favorite books for preschoolers and primary schoolers. I've included questions and conversation starters for use at home with your child.)

Before Reading

You can prevent confusion, loss of interest, and sidetracking if you talk with your child about the contents of a book before she reads it.

Whenever you can, you should read in advance any book you want your child to read. If you don't have the time to do a careful job, at least read the first and last pages, flip through the others, note the characters and language, so that you have a general idea of what the book is about. Don't assume that because a book appears in the children's library it's automatically appropriate for your youngster. There's lots of junk out there, books that might be too complex, too tedious, too realistic, too sad, or too strange to share with your child.

Then consider these pointers:

- *Talk about the title and the cover.* Use the words and the illustration on the cover to find a path of entry for the book. You might ask, for example, "What is the little boy doing on the cover? Why does he look so happy, do you think? The title of this book is *The Marvelous Mud Washing Machine* by Patty Wolcott. [You always want to name the author to make connections between books and the living spirits who wrote them.] Why is the machine marvelous, do you think?"
- *Talk about some of the ideas or characters in the book and try to connect them with your child's own experiences.* "In this book a little boy gets very, very dirty. When did you ever get very dirty? How? How did we clean you off? In this book the boy gets cleaned off in a very strange way. Let's see if you can figure out how he cleans himself." With questions like these you set the stage for attentive reading. You help to focus the child's eye and ear on the details that you believe are most important in the book.
- *Alert your child to new words and concepts.* Focus attention on both language and ideas. Is there an important word whose meaning may stump your child? In Wolcott's book, the mud-washing machine washes mud off a little boy. It's

not like a washing machine your child is apt to associate with such a label. Wolcott's machine is more like a car wash. Raising questions about the word prepares your child to pay attention to it as he reads. You might say "These words say 'washing machine.' Do you remember the washing machine we use down in the basement? What do we use it for? What kind of washing machine do you think a mud-washing machine will be? What could it be used for? You're going to be surprised in this story!"

- *Invite questions.* Your child may be bursting with questions himself, and you should encourage them. Perhaps something on the cover will stimulate a question; perhaps one of your inquiries will dislodge others. In some cases answer directly; in others, you'll want to say, "Let's read the story to find out."

During Reading

Here your intent is to establish interaction between the child, his thoughts and ideas, the illustrations on a page, and the words that accompany them.

- *Read the words on the page and call attention to their meaning.* The text of *The Marvelous Mud Washing Machine* is very simple—there are only ten words. For example, one phrase repeated on top of several pages is "Washing, washing, washing, wash." You could point to any of those words and tell the child quite specifically what the word said. An older child might enjoy finding the word *wash* within the word *washing.* Also, on a typical page of text you might see other words, not necessarily part of the author's sentences but part of the illustration. Thus, on a page from Patty Wolcott's book, you'd see the word ON on a neon sign to signify that the machine was running. On a structure attached to a huge brush appears the word SOAP. Be sure to look at those words with your child.
- *Talk about the illustrations on the page.* Very often the illustrations tell a separate tale, one that supports the text

the writer has produced, certainly, but one that goes beyond the main story-line. In *The Marvelous Mud Washing
Machine*, the pictures tell most of the story. Unless you
talk about them, you miss much of the delight—and most
of the information. For example, one page shows the boy's
mother holding a garden hose; her son, splattered with
mud from head to toe, turns his back to her and walks off.
A big question mark hovers over the mother's head. No
words appear on the page. You're going to have to help
interpret that page for your child, who, depending upon
age, may not know a quesiton mark from a bagel. "Where
is the boy going, do you think? What is the mother thinking? With the question mark—that's what we call the squig-
gle over the mother's head—the writer is showing that the
mother has a question about what the boy is doing. What
do you think her question is?"

As you talk about individual pages, you want to draw upon
your storehouse of *why* and *how* questions to arouse critical
thought. "Why does the boy take a bath in the marvelous machine? Why does the boy say 'Beautiful marvelous mud. Marvelous beautiful mud'? Why does the boy's mother say 'Beautiful
marvelous boy! Marvelous beautiful boy!' when she sees him?"—
these are wonderful questions to ask about Wolcott's book.

Many books, especially for very young children, have no text
at all. You and your child should delight in telling these no-
word picture-book stories yourselves.

- *Talk about what might possibly happen on the next page, before
  you turn to it.* A very important skill that your child must
  learn in order to participate in the adult world of literacy
  is to anticipate outcomes. One of the hallmarks of critical
  thinking, the skill of predicting outcomes, is one you can
  practice early. Simply put, you just have to ask, "What do
  you think is going to happen next?" When your child responds, say, "Why?" or "What else could happen?" Such
  questions will release the floodgates of creative, original
  responses.
- *Relate events on a page to your child's life.* When you ask your

child to compare how he himself cleans off mud and how the boy in the book cleans off mud, for example, you are practicing a paradigm for thought—the comparison-and-contrast paradigm—that underlies much adult thinking activity. In addition, by helping to establish a new context for an event represented on a single page, you demonstrate another key skill for critical thinking, making connections between print and real life.

After Reading

When children talk about what they've read, no matter how young they are, they start developing skills that are among the most important for reading excellence. An informal chat with your daughter after you've gone through a book together will sharpen her ability to recall details. Every primary-school reading test I know tests for this skill, and the two of you can nurture its development simply by discussing a book you've read. In addition, talking about one book lays the groundwork for future explorations of other books. You're setting up a model of thought and inquiry that we hope children learn as they expand their abilities: part of the joy, appreciation, and learning that books give us comes when we talk about them and make them part of our lives.

- *Talk about the people, events, and ideas in the book.* Don't think of the discussion of a book after as a test! Don't bother with niggling details. What you're interested in is seeing that your youngster understands the story line and can recall some of the essential features of the narrative. About *The Marvelous Mud Washing Machine* you might use questions like these to spark conversation: "How did the boy get dirty? How did the boy's mother want to clean him? Why was she surprised when he walked away? How does the washing machine clean him off?" That last question is especially interesting: It might be tough for your child to recall the sequence of events that lead to the boy's final, neat-and-clean appearance. Don't hesitate to dip back into the text to find forgotten information.

- *Link items in the book to items in your child's immediate world.* Placing an object or an idea in a new context is an important thinking skill. (I'll expand on this idea in a later chapter.) In regard to Wolcott's book, for example, most children today have seen automatic car-washes. I would want to compare the machine in the book with the car-wash machine that my son or daughter may have experienced inside my car as it passed through suds and spray. Could a person really be washed in such a marvelous machine? Also, I'd talk about feelings and values reflected in the book and mirrored or refuted by my child's experience. "How do you think the boy felt playing in the mud? How would you feel playing in the mud? Why didn't the boy's mother yell at him when she saw how dirty he was?"
- *Stimulate your child's imagination and fantasies.* Use story talk (look ahead to Chapter 5) to stimulate your child's imagination. "How would you like to have a wash in the marvelous mud-washing machine? When would you be dirty enough to need to use it? What other marvelous machines can you think of?"

PAGE TALK, BOOK TALK

I've been making the point in this chapter about how important it is to talk with your child about books. Let me give you some specific examples of how a typical word-and-picture book is a key that unlocks conversation and welcomes language building in young children. Look at these pages from a favorite Stan and Jan Berenstain book, *The Berenstain Bears' New Baby*.

Clearly the authors designed these pages for conversation. The text accompanying the illustrations makes a generalization without any reference to specifics that support it. After reading aloud the words "There were all sorts of interesting things for a small bear to do and see in bear country," you'd want to ask, "What are some of the things Small Bear does here?" You could let your child pick at random from the pictures on the page and talk about them. Or, and I think that this is a better idea, you could start with the scene at the upper left corner of the

There were all sorts of interesting things for a small bear to do and see in Bear Country.

page and move straight across one by one until you reached
the picture of Small Bear gazing at the moon; then you would
return to the left again, this time at the bottom, looking at the
snorkeling scene and moving across the page from there. Going
from left to right in considering the sequence of pictures is
helpful practice for youngsters at a prereading stage; ultimately
when they read English words, they must learn to move their
eyes from left to right, and you should try to encourage that
movement (even when you're looking at pictures) any
time you examine a page.

Asking a question such as the one I've indicated stimulates
the child's descriptive language skills. I call these "Look-Say
Questions": The child looks at a scene and draws upon his or
her own linguistic resources to say in words what the picture
says visually. These kinds of questions are simple in that they
do not demand any higher-order thinking skills. Simple though
they may be, they are not simplistic. They are dipping into the
well of language deep in each child and can draw lively creative
responses and build confidence in your youngster's ability to
use his mind.

One October morning I asked my youngest son, Saul, what
Small Bear does in Bear Country. Guided to look at the pages
from left to right, he took obvious delight in ticking off the
scenes.

> "Catch a butterfly.
> Go fishing.
> Watch a spider spin her web.
> Sit outside in the nighttime and see the moon.
> He can swim underwater and see all the fish.
> He can go on a log and catch frogs.
> He could go rowing in his little canoe.
> He could fly a kite."

When I asked which Saul thought Small Bear liked best and
why, a lively conversation ensued. "I think he likes to go fishing
best because he could catch a lot of fish and it's a very good
sport to do."

"Which would *you* like to do best?" I asked.

"I think I'd like to go fishing also."

"Why?"

"I never went fishing before and I want to try it. But first I have to get a fishing rod."

"But why fishing of all the things he's doing?"

"When you catch fish, you're really happy."

"What else would you like to try?"

"I'd like to go underwater. It would be fun to watch the fish when they swim. [*pause*] I sure have a lot of things in my mind!"

"What wouldn't you like to do?"

"I wouldn't really like to go out and watch the moon because I'm afraid, it's dark, you know why, because if I'm sitting on a tree and someone might yell, 'Saul, come down!' and I might fall down!"

"It's scary to be outside at night alone, isn't it? Even with the moon shining, you could fall if you had to climb down a tree quickly."

I think you can appreciate the value of such a dialogue between parent and child in stimulating and stretching a youngster's language and thought skills. I want to point out some of what I believe are the most important qualities here. First, you can see parent and child as "communicative partners." (This phase, coined by sociologist Shirley Brice Heath, is one she uses to identify the goals of parents in Roadville, North Carolina, who want to help their children get ahead.) As communicative partners Saul and I fully explored a dimension of his world, stimulated by the words and pictures in a book.

In this type of conversation, however, Saul and I go beyond simple identification-responses. You know about these because you undoubtedly use them with your very young children now or have used them in the past. Remember? You're reading *The Berenstain Bears' New Baby* to your two- or three-year-old and you say, pointing to the picture, "Who's that?" expecting the child to name the character. Then you might say again and again the name the child gives you, describing the scenes as you go along: "Right. That's Small Bear. There's Small Bear chasing a beautiful butterfly. Where's the butterfly? [*Child points to it.*] Good. And there's Small Bear—well, look how he's watching that big fat spider. . . ." You might even turn the pages, saying, "Let's try to find some more pictures of Small Bear."

In this identification-response activity you would welcome any observations about the pictures from the child, but your essential goal is to provide language that a child who is developing speech can imitate sometime later; and to stimulate your child both to give and to receive some simple information about the book you're examining. This is all very good practice and very important as an early language-giving activity for your toddlers.

Unfortunately, many mothers and fathers abandon these kinds of questioning games after the youngster reaches the age of four. Although reading aloud to four-year-olds and older children is a new practice in the home nowadays, you need to develop similar, though more advanced, and equally enjoyable, conversation strategies about the books you share with your child. In this way he can integrate the books fully into his consciousness and can practice his own emerging language skills at a vital stage of learning in his life.

At the time of our excursion into Bear Country, Saul had not yet received any formal classroom instruction in reading. I helped him only to formulate approaches to books—we question them, we interact with them, we connect them to our own lives—that all competent readers must take. Also, these conversation strategies are very important in getting children to probe their own minds and feelings, to make observations that parents can validate and support. Our goal in this last case is, of course, to encourage such probing as a means to advance critical thinking. You can imagine how wonderful it was to hear Saul pat himself on the back—"I sure have a lot of things in my mind!"—as a grin like a slow wave spread joy and confidence over his face. Daddy, he was saying at that moment, I can think and I can say what I think.

But there is more than just language-building at play here. A relaxed conversational format allows your child to bring up informally the thoughts and ideas that are important in his own life. Here Saul delivered some messages about himself in the context of a talk about a book.

First, as he chatted about Small Bear, Saul told me indirectly how much he wanted a fishing rod. His brother Joseph is a ten-year-old fisherman and regales his younger brother with the joys of casting a line off the dock not far from our house. We think Saul is still too young to risk this adventure. No one in this world is happier than Joseph when he returns with a small catch of snapper, and Saul's enthusiasm for the sport clearly derives from his brother. We're thinking about a fishing rod for Saul's birthday and a family excursion to the pier.

Perhaps more important, in this moment of rational discourse about our sojourn through Bear Country, Saul had a chance to air his lingering fears about the dark. How often, I ask myself, does a child have the chance to introduce obliquely such a pressing concern? It's hard drawing youngsters into direct discussion about their fears. You know how embarrassed, self-conscious, and vulnerable they feel. But because of our conversation, Saul brought his anxiety into the open without the slightest prodding from me. In a quiet, intimate moment he confessed a weakness, and I had the chance to reassure him gently and without fuss that fears are normal and often appropriate. By entering the story in a book and by relating to one of its characters, Saul found an indirect sounding board for his own psychological musings.

Now that Saul is of school age these book conversations have not ended. Last summer, just before he became a second-grader, we took a long drive during a visit out West. A tireless reader, Saul chose at a Santa Fe Bookstore earlier in the day one of Jane Yolen's Commander Toad books. Both my wife and I felt that *Commander Toad and the Intergalactic Spy* was a bit too tough for Saul at this stage of his ability—although the publisher, Coward McCann, recommends the book for primary grades—but Saul insisted and we gave in. As I encouraged you to do, we first looked at the cover together:

Despite the charms of Bruce Degen's drawing, the illustration accompanying the title here is not much help for a parent who wants to talk about the book in advance. This was Saul's

COMMANDER TOAD
and the
INTERGALACTIC SPY
by Jane Yolen

pictures by Bruce Degen

first Commander Toad book, but the cover doesn't say much about what's under command! The star on the shirt implies some kind of space travel, perhaps, but this is an altogether too subtle clue for a recent first-grade graduate. And I suppose that the eyes peering through the oversized foliage also imply something, maybe about spying. But we find this cover particularly weak in achieving one of the important goals for book covers for young children: Not only must the cover pique the child's interest, but it must also open a window on the content of the book. For us as parents, the problem was trying to talk about both *intergalactic* and *spy* from the clues on the cover, but we had little help from the author-illustrator team here. Fortunately, the page facing the title page set a broader context in the interstellar travel business. Saul didn't know what intergalactic meant, but we used "space" as an expedient image-maker. It's easier to establish Commander Toad's work from this picture than from the cover.

Before we left the bookstore, we had talked all about spies and the nature of that word—a mouthful, to be sure—*intergalactic*. Saul shared some of his thoughts about galaxies, planets, stars, space travel, and how spies might fit into such a scheme. We flipped through the book, admiring and commenting on some of the drawings. Our purpose was to connect his prior experiences and thinking with the book he was about to read so that he might deal successfully with any difficulties that arose in the text.

Before long, sandwiched between his older brother and sister in the backseat, Saul announced that he would read aloud from his current place in the book. We all loved the idea; we look forward to something that will set us talking on these long trips. We allot time during our drives for talking and listening to each other, time when the radio is off and we have conversation. What ensued was another kind of informal language-learning activity based on a book and rooted in the light and friendly banter of a family at ease. This time we used a read-and-talk moment to examine the meaning of a word.

Here's the page that started us going:

"I am your cousin,
Tip Toad,
master of disguise,"
say all five monsters
together.
"These other monsters
are imposters.
They are evil spies
who want to
get on board your ship
and steal it
and all its secrets
away."

Saul stumbled a bit when he read *imposter*. That was my clue. Did he know what the word meant?

"No," he replied sheepishly.

"That's a tough word. Let me give you a hint. I'll use it another way and see if you can figure it out. 'The imposter at the door looked just like my father.' " A good clue, I thought.

"Does *imposter* mean '*man*'?" An even better response! How well it showed up the weaknesses in my clue! "Man" was certainly not the meaning I'd hoped Saul would surmise from my sentence.

Melissa, sixteen and pretty experienced at these talk-about-reading encounters, took up the cause.

"The imposter *pretended to be* my father," she said. "Now what do you think?"

From the rearview mirror I saw Saul thinking, his intense brown eyes narrowed into little slits. But Melissa couldn't wait for a reply. "An imposter is someone who pretends to be someone else. You have it now?"

"It was such a good clue, Melissa! Why didn't you wait for Saul?" I pouted.

"I would've gotten it!" Saul said.

"There's a little more to it, though," I said. "It's not just pretending for fun alone. An imposter is a fraud, you know, somebody deliberately trying to trick other people."

"Okay, Saul," my wife, Barbara, injected. "See if you can explain it now. How could *you* be an imposter?"

"What do you mean?"

"Suppose you wanted to be an imposter for your friend Flynn. How would you do it?"

"If I pretended to be Flynn?"

"Yup. Like Flynn. Your friend Flynn."

"I'd need glasses. I don't wear any glasses. Flynn wears glasses."

"Good. What else?"

"He always wears Oshkoshes. I'd need Oshkoshes. And"— Saul was really enjoying this now—"and, I'd need to shrink myself, and curl my hair up, and get his voice."

"Then you'd be an imposter all right. People would think that you were Flynn."

"You don't have to look like someone to be an imposter, though, do you?" This was Melissa talking. "You can pretend to be something you're not, like a surgeon or a lawyer. You wouldn't have to look like a particular person. You'd just need to convince everyone that you were what you said you were."

"Why would you want to be an imposter for Flynn? Why would you want to trick anybody into thinking you were Flynn? Yuk! Sounds pretty dumb to me." This was eleven-year-old Joseph, distracted no more than a minute from his book, but just long enough to sound the alarm.

"You don't know everything, Joseph. I could go to a Halloween party and pretend to be Flynn. Maybe I'd want to do it then."

"That would be just-for-fun pretending. That wouldn't make you an imposter, would it?"

"But if I tricked his parents good enough, maybe I could ride off on his new bike."

"That would do it, you little imposter! That would do it all right!"

It's not hard to see what we tried to achieve here, the whole family chiming in for this conversation. We were tuned into Saul's reading carefully enough to note a word that he might want to explore a bit. We didn't leap to define the word immediately but tried instead to draw upon Saul's analytic skills to get him to figure out the meaning from information connected to his own world. The best of intentions don't guarantee success, however; I'd hoped that my sentence would lead Saul to see that an imposter was someone who assumed somebody else's identity, but my clue was too general. Sure, *man* fit that sentence perfectly. After Melissa had explained what the word meant, we didn't leave things there, however. We wanted Saul to see the word from different angles, to incorporate it into his own experiential reality. Hence, we asked him how he could be an imposter himself.

I don't think of this little exchange as a reading or a vocabulary lesson. We were talking about a book; we were talking about words; and we connected them to daily experience. I can't imagine a better way to couple print with life in a more enjoyable context, a relaxed, unpressured conversation between children and adults about our greatest source of information and pleasure, books. Books communicate serious ideas; they teach us; we enjoy them. If that's the only notion and no other that you give to your child about the printed word you'll generate literacy in ways that no formal home program of instruction could ever achieve.

PICTURE TALK

An important source of good conversation with children is pictures, illustrations, photographs—whatever two-dimensional non-print representations on a page draw your child's interest. You saw the part pictures played in our discussion of Saul's books in the last section: the words and pictures in *The Berenstain Bears' New Baby* and *Commander Toad and the Intergalactic Spy* together fueled the conversation. But I don't want to end this chapter without considering illustrations in their own right, apart from the words that often accompany them in a book or magazine.

Looking at and talking about a picture is visual reading. For a youngster who cannot read, examining a picture stimulates the imagination and, based on good questioning and discussion strategies by the parent, invites early application of those thinking skills that lead to success at school. Not words but lines, shapes, and colors provide clues to meaning.

When you look at a picture you tap all those reading skills we struggle to instill in beginning and advancing readers. You have to try to identify the main idea of the picture, what it's all about. You draw on the major details in determining that main idea, and you reject any minor ones. The details give you factual information about the scene.

They also give you the basis for inferential meanings. You can tell, for example, whether a figure in the picture is happy or sad, lively or dispirited, weak or strong. You can compare and contrast and make determinations of cause and effect. You can draw conclusions, generalize, predict outcomes. You can make judgments. And you can do all of these without recourse to written words. By looking at and talking about pictures in children's magazines, family magazines, newspapers, picture books, photograph albums, you practice reading skills. As your child starts focusing more intently on words and sentences, you'll want her to transfer to the printed page just what she does here.

I've selected the lively cover illustration of a familiar and well-regarded magazine for children, *Highlights*. If it's not a magazine you subscribe to, you've surely seen it in your pediatrician's or dentist's waiting room—a good place for sustained talking with your child as you kill time until your turn to see the doctor. This cover explodes with action that you can chat at length about. I chose it deliberately to point out a wide range of strategies you can use to talk about such a picture and the particular thought and language skills your discussion can strengthen. They include identifying, locating, and expanding on people and objects; finding, highlighting, expanding on, projecting, recalling, and evaluating actions; describing, comparing, classifying, and expanding details; explaining a process; explaining causes and effects; and using logic. Also, you want to make the scene personal by relating it to your child's own experience and to establish new contexts by changing one or two features of the setting.

Some of the strategies challenge your child's powers of observation and recall. In other words, can he represent accurately in language the key features of the picture? In talking about these features he may provide one- or two-word responses. Other strategies will stimulate more sustained conversation that you'll be able to build on your own.

After you look at the picture yourself and consider the strategies I'm using, try the activity with your child. Show him or her the illustration and start talking! I expect the questions and conversational starting points below to serve also as models for discussions you might hold about other illustrations or photographs. Don't expect to use all of these suggestions for a single picture. Let the content and your good judgment guide your dialogue.

I'd begin with an overview here. Just what does your child think is going on in this picture? What is the *story* of the picture? (We'll look at story-telling in greater depth in Chapter 5.) Listen to the narrative your child tells. Then, use some of these questions and conversational prods to talk about the page in depth. Remember that I'm trying to offer guidance for children in a broad age range, so that some of my questions may be too easy or too difficult for your youngster. Depending on the age of your chiild and his or her skills level, you might want to move from left to right (the direction in which we read when we look at print) as you explore the picture.

Identifying, Locating, and Expanding on People and Objects

[*Pointing*] Who is this? What is that?
Where is the lifeguard? Where are the bench and towel?
Where do you see grown-ups? Where is the man with the moustache? [*Child points*]
What is the lifeguard wearing? What is the woman wearing on her head? What does she have wrapped around her shoulders?
Whose towel is this? Whose goggles are these? Whose feet are these?

Finding, Highlighting, Expanding, Projecting, Recalling, and Evaluating Actions

What is this boy doing? What is this girl doing?
Where is the child jumping into the water? Where is a child waving her hand?
What is the girl sitting on? Where are the two children holding hands in the water?
What has this child just done? What is this child going to do next? Why are the children talking to the lifeguard?
Which other children do you see swimming?
Which children look happiest? Do you like this girl? this boy? Why?

Describing, Comparing, Classifying, and Expanding Details

What color is the ball?

Talk about this child—what is she wearing, what color is her hair, how is it done up?

Which child can swim? Which child cannot swim? How do you know? Which children are in the water? Which are outside the water? Where are the white children? Where are the black children? Let's find all the big children. The little children. The grown-ups.

What's going on here? What is this child doing? Why is she doing it?

Explaining a Process

How did the boy dive into the water? How do you think the children play the game with the ball? How is the man teaching the little boy to swim?

Explaining Causes and Effects

Why is this girl sitting with a towel around her? Why is the lifeguard wearing sunglasses? Why is the mother holding the little boy? Why does the woman have a towel wrapped around her head?

Using Logic

Why does the lifeguard have a whistle around his neck? Why is there a tube under the lifeguard's stand? Why is this boy holding onto the ladder? Why does the boy want the goggles? Why is there a fence around the swimming pool? Why is the towel on the bench?

Changing Contexts

What if it starts to rain? What will the children do?

What if the children were at the beach instead of in a pool? What would they do? What other games could they play?

Making the Scene Personal

What do you do at the swimming pool? Which friend do you play with? How did you learn how to swim? What do you talk to the lifeguard about?

Visual reading and word-and-senence reading demand conversation. "The conversation that goes with reading aloud to children is as important as the reading itself," advises the Department of Education and Secretary of Education Bennett. "When parents ask children only superficial questions about stories, or don't discuss the stories at all, their children do not achieve as well in reading as the children of parents who ask questions that require thinking and who relate the stories to everyday events. Kindergarten children who know a lot about written language usually have parents who believe that reading is important and who seize every opportunity to act on that conviction by reading to their children."

Enough said.

5

Panning for Gold:
Story Sharing

Joseph, our eleven-year-old son, is a selective eaves-
dropper. As you may know, the word *eavesdrop* at one time
meant, literally, the ground outside a house where water dripped
from the overhanging lower edge of the roof. You can see
furtiveness in the original definition. Someone is so bent on
overhearing your conversation that he risks rain and damp feet
to stand outside your house with his ear pressed to the window
or door.

Little in this literal meaning applies to Joseph, however, because there is nothing clandestine about his listening-in. He
stops everything when he hears talk. Piano practice ends mid-
note; a fork stops halfway from the table to his mouth; a pencil
poises inches from a homework page. He wants to know who.
He wants to know why. He wants to know how. Joseph spares
no questions: Talk rivets him.

But it's not just any kind of talk that steals his attention, and
that's why I said he was selective. He listens in on stories. I
don't mean invented stories that parents tell children to amuse
them (although he loves these too). I mean the narratives of
daily life, the unprofound events that mark our days. When
recounted at dinner or in the living room after they occur, daily
events engage him totally. When my wife tells of an incident

with her first-graders in reading class, when Melissa reviews her English teacher's latest saga of his alternate life as a Big Mac maker at the mall, when Saul tells the story of the lost point on the soccer field—whether or not these stories are directed to Joseph, he is taking them all in, every last word.

And why not? Who doesn't love stories? They give us pleasure. They give us information. They are a major vehicle for conversation. Stories real and imagined play an essential role in our cultural history. Homer's epics—elaborate, romantic narratives—were recited to genial audiences in social settings. In another age troubadours carried their tales of love and battle from town to town. Tribesmen in nonliterate cultures preserved the history and mythology of peoples and nations through oral stories passed down from generation to generation. From the beginnings of humanity's social relations stories obviously had a cherished, central role. Stories instruct; they reflect models of human behavior; they record a speaker's special vision; they link related, logical events, affirming continuity in an often illogical, discontinuous world.

As you might have suspected, Joseph doesn't stint on telling stories either. No one in our household holds back here. I can remember as a child being fascinated by the tales my father told about his younger days on Manhattan's Lower East Side, about adolescent life in East New York, about the routine events (to me, adventures) of workingmen and -women on Seventh Avenue and Thirty-eighth Street. My wife echoes similar memories of storytelling and story-listening in her childhood. The outside observer to our house now would note a favored place for stories amid the regular din of conversation.

We all know about the value of stories in written form. We're always trying to expand our children's libraries, and we are committed to reading stories aloud—now, I'm hoping, of a kind much more coversational than in the past and reflecting some of the issues I addressed in the last chapter and will expand upon in Chapter 9, "Fifty Talk-About Books for Young Children." In the present chapter, however, I'm highlighting *oral* stories. I think we can easily miss their value and impact as language builders for our youngsters.

At the Ontario Institute for Studies in Education, Gordon Wells connects stories with the basic cognitive processes of human biology. He insists that building stories in the mind is fundamental to the ways that we learn to make meaning. We construct stories almost as a biological need in order to understand perceived information. But storytelling is also "the means whereby we enter into a shared world, which is continually broadened by the exchange of stories with others." Wells believes that through conversation (it's that key word again) children link the stories constructed in their minds with the forms of oral language. As such, "storying," as he calls it, permeates every dimension of learning.

If you're living with a lively preschooler, you know what an essential role storytelling plays in his life. He's constantly bursting into the room to tell you about a toy, a television program, a friend, a little sparrow he's watched form the window. You hear him tell stories to himself—*create* stories is a better term—about the stuffed bear beside him at lunch or about the blocks on the floor of his room or about the family of rubber ducks that join him in the bath. Your child is also begging for stories by now: You've heard the ringing request that resonates delight through centuries and cultures, across languages and geography—"Mommy, tell me a story."

The connection between speaking and writing is very important when you consider narratives. Narration is an essential writing skill for the schoolchild. It contributes to many other types of writing, such as scientific or historical reports, explanations of processes, and argumentation. In its most simple form, narration is the review of time through language. As such, it may unveil an event that occurred over a long period. Reporters and historians do this when they write about the instances that characterize a crime or a battle. With an enormous base of data at their fingertips, experienced writers, by using details, can present an account of an extended occurrence so that readers feel that they are living through the times described.

But the kinds of narratives that are most productive for beginners are narratives that cover a limited time frame. Your child will learn most efficiently about chronological sequencing if he's telling an event that's not too broadly drawn. Encourage him to tell stories limited in time and geography. Use creative questioning to help limit the event to a brief moment and to stimulate your youngster's memory for details. Ask when the event took place and encourage your child to name the month or season of occurrence. Did it happen in the morning or afternoon, in December or sometime during the summer? Ask about colors and sounds, about what people said and how they moved. Say, "How did you feel about what happened? Were you scared? Were you happy? Were you annoyed?"

Any occasion that impresses your son or daughter is ripe fruit for successful narration. A moment at the breakfast table, at the street corner, on the yellow school-bus, in the playground covered with leaves, on the stairs to the library, in the gym, during snack, at the chalkboard, in the lunch room, at the shopping mall—all these are strong possibilities.

To get your youngster talking, you might ask first for a subjective judgment of an event in order to focus his or her insights:

- "Did you have a good day at nursery school—what was the best thing that happened to you there?"
- "What do you like doing most with your baby brother?"
- "When did your friend Karen make you angriest?"
- "When were you embarrassed?"
- "What was the most exciting thing you did in the snow?"
- "What was the best part of the picnic?"

Have you stopped to realize how important storytelling will be in your boys' and girls' preschool and primary-school setting? Telling stories is probably one of the few opportunities in school for your child to talk and be heard at some length, without having to worry about someone scolding him for talking out of turn. (Why must the classrooms of America be so quiet?) I don't want to appear overly enthusiastic about these stories, the formal "presentations" children make at the front of the room, however, because so many other strong possibilities exist for regular classroom interchange. Nevertheless, kids at least are rubbing shoulders with conversational possibilities when they get to tell their stories publicly.

As you may remember from your own experiences, extended conversation in the teacher's presence is very often limited to "onstage" storytelling episodes. These are generally undynamic affairs. A child steps to the front of the room, typically holds up a picture or a toy or some exotic object—you know the "show-and-tell" routine from your childhood—and is expected to talk coherently, logically, and succinctly about it to a group of fidgeting youngsters. Questions may follow, but very little exchange occurs, not much you could call conversation, to be sure. Perhaps your child must tell about an incident that happened on the way to school or at home. Perhaps she must recount an event that the class participated in together—a police officer's visit to the kindergarten room; an experiment with a celery stalk, a glass of water, and red ink; a puppet show in the auditorium. Or perhaps your child must invent a story by pretending to be an inanimate object, an animal, or a character in a book or on a TV show.

Stories are fun to tell and listen to at home. At school they may be fun, but they're always important, and that importance can steal some of the joy out of the experience. That is, unless your child knows some storytellers' conventions, however slightly. Even with the informal stories kids have to tell in small groups when an adult is present, teachers have certain expectations from children when they relate stories. Some traits are valued; others are not; and children are expected to reflect their control of the formal elements of conversational storytelling.

What are they? I'm going to enlist the help of some really good teachers and researchers later on to review with you some of the qualities that teachers often look for in children's stories. Once you know these qualities, you can start encouraging your youngster to think about them and to address them in his or her home narratives. You can bet that I won't be talking about any rigid schema or drills—just some easy comment-question-answer activities that will help build some of the skills your child will need in school and beyond.

STORY TALK

As we explore the role of the parent in nurturing the child's storytelling skills and opportunities, I want to propose the term *story talk* to place the activity in its appropriate, interactive context. The more familiar word *storytelling* implies a performance, one speaker, one or more listeners, a job well or poorly done. But the kind of "storying" we're interested in, the kind that builds linguistic awareness, stimulates thought, and reflects acceptable story formats, is much more dialogic. With the loose narrative elements provided by one conversational partner, the other partner (the active listener) first helps to shape them and then integrates them into his own consciousness through questions, supportive comments, summaries, and other features of oral exchange. Like the first draft of a piece of writing, story talk is thought in progress.

Remember scaffolding from Chapter 3? Scaffolding is the technique of both drawing language out of your child and providing feedback on his observations. Story talk draws upon all the features of scaffolding, focused now on helping to advance your child's narrative. When Michael Halliday used scaffolding to draw out Nigel's zoo story, he was using story talk. Not all scaffolding focuses on stories however, so varied are the language-sharing episodes in the resourceful household. Hence the distinction that *story talk* aims for is of value here as we consider ways of developing your youngster's narrative skills.

Children need story talk, not storytelling performances. When you are relating a story or when your child relates it, you want to make the moment conversational. Your purpose? To tease out language and meaning. To validate experience. To model story conventions and to encourage their application. We don't want simply to listen as our child tells a story or to have our child simply listen as we tell one.

Although they enjoy stories, almost cannot avoid them, children benefit from our help in learning to use stories as part of the spoken language repertoire. Because of our own mature conversational instincts, for example, we know when to speak

and when to interrupt as we exchange narratives with other
adults. When someone is sharing a story with us, we usually
listen more than we talk—so adept can our partner generally
be in the conventions of storying. He or she can anticipate
many questions by connecting events carefully, reflecting on
them, and identifying details even before we might think to ask.

We can help children learn these skills. Teachers often expect
them right from the start of a child's experience at school—
perhaps too early, you might think. A good teacher knows how
to nourish and train the skill so that it emerges when the child
is ready for it. But it's not worth taking the chance that your
child will have such a teacher, when you easily can provide the
same kind of support at home.

Even when we think we're simply listening attentively to a
story, we are not at all passive. We do raise questions and make
comments. The conversation, the social interaction in a storytelling moment, actually helps produce the story. "Like all conversational meanings," says Gordon Wells, these kinds of stories
are "jointly constructed and require collaboration and negotiation for their achievement. In this way, members of a culture
create a shared interpretation of experience, each confirming,
modifying, and elaborating on the story of the other."

MOTHERS, FATHERS, STORIES

How do we create story-talk opportunities at home?

First, let us again acknowledge that many kids are instinctive
story engines, so you're not going to meet with enormous re-
sistance in revving them up to get stories going. But you do
need to reflect in your attitude toward stories a belief in the
riches of experience in every child's world, riches that language
will shape and make available for others to hear. Thus, our
children must know that as much as we want them to listen to
us, we also respect *their* narratives and are willing to listen
carefully to what they have to say.

The parent sets the stage in the home for children to share
their experiences comfortably and without fear, ridicule, or
criticism. You need to encourage your son or daughter, without

prying, to talk about moments he or she wishes to share. "What did you do at play school today?" "What did you do in the playground?" "Whom did you talk with at snack time?" "What happened today on the bus?" Questions like these will start things off. You'll be providing a pressure valve for the complex events in your child's life. In homes where children feel free to examine their experiences, deep, underlying questions and problems can surface in the course of easy conversation. Sadly, in many homes there is not even a possibility for interchange about daily experiences.

If you've tried regular story-talk sessions with your youngsters, you know, however, that you can sometimes draw a blank. You might get a one-word response: "Nothing" or "Nobody" or "No." Or, you might get a brief answer without much substance: "I had a fight with Johnny"; "We drew pictures"; "Lisa brought in a frog"; "Mrs. Harris showed us an experiment." What do you do then?

Your first effort should be to draw out the details, to have your child flesh out the story in his or her own words. First show your interest, framing questions whose answers will draw out the experience and its emotions in your child's language. "A fight!" you might say. "Where did it happen? What about? You must tell me all about it!" or "Well, I can't remember when I last saw a frog! What did it look like? What sounds did it make?"

Taking cues from your son or daughter's narrative, you can ask occasional questions. Show great concern for the details, especially those that demand the child's recall of the sensory experience; ask questions to elicit those details. You want to know about colors, about sounds things make, about movements and actions, smells and touch sensations, about the exact words people say. Ask when things took place—afternoon, morning, before lunch, at recess—because it will help the child's inner eye to focus upon the moment that he is now putting into language. The youngest child thrills in giving these details, and with a little encouragement will even act out responses. A child who hops about the room with glee when asked how the frog moves would earn my applause; and then I would ask,

"How would you tell someone who couldn't see you just how it moves?" I'd hope to hear "He hops" or "He flip-flops" or "He bounces." What solid, sharp actions! If I heard "He moves" or "He walks," I'd try to reach out for more exact words.

As soon as your child can speak about experiences, you'll want to begin this kind of creative questioning. At two or three or four years, your child begins to sharpen the powers of observation that are so critical to effective storytelling.

I've already talked quite a bit in Chapter 3 about creative questioning. It is the very heart of enlightened conversation with your child, especially when you examine books together to stimulate active reading. But you should also realize that your child may not easily communicate an experience you've asked about, no matter how carefully you've tried to establish a comfortable home conversation scene.

In that case, you yourself must turn storyteller. This will take pressure off your child, who suddenly may feel intimidated even by the gentlest request for a story. Sometimes the emotions evoked by an experience arouse more pain in recalling it than it did during the actual occasion. Back off. Tell your own story, alive in action and setting. "So you saw a fight, too! Well, I saw two men screaming at each other this afternoon, right in front of Macy's. The rain had turned everything wet and sticky. Well, an old man backed his Chevy into a new white Oldsmobile. Then a teenager in a plaid shirt leaped out of the Olds and slammed the door. 'Why don't you watch where you're going, you old goat!' he boomed. 'You little dummy,' the driver of the Chevy screamed from behind the steering wheel. 'Why did you park in front of the hydrant?' Fortunately, a police officer arrived to settle things before they got ugly!" As you speak, call up your own dramatic energies, changing voices to show how people talk, lacing the tale with whatever excitement or sadness or joy it might evoke.

In this kind of telling, concrete details set an example for similar experience-sharing by the child. Name places and people (where you can) carefully. Use words that suggest clear actions. Mention colors and sounds and use words for touch sensations. These stories establish a framework and act as models for your child. Using the kind of questioning I recommended when your youngster offers his story, you can establish a general sense of the quality of details that a good narrative retelling usually advances. By supporting the value of your child's experience, you will help avoid these painful self-judgments we hear so often from our children: "Nothing interesting ever happens to me" or "I have nothing to talk about."

STORYTELLING FORM

So important and frequently used is our storytelling impulse that a kind of format for stories has evolved. Think about the worst storyteller you know, think about what you wish he'd do to make it easier for you to listen without wanting to tear out your hair, and you'll be able to define some of the conventions most adults follow when we deliver our version of events we've seen or heard or invented. Of course, you don't think of the qualities of good stories as *rules*. *Conventions* is a much better word. Yet no matter what you call them, they do exist, guiding our judgments about the oral discourse of our friends and associates, and, surely, guiding the judgments teachers make about our children in formal classroom settings.

Certainly one can argue about how important it is to preserve the special role of everyday speech in children's language experiences, speech unhampered by the "rules" of "grown-up" or "educational" models. Nancy Martin, one of the major researchers on literacy in England, makes a convincing point. We often push children too hard and too soon to imitate adults' language "without regard for the needs of the actual situation, which is of their learning." We want to preserve the original, unconventional language creations of our children without shackling them to a rigid system of rules. That's not our purpose in language-building activities.

Opportunities do exist in the home, however, for a loving parent to explore some of the givens of adult language without too hard or too soon a push. By the time your child reaches formal schooling, you want him to have practiced language on the adult's playing field, so that he will not feel suddenly oppressed by the regulations of what seems like a whole new ball game.

Since *story talk* as we're using the term depends upon the conventions of both storytelling *and* conversation, let's look at some of the expectations teachers will have of your child's skills in these areas and at some of the steps you can take to stimulate their development without pressure in the home.

First, let's distinguish the major kinds of stories that kids are expected to tell, factual narratives and imagined narratives. It's unfortunate for youngsters starting to share their stories publicly that the word "story" has some opposite connotations. Children have to learn that when teacher says, "Tell the story of our trip to the pet shop" she means one thing; when she says, "Pretend that you are this leaf and tell the story of your life" she means another; and when she says, "I'm going to tell you the story of the Hungry Caterpillar" she means something else. Stories mean facts; they also mean imaginings.

Factual stories are stories of real events—real in the sense that they are perceived by the senses and reflect actual occurrences. At the corner of Oak and Sunset we watch a man in a yellow cherry-picker twisting telephone cables high above the street. Our story here is the event revolving about this man— what he did, how he did it, what happened as he worked, what consequences followed his actions. In such an instance, listeners expect the facts; whoever tells the story provides sensory images anchored in narrative sequence. "There was a man in a yellow metal box at the end of a crane, and he was high over the street fixing the telephone wires. First he cut the wire; then he took more from around his waist, and. . . ." Questions from listeners might draw out further details. Such a telling recreates a moment as someone perceives it.

In the factual stories your child retells in school, the teacher has often witnessed or participated in the events for which she's eliciting a narrative. Unlike events your child sees on his own and reports to an unfamiliar audience, the teacher here has her own mental image of the story. In her mind she sees how it should be structured, which events stand out, which characters need introduction, which actions require embellishment. To gain approval, your child's story will have to reflect that pre-conceived notion that the teacher has developed. She wants to see if your child can remember events accurately, can sequence them correctly, can connect details logically, and can evaluate the characters, ideas, and actions.

Imagined stories are stories invented in the creative faculty of the mind, the imagination. They may be rooted in specific events. A child telling a pretend story could start with the man in the cherry picker and take us into fantasyland. Or these stories may be based solely upon made-up characters or situations. Here realism is not an issue. With imagined stories, listeners often prefer some cue that the story is not factual, that the child knows that the events are fictions. A good listener can easily pick up clues as the story proceeds, but teachers are especially concerned that your child know the difference between real and imaginary. Often, the teller relies on formulaic structures: "Once upon a time. . . ." Even with imaginary stories, we expect certain conventions similar to those in factual stories. We want to know what the story will be about, even if only roughly. We want to learn about the characters as soon as we can. We want a framework of sensory details. We don't want to struggle with narrative sequence.

When a child summarizes a fictional story just read to her or a television program she's just seen, we have another cate-gory, a kind of cross-breed with characteristics of both factual and imagined tales. In this kind of narrative retelling, a child must stick to the facts of what may be wildly imaginative events. The story's fiction coheres about narrative and dialogue; an internal logic exists that holds the pieces of the story together. Try retelling *Green Eggs and Ham* or an episode of *Max Head-room* and you'll understand this story category. Experiencing a piece of imagined literature (most of the stories you or the teacher read to children fit this category) and narrating it for an audience places special demands on the child storyteller. She has to keep the events straight—logical, coherent, sequential. She also has to deal with the imagined world of the story.

And, as Shirley Brice Heath points out, your child often has to "negotiate" the meaning of a story with an adult. Children in two of the North Carolina communities she studied so carefully had very limited experience in these negotiations. When the primary teacher read the class the story of "Curious George," H. A. Ray's little monkey who is always in the thick of trouble and mischief but who always prevails, children from both groups had trouble. Some had very limited experiences with improbable fantasies; some had never heard such animal stories read to them; most were unfamiliar with strategies for dealing with the teacher's questions, such as "Isn't he crazy?" "Do you think they'll catch him?" "What would have happened if . . . ?"

Heath observes dramatic differences in the features of stories told by socially and culturally different groups. We see again the important relation between home language experience and school language use. Teachers had one set of expectations; the children, depending on their linguistic and cultural backgrounds, had other expectations. Thus, groups of youngsters "meet very different notions of truth, style, and language appropriate to a 'story' from those they have known at home. They must learn a different taxonomy and new definitions of stories. They must come to recognize when a story is expected to be true, when to stick to the facts, and when to use their imaginations."

In the preschool and elementary classroom, a story is one of the few alternatives to "short take" talking, those typical one-or-two-sentence responses kids must give in the occasional school exercises that draw on conversation. What storytelling features do teachers value? Bringing the notion of story talk into the classroom arena, we want to consider not only the details of the story itself, the content if you will, but also what Heath calls "interactional" features, qualities related to the social conditions of the story. I've tried to capture some of the elements of school storytelling in the list below. We'll take up each one in turn.

Characteristics of Stories Teachers Value

1. Wait until stories are asked for.
2. Tell single narrative moments.

3. Get to the point right away.
4. Introduce characters; identify them; set temporal and geographical contexts.
5. Stick to the facts; use a sequence that listeners can follow.
6. Respond to questions; provide evaluations of events; listen to reactions, analyses, evaluations proposed by others, and so on.
7. Provide sensory details.

1. *Wait until stories are asked for.* My favorite stories from children are the spontaneous flowers that bloom without advance warning, the little blossoms that unexpectedly open rare new worlds to us. Unfortunately, teachers charged with many children in a single class often see those unrequested stories as distractions from other learning. I wouldn't want you to discourage spontaneity at home just because the unfortunate realities of class size may not favor it at school.

However, it's a good idea to request stories at home so that your child gets the knack of responding to those requests when teacher makes them. Thus, from all the events in a child's day you can ask for a narrative retelling: "Tell Daddy the story of the man in the cherry picker"; "Tell Grandma about the squirrel we saw in the park"; "Tell Mommy the story I read to you before your nap." Or, you can ask for stories in the imagined category: "If you were that squirrel, what would you be doing now?"; "What do you think Goldilocks will do tomorrow?"; "If you were Curious George, what would you do next?" With gentle promptings like these you can build experience in important storytelling skills.

2. *Tell about single narrative moments.* What is a moment? A moment is a single instance, a flash of time that the speaker recreates in vivid language so that the events come alive. When your child *writes* a narrative, she will expand a brief scene with concrete sensory details (see 6 below). To prepare for writing activities and formal storytelling exercises, help your child concentrate on a brief span of time. Any occasion that catches your child's fancy has rich narrative possibilities.

3. *Get to the point right away.* As children learn storytelling

skills, they have to learn how to frame their stories for the listener as soon as possible. This convention imposes a planning activity on storytelling. That is, your child will be expected in the early school grades to have thought out the narrative before she tells it rather than simply to tell it as she composes the words on the spot. You know if you've listened to your very young child that she generally weaves her stories from language she produces at the moment and with little, if any, prior thought. Even if she's recounting actions that she's seen recently, she may not have constructed them in a story format before she actually begins talking. This lack of prethinking—it's quite normal—helps explain many of the inaccuracies, the omitted or embellished details, the imaginative forays amid the retelling of factual events.

Advance planning helps your child develop skills at generalizing. When your child generalizes, she establishes a broad context for the story at its outset. In short, she tells the main point of it right away and draws the chronological events into service of the generalization. Heath calls this "abstracting" and gives a compelling argument for its importance in a classroom setting. Teachers often extend an invitation to the whole class at storytelling time, and a child who steps forward must do more than just introduce herself or announce her intention to tell a story. If children do not make their points quickly—"tell what their story is about in a brief abstract"—some other child may steal the floor. The scaffolding strategies we discussed in Chapter 3 will help you elicit generalizations or abstracts from your child. Below I'll offer an example of creative story talk, and you'll see how your questions can help put together the necessary narrative skeleton. Also, I'll give more examples of generalizing in Chapter 8 when we look together at television's role as a conversation starter in the household.

4. *Introduce characters; identify them; set temporal and geographic contexts.* Little is as distracting in a story as the assumption by the storyteller that the listener knows the characters and the scene. You want to help your youngster learn to identify the people in the story and its surrounding physical place. Thus, by your questions and advance suggestions, you can elicit the

names of people or animals, the details of appearances and actions, the general time of the event being shared, and the setting of the story.

I'm not suggesting these as formal touch-points that your child should address as she must, soon enough no doubt, in those dreadful book-report formats most of us had to write in grade school. Glued together by roman numerals, the formats tortured us with categories: I. Author and title; II. Setting; III. Characters; IV. Plot, and so on. Instead of rigid requirements, I'm asking you to consider the key elements of narratives that we enjoy and that condition the mind of the listener to follow the story's thread. It's the reporters' *W*s—Who, What, Where, and When and Why (and How, too)—that frame narratives and help listeners follow along. As your child tells an imaginary tale or recounts the events in a real moment, you want to tease out language that elaborates the story and makes it interesting and full of meaning for the audience.

5. *Stick to the facts; use a sequence that listeners can follow.*

When your child retells an event (a factual story) or when he retells a fictional story that the teacher read to him or that he saw on television (a combined factual and imagined story), his teacher will expect him to represent the scene accurately and to follow an appropriate sequence.

Factual accuracy does not mean exhaustive completeness, however. It means a faithful representation of important events without unnecessary embellishments or digressions that can easily divert a listener's attention; and without imaginative flights that can inappropriately diminish the story's reality.

Sequence—that is, order of events—helps control a story. It is the set of road signs that point us in the right direction. Most stories are chronological: They proceed from one event to the other in time order. First this happened; then this happened; finally that happened. Chronology establishes a temporal sequence so that the listener understands how events are related.

Seemingly simple, chronology has its subtle complexities. For example, a storyteller may have to establish background by referring to a previous event to help the listener. These necessary digressions can trap an unaccomplished storyteller. Interesting in their own right, they can overtake the main story and thoroughly confuse the listener. Stories can also proceed through spatial sequence. In telling a story about the kitchen or the playground a child may relate events as they happened in time; but she also could talk about events from front to back, left to right, top to bottom, far to near, depending on her point of view. In addition, events may be ordered according to importance—least important first, most important last—to hold a listener's attention.

You know that, left to their own designs, children can run all over the place when they tell a story, bouncing back and forth in time like little rubber balls. You know that some children digress easily, focusing on seemingly insignificant events, overlooking others of apparent importance. Some children, on the other hand, strip a story down to its bare bones, a few emaciated sentences without details and without ideas connected explicitly, either through logical or temporal patterns or through syntax—subordinated phrases or clauses that establish linkages. You know further how some kids love to invent pieces of a story. The fiction mixes with the facts in a delectable, if inaccurate, fruit salad whirled together in the blender so everything runs together.

How is your preschooler to learn to adhere to the specific details of a real event or of a story she's read or heard? How is she to know how to elaborate important details and skip unimportant ones? How is your child to learn to follow temporal sequence?

Here, Mother and Father step front and center again. When you talk regularly with your child you can stimulate these skills. Use story talk. The way in which you invite stories at home and respond to them with your questions will help your child shape narratives that adults and other children value.

6. *Respond to questions; provide evaluations of events; listen to reactions, analyses, evaluations proposed by others, and so on.* Among the qualities of storytelling that teachers support is your child's ability to respond to comments and questions during the story and after it is over. By using story talk in the manner suggested

here, you're giving your youngster a significant advantage in developing valued skills. Asking questions throughout the story and providing bits of analytic detail—interpretations and evaluations included—underscore the interactive nature of story talk. You may have to fill in bits of important information that your child doesn't remember or couldn't know in the first place. Here's the opportunity for painless teaching: As you perceive the need to provide more information you can offer it in the relaxed setting of a shared story. Thus, in talking about the man in the cherry picker, you might explain why we call the vehicle a cherry picker or how the man learns how to use it or the principles of safety he follows in order to do his job without injury.

Your child will learn to be analytical as he listens to your analysis of his story. He'll see how thoughtful listeners bring their own visions and outlooks to a narrative. He'll see how to respond to questions that help the listener sharpen understanding. He'll also learn that a factual retelling is in many ways a public act; other people may have witnessed the event, and they will be checking their perceptions against the perceptions of your child. The factual story in the classroom becomes a kind of community expression, told by one child, perhaps, but validated by group response.

As I've said before, the teacher has often shaped the story in her mind before she asks children to tell it. She's listening for how well your youngster's version of events matches what the teacher herself perceives. At home, with story-talk activities that follow an event you and your daughter have witnessed, you'll be doing the same kind of thing. You've both seen the man in the cherry picker; you have the events laid out on a storyboard in your mind; and when you ask Johnny to tell Dad or Grandma the story of the cherry picker, you'll be measuring Johnny's version against your own. Good experience, don't you think? In a simple, relaxed conversational setting, you're helping your child master important skills that he'll be expected to know soon after starting school.

You want to consider another point. Many children cannot flesh out a story and hold a listener's attention. Your question-

ing and commentary help make the child aware of the possibilities for expanding ideas (more of this in item 7 below). Call
upon your son or daughter to evaluate events and characters
in the story. "What did you think about what that squirrel did?"
"How do you think the man in the cherry picker felt?" Encourage your child to connect events. Did one thing happen
because something else happened? Did one thing happen as a
result of another? What *might* happen as the result of some
action? "Why did the squirrel bury the Cracker Jacks? What
do you think he'll do if he comes back and finds they're not
there?" "Why does the man have to fix the wires on the pole?
What do you think would happen if he doesn't fix the wires?"
Making these linkages, even a very young child starts to sharpen
critical thinking. Events do not simply occur as functions of
time. Causal relationships do exist, and we can start calling
attention to them early.

In helping children focus attention on details of a story, have
fun with a tape recorder. Get your youngster to speak into the
microphone, then listen together, stopping the tape at relevant
points in the story and asking questions that will tease out more
information. Also, some parents like to ask their children to
draw a picture of an event and talk about it together. A child's
illustration is often the magical key to unlock conversation.
Later in this chapter we'll look in more detail at the value of
pictures in stimulating talk at home.

7. *Provide sensory details.* A key element in successful written
narrative is *concrete sensory detail.* In the early grades, teachers
will be asking students to speak and then write their little stories, and one of the mainstays of appropriately elaborated narratives is words to convey sensory impressions. I'm talking here
about description. Our language is rich in words that convey
sense impressions: sound, smell, sight (color and action), touch,
and taste. Words like *boom* or *whisper, musty* or *piney, squirm*
or *leap, orange* or *violet, dry* or *wet, sweet* or *salty* appeal to the
reader's senses. For some of the senses it's a simple matter to
find word-equivalents for real sensations. Perhaps sound is the
easiest to capture because English has an enormous variety of
words for naming sounds. There are not only words like *shout*

and *explode* and *cough*—words for sounds—but also words that make the sounds they name, like *whoosh* and *buzz* and *bark* and *click*. Words for color and action similarly fill the language, as do words for touch sensations, though to a lesser degree. Words that name smells are less abundant, and those for taste sensations are the least available.

When I speak of *concreteness,* I mean the degree to which a word names, specifically, the thing it represents. It's clear among these three word choices which is most specific: plant, flower, rose.

Plant names a large and very general group. *Flower* helps narrow down the plant group by excluding vegetables, non-flowering shrubs, many trees, vines, weeds, and so on. But *rose* is the most exact of the words, the most "concrete," the word that has the sharpest visual quality. Say *flower* and listeners need to make their own choices—one person sees a daisy, one a chrysanthemum, another a tulip. Good storytellers want listeners to form exact visual connections, to see things precisely in the way that the person telling the story sees them.

Children are awake to the sensory world; they respond to it and internalize images of it long before learning the language that will recall it from memory. When naming things for your toddler, know how to find the exact word for an object, *le seul mot juste,* as Balzac would say. When reaching out and touching a *leaf,* a child should hear that word along with *flower* or *plant.* Your child should hear you say *robin* or *sparrow* as well as *bird,* when he or she hears and sees the flap of wings outside his window. As you help your youngster of five or six to identify an object, help her find the most precise expressions: *elm, First National Bank, Park Road,* and *skirt* all name more specifically than *tree, building, street,* and *clothing.*

In writing, there is a magic about naming—especially proper names—that involves the reader instantly: *Cricklewood Drive, Kings Highway, Hout's Department Store,* and *Grand Central Station* weave a spell that *street, highway, department store,* and *train station* cannot. In writing, of course, as opposed to speaking, a child can concentrate more fully in choosing sense words that bring narrative to life. Yet you can lay the foundations for developing skill with imagery by asking your child to provide sensory language as part of the story-talk scene. You'll also be giving clues to a child who is reluctant to expand a story. Ask questions like, "What color was the truck?" "What was the man wearing?" "What did the flower smell like?" "What sounds did you hear the squirrel make?" These questions underscore the value of sensory detail in any experiential narrative and will help your child integrate such details in stories she tells and writes at school.

I don't want to leave this discussion of important details without mentioning the value of dialogue. Listeners—teachers included, certainly—always like to hear snatches of conversation in stories. I'm not talking of verbatim dialogue. Nothing is as tedious as a storyteller who tries to recreate every word of conversation accurately. I am talking about snippets of language, a word here, a phrase here, that capture the mood of the moment and show the story's participants in a realistic light. Dialogue injects life; the characters breathe when we hear the storyteller's version of the words people speak. As your child tells her story, ask, "What did the man say?" "What did you say to him?" "What did Mommy say to the newspaper girl?"

Let's see how some of the pointers we've been considering converge in a typical story-talk moment between parents and their four-year-old child. You'll recognize familiar elements of scaffolding here, but remember that we're applying them in a storytelling context.

Mother: Tell Daddy what we did today. (1)
Allison: Nothing. What? What did we do? (2)
Mother: Tell Daddy about that funny squirrel we saw. (3)
Allison: We saw a fun-nee squirrel today. (4)
Father: Where? (5)
Allison: By the swings. (6)
Father: The swings? Where? (7)
Mother: Tell Daddy where you were at the swings. (8)
Allison: The park, Daddy. We were at Marj-ree Post Park and we saw a squirrel. (9)

Father: When did you go to the park? (10)

Allison: The morning. Before nursery. (11)

Father: What did the squirrel look like? (12)

Allison: A big furry tail. (13)

Father: Just a tail? No wonder he was so funny! (14)

Allison: [*Laughing.*] No! He had everything. Feet. And claws. And a teeny-tiny nose. And a tail. (15)

Father: What color was the squirrel? (16)

Allison: It was a gray squirrel. And he had whikkers. (17)

Mother: Whiskers. He had whiskers. (18)

Father: Well, what was he doing that was so funny? (19)

Allison: Eating Cracker Jacks! (20)

Father: Why is that so funny? (21)

Allison: Squirrels don't eat Cracker Jacks, silly! They eat nuts. (22)

Mother: That's right, sweetie. They do eat nuts. They eat other things that grow, too. They eat buds off trees and they eat vegetables and berries and flowers. Remember that squirrel who ate the top of the tulip in front of our house? (23)

Allison: Yes, but Cracker Jacks don't grow! They come in a box. (24)

Father: Cracker Jacks are sweet popcorn. Maybe the squirrel likes the corn. Corn grows. (25)

Allison: He probly likes the sweet. (26)

Father: The syrup on top? (27)

Allison: The syrup. That's what I like. (28)

Father: You're right. I bet he does like the sweet syrup. What did the squirrel do after he ate the Cracker Jacks? (29)

Allison: He ate the Cracker Jacks. Then he took them to the sandbox. He made a hole. (30)

Father: How did he do that? (31)

Allison: With his little feet. The ones in front. He was kicking sand. Mommy said, "Sh, sh! Don't scare him away!" (32)

Mother: Allison was laughing, and I was too. We were watching this squirrel bury Cracker Jacks. (33)

Allison:　He was burying the Cracker Jacks. He put them in the hole. (34)

Mother:　Why do you think he did that? (35)

Allison:　He didn't want me to take them and eat them all up! (36)

Mother:　You wouldn't do that, all those sandy Cracker Jacks! But you're right, squirrels hide food so no one else can get at it. They also hide food for the winter when it's hard to find. (37)

Father:　What else, honey? Is there more to the story? (38)

Allison:　He was singing, *chip-chip, chip-chip, chip-chip.* Then he ran away fast, away, away, over the trees, up, up, into the sky! He was a star. (39)

Father:　A wonderful make-believe ending! (40)

Allison:　[*Giggling.*] Just a pretend star. He didn't fly into the sky. But he ran away. And that's all. (41)

Using scaffolding in a story-talk context, the parents tease out the narrative and its details from their daughter's perception of an experience in which Mother has also participated. Mother invites Allison to tell a story (1). In school, children are expected to respond to the teacher's request for a story and this is good practice. But you notice that the request does not have its desired effect (2). Allison is confused because the remark designed to prompt story talk here is too vague. Of the innumerable activities in the day, which one, in fact, should the child identify? She doesn't know. You see here a basic problem with preconceived stories, those that an adult has in her mind and expects a child to mirror accurately. Unless your child is a mind reader, she may have trouble knowing what you're asking her to do.

In 3, Mother rephrases the request and provides a more specific context. She highlights the particular occasion she has in mind, thus moving her child to consider a single narrative moment. The new cue to Allison is not "Tell Daddy what we did at the park" or "Tell Daddy what you saw at the park." Those requests might have produced interesting narratives, but they might not have generated the story Mother wanted. Further, my guess is that these last requests would have drawn out a very diffuse story, a hodgepodge of little details that stuck in Allison's mind from the time she spent at the park. Mother's intent here is to get Allison to focus on a specific set of events.

It's important to notice here how Mother helps focus the story. The words "that funny squirrel" generalize the event at the outset; they give an attitude or opinion so that a listener knows the point of the pending narrative. It's like a coming attraction in a movie house: You see a little bit in advance of the main show. Because her child will have to learn how to come to the point of a story right away, Mother is modeling an important skill. Note how Allison restates the words in her own sentence (4). Our hope is that with lots of home practice, she will know how to generalize a story on her own before she gives its full details.

Father's questions 5, 7, and 10 build on Mother's focusing efforts and get Allison to state the temporal and geographic limits of the moment. We can only imagine how the child's inner eye is shaping and reshaping a version of the reality she experienced earlier. Her parents' questions help Allison illuminate essential details and block out irrelevant details.

The playful banter in 12 through 18 shows how, in a relaxed setting, a mother or father can help a child generate sensory details. Here, questions and comments encourage Allison to introduce the main "character" of this story—the squirrel—and to shape a visual image in the listener's mind. Father hasn't seen any of this, remember. For him to imagine the moment, Allison must supply sense words so that he will see the scene just as she saw it.

(We are at the true boundaries of creative expression in this exchange between parent and child. Do you know Tolstoy's definition of art? "To evoke in oneself a feeling one has once experienced," he says, "then by means of movement, lines, colors, sounds, or forms expressed in words, so to transmit that feeling that others experience the same feeling—this is the activity of art." With their gentle yet directive conversation, Allison's parents stand with their daughter at art's border. Who knows what stimulates creative expression, what makes the

Michelangelos, the Virginia Woolfs, the Tolstoys? Perhaps it is a compulsion to share the special vision of experience. By drawing out that vision in language, a parent helps a child validate perception and acknowledge its worthiness as a shared, communal enterprise. Do you see the point I'm trying to make? An experience registers some feeling in your child and makes its imprint in her mind and body by means of the senses. The sounds, the smells, the colors, the actions, the sensations of taste and touch provide the passageways for the emotional experience she stores as memory. To transmit that experience, a child must use language to convey those sense impressions. By stimulating that language, parents fan the same embers kindled by the artistic impulse.)

About halfway through this story talk, then, we have information that will keep listeners attentive. We have a preview of the moment in the focused generalization about the funny squirrel. We know the time and place of the action. We know some of what the squirrel looks like—words like *gray* and *furry* help evoke the scene with their appeal to our senses. The details of time and place, color and action, are not tangential to the narrative. They establish its viability.

I want to call your attention to Allison's mispronunciation of *whiskers*. Mother corrects *whikkers* in 18; and Allison apparently ignores the correction, or perhaps Father's next question prevents her taking any action to pronounce it again if she wanted to. The point, though, is that there's no fuss here. A word is mispronounced; someone corrects it; and we just move along to other things. I'll have more to say about the issue of error in Chapter 6.

Notice in 19 how, once Father knows some details, he refocuses attention on the narrative events. In 21 he challenges critical thinking. Allison must evaluate her perceptions. She must offer an interpretation: What's so funny about a squirrel eating Cracker Jacks? Notice how Mother provides some extra information to correct what may be a too limited view of what squirrels eat (23). Relating this added information to a prior experience—Allison saw another squirrel eat the head off a tulip—is an excellent strategy. Teachers will expect your youngster to make connections between current moments and past events, between unfamiliar characters and familiar ones, between real-life moments and scenes in books.

Conversation in 24 through 29 gives Allison a chance to integrate her understanding of these new details of squirrels' eating habits. Father is sensitive to language growth: He guesses that his daughter probably can't come up with the word *syrup*— she uses *sweet* in 26—and he provides it naturally in his conversation.

When Father asks "What did the squirrel do after he ate the Cracker Jacks?" (29), he not only calls Allison back to the narrative, but he also zeroes in on sequence. Words like *after, then, before, next, later, earlier,* and many other time markers in our language, will help move your child's narrative along appropriate temporal lines. Note how Allison repeats the first event in time, uses the marker *then,* and indicates the next event in the chronology. All this is in direct response to Father's encouraging questions. Asking for more information that checks on Allison's observations, Father stimulates the wonderful statements in 32. The line of quoted detail adds spark to the story, don't you think? "Sh, Sh! Don't scare him away!"

It strikes me that Allison is unsure of the meaning of the word *bury,* or at least she feels a need to define it in her own language (34). Mother presses for critical thinking with her question in 35. After Allison's delightful response in 36, Mother keeps the mood light with her little joke, then takes the opportunity to provide useful analysis that models the mental connections we want children to make on their own. Note in 37 how she links events causally; squirrels do this because of that. Causal thinking is not easy. We can get trapped in teleology (the doctrine of final causes, of design or purpose in nature) and the *post hoc, ergo propter hoc* fallacy (because this thing happened first in time, *therefore* this thing happened as a result of it). Nevertheless, seeing causes and effects is one of the hallmarks of critical thought, and we can try to demonstrate it at home in these storytelling episodes.

Father returns Allison to the chronology in 38, and his request is an effort to move toward closure. Allison's attention is flagging. After her wonderful onomatopoeia *("chip-chip, chip-chip, chip-chip")* in 39, she flies off into fancy. But note how well Father handles this in 40. He makes clear that he knows that the ending is pretend, and Allison acknowledges it herself in 41. There are no admonitions—"Stick to the facts!"; "That's a lie!" Instead Father describes the ending as make-believe and judges it favorably. Allison's formulaic ending in 41, "And that's all," closes the story. The closing shows Allison's experience with storytelling formats, probably from books her parents and nursery-school teacher read to her. Bringing a story to an end is a trait teachers favor in the classroom.

Conversations like the one you've read between Allison and her parents require no special training. The principles I'm laying out will help you engage your youngster in productive storytelling, but you don't need an advanced degree in psychology or linguistics to tap your child's emerging language skills. Remember your own good instincts, be loose, and honor your child's mind and language. And don't forget to have fun. Don't make your living room a classroom.

PICTURE TALK REVISITED

A child's early attempts at conveying sensory impressions spread out as splashes of line and color on a page. In crayon, pencil, colored pencil, or ink, youngsters portray a vision of reality unique to their perceptions and their talents. At first the scribbles and scrawls, the wide arcs, the concentrations of design propose a shapeless landscape of color and texture; then, bit by bit, the components fit together into some partially recognizable whole. There stands a bird with an oversize wing, one leg, a beak like a broomstick; here stands a house beside a child who is twice as large as the building and extraordinary for the arm that shoots from her neck. Next, in a sunburst of light and swirls of red, yellow, green, orange, and gold, there is a thing with ears whose crossed eyes look gloomily beyond your shoulder.

When, with a flourish, your young artists present their latest works, there's another opportunity to talk with your child. Don't be one of those parents who, afraid of hurting a child's feelings, only praise and never venture a "What is it?" about the latest artwork. Of course, it's the way that you ask the question that will determine the response. Asked without impatience and without a suggestion that the child is either wrong or untalented, a "What is it?" often unlocks a glorious stream of narrative, filled with colors and sounds and glimpses of action that only a child can see.

You saw earlier how questions draw out conversation about printed illustrations in books and magazines. About a picture your child herself draws, questions that show interest and urge a solid attention to details help your child sustain the narration and your mutual delight in conversation. "Why is this boy bending over?" "Where's the driver of that bus?" "Why are there no leaves on that oak tree?"

As I've said before, listen carefully to the responses. Show no disappointment if the person or object looks strange. Here in the explanation of a picture, your child is sharing an event that marked his consciousness. Your youngster's pictures and stories offer snapshots of his vision and psychology. Trained counselors can learn a good deal about a child's personality— his problems, talents, fears, and successes—from the pictures that he draws. For you the pictures are yet another starting point for story talk.

In your talks about a drawing, you establish a critical connection between the picture and the word as a means to convey experience. These little pictures can engender lively conversation, which invariably moves into storytelling, and you'll be able to apply what you've learned in this chapter. Whenever you can, encourage your sons and daughters to talk about the idea behind the pictures they have made. I mention drawings here because they often grow from a child's spontaneous doodling. More formal attempts, such as finger painting, watercolors, and cut-and-paste creations are also good starting points for written language, especially for the child who draws reluctantly or too self-consciously.

Every child enjoys cutting pictures out of newspapers and magazines and then pasting these cutouts on sturdy paper to make collages. You should encourage this activity. "Why don't you cut out the prettiest room you can find?" or "Cut out as many pictures of red things as you can" or "Go through the magazine and cut out the things you find that start with the *b* sound." After the child's artistic effort is complete, encourage talking with a "What is it?" question. You might help your child write a sentence underneath his work: "This is a large, happy room" or "These things are all red" or "All these things start with *b*." You can relate this activity to holidays, seasons or months of the year, parties or celebrations, special events at home or at school.

I recommend the photo essay as a wonderful activity for parent and child on a rainy afternoon. It's the kind of creative play that, once begun, holds a boy's or girl's interest. First talk about some overriding theme for the project—"spring is here," "Christmas is a happy time"—and then suggest that the child tell one sentence to offer the main idea of each picture. If you have an old tin box of family pictures, or if you encourage your youngsters to use cameras to take their own photographs or slides, this creation will be great fun!

If you have preschoolers or elementary-school children at home, once you put into action some of the ideas I've asked you to consider here, you probably won't be able to stop the flow of story after story, little narrative jewels, some fanciful, most real, all told with intensity and animation. Enjoy them. Feel confident that in tapping your child's instinctive gift for storytelling you are also interacting with your child in important ways. You're helping to build language skills that will make your youngster ready for the demands of learning in school and in the world beyond it.

6

Language in Play

How can a parent help expand a child's word resources and a child's options for using those words? Here, as in other areas of language growth, you can use your home environment to tap children's native talents. Children enjoy playing with words, and in this chapter I'd like to suggest a few language games so that you can have some fun with your youngster as you heighten his vocabulary and broaden his thinking. I also want to talk about the correctness bugaboo. I'm sure you're wondering about how to handle your child's errors in syntax, word choice, and pronunciation, and I have some ideas that you may find useful.

To the fun first.

BUILDING VOCABULARY

Experts agree that a child's vocabulary relates to the nature of his experiences and to the language he hears and uses to explore those experiences. Children have an innate love for words. Just think a moment of your child's delight as you read aloud the improbable rhymes in Dr. Seuss books or as your child invents nonsense words. Never lose sight of the pleasure and fun of saying, using, and playing with words in moments of shared experience with your youngster. A parent accompanied by a four-year-old who watches snatches of activity in a supermarket can direct and influence his child's vocabulary by observing and discussing the words that apply to that scene. A child may hear and use: *unloading, supplies, stack, crate, special, discount, coupon, container, margarine, aisle, sawdust, manager, refrigeration*, and countless other new or only vaguely familiar words. In a natural way you should talk about objects and events, and encourage questions and observations.

After your child reports an exciting experience, you can aid vocabulary growth by guiding her use of words to describe that experience. A three-year-old rushing in and announcing, "It's snowing" has opened a door for word exploration. You might say, "Snow? How wonderful! Let's see how many words we can use to tell about snow." Parent and child can enjoy coming up with words like these together:

icy	dancing	lazy	like white paint drops
cold	white	flaky	playful
wet	swirling	fluttering	like falling sugar
soft	blowing	tickling	fluffy
frozen	shivery	powdery	slippery

All the vocabulary-building books and exercises and all the attempts to commit long lists of words to memory pale beside the invaluable connection of language and experience. Mother or Father acts as a child's dictionary of word resources by naming, constantly, the items that are part of a new or familiar experience. A visit to the doctor yields: *examination, throat culture, patient, prescription, stethoscope, injection, blood pressure, vaccine, inoculation.* The child who helps with cooking hears and uses: *simmer, steam, blanch, blend, pot, pan, carving knife, dice, beat, mold, cinnamon, yeast, broil, bake.* The youngster who likes to wash the car with Mother or Father considers: *filthy, sudsy, scrub, hubcaps, grid, hood, taillights, headlights, windshield.* A talk about a picture in a magazine will release a jet stream of language. The bedtime story, the program on television or radio, and the motion picture all are ample sources of new words too.

In moments of language experience, children will often signal when they don't know the definition of a word. The question "What does that mean?" from a boy or girl of any age is an invitation for a conscientious parent to help with vocabulary. Later in this chapter, I'll provide some tips for dealing with the questions your child will doubtlessly raise about words he doesn't know. In the meantime, you should attend to the unfamiliar word by talking about other words that mean the same or nearly the same thing and by eliciting or giving an appropriate example of how to use the word. Often I will "plant" what I'm sure is new vocabulary, using a word my child might not know, and then I'll wait for his question about its meaning.

Even with simple words, such as *pot* and *pan,* you should be sure to identify distinct meanings so that the difference between such familiar objects stays clear in your youngster's mind. Selecting the most specific word from among several and attempting to find more specific words for general ones are other techniques that help children focus upon the *exact* meanings of words. Helping your child name opposites to words also fixes meanings in her mind, although this is often difficult because not all words have true opposites and because in many cases several opposites exist with subtle differences of meanings. However, antonyms for words like *day, black, sweet, weak, boy, cold, sad, light, woman,* and *enemy* are simple to find, and children love and learn from the game.

Concrete language comes strongly into play in vocabulary growth. Several years back my wife overheard an instructive interchange between a child and an adult as they waited to see a performance of *Snow White* at the Westerly Parkway School. One mother, accompanying her young daughter and a group of the daughter's friends, tried engaging each child in conversation. To one little girl with brown hair and smooth skin, she said, "Those are really cute shoes you're wearing." The child shook her long brown hair and said, "Uh, uh. They're not cute." "Oh, yes they are, Mary," her friend's mother replied. "They're very cute." "Nope. They're *attractive*." The woman laughed. "Well, I still think they're pretty neat."

Here the child brought a precise word from her own storehouse of vocabulary, one much more valuable in suggesting the grounds for judgment than *nice* or *neat* upon which the older woman insisted. *Attractive* is not as precise as *new leather shoes* or *brown suede shoes*, but it's an improvement over time-weary choices such as *neat* or *nice*. *Cute* and *neat* and *good, interesting, nice, swell,* and *bad* are vague words, and are as poor for describing as the words *thing, item,* or *object* are for naming, and as *went, walked, was, appeared,* and *seemed* are for showing action.

When you have the chance to explore words with your children, try to select words that suggest qualities as precisely as possible.

"Well, Nicholas, how did you like the book Aunt Clara gave you?"

"It was good."

"Good? What do you mean? I don't think I know what you mean."

"It was good. You know. It was good."

"Do you mean funny?"

"Oh, yes. It was funny. It was even silly."

As soon as the child taps her vocabulary for a precise word, help her explore the wide variety of words that can replace the vague one. Make lists of precise words according to your child's interest and age.

Instead of *good* (for a book)		Instead of *nice* (for a person)	
funny	fanciful	friendly	happy
exciting	realistic	helpful	funny
silly	tender	gentle	peppy
unusual	challenging	warm	relaxed
scary	suspenseful	inspiring	lively
dramatic	humorous	good-natured	thoughtful
heartwarming	tense	kind	cooperative
truthful	romantic	generous	fun-loving
adventurous	lively	cheerful	adventurous
imaginative	frightening	loving	strong

Instead of *went* or *walked*			
rushed	hustled	drifted	limped
scurried	scampered	strolled	galloped
skipped	marched	hopped	eased
sailed	slipped	flew	rolled
jumped	paraded	stormed	hobbled

All these activities encourage the exploration of options and help your child avoid overusing "standard" words—old reliables that are a weary part of our linguistic grab bag. In a subtle way, you are discouraging the common, imprecise favorites: *thing, idea, way; give, make, get, be put, walk, have, cause; a lot, interesting, important, big, much, many, good.*

The following games will help you develop your own resourceful approaches in expanding your child's vocabulary. If you arrange to share exciting experiences—better still, if you and your child train yourselves to see excitement in even the most ordinary experiences—the language that grows out of such occasions builds and reinforces a valuable word supply. As you know, your own sensitivity sets the pace for your youngster's lifelong attitude toward language.

WORD GAMES

Part of a home word-building program is to point out to children the way words change to mean different things.

Even a simple shopping-trip excursion with a sensitive parent can inspire a boy or girl to look at the magical, quick-change artistry of words. You visit the *bakery* and see the *baker baking;* as *shoppers* you go to the *shop* to do *shopping;* see *drivers drive* into a *driveway*. By saying the words, talking about meanings, and enjoying the fun of hearing changes in word sounds, you and your child become aware of the immense flexibility of language.

Help your child see the versatility of language by examining related words. You might want to prepare a list together. If your youngster isn't writing yet, you jot them down, just to keep track. Or, have your child speak the words into a tape recorder. Look at all the words we can generate from *play:*

Play

plays	playful	plaything	playbill
player	playfulness	playpen	playboy
played	playtime	a play	playfellow
playable	double play	playact	play-by-play
playing	playhouse	playback	playgoer
	play-off		

By offering your child a group of unfinished sentences, you can ask him to fill in the blanks with words from the list you just prepared. This will show you if he understands the vocabulary.

1. The children were _____. (playing, playful)
2. He _____ all afternoon. (played)
3. The pitcher helped in a _____. (double play, play-off)
4. The kitten was _____. (playful, playing)
5. At school I like _____. (playing, playtime)

Another way to help a youngster see how words change is to start with a base word and ask your child to create words from it, words that suit the blank space in a sentence. Help out with the tough ones!

Sleep
1. I feel _____. (sleepy)
2. Two puppies were _____ on a rug. (sleeping)
3. She spoke _____. (sleepily)

I promised to consider some strategies for dealing with questions about new words. I think it's very important for you to resist telling your child the meaning of a word she doesn't know straight off. At the early stages of vocabulary growth, you will provide meanings as needed, of course. That's one of your most important roles as an aide in your child's advance to linguistic excellence. Yet as soon as you can, free your child from dependency on you as the only source of definitions. Suggest the patterns you follow when *you* stumble on words you don't know.

Most people first use informed guessing as a means of un-puzzling a new word. Don't you try to figure out meanings from the sentence you hear or read in which the word appears? Most times you can come up with a definition that's accurate enough to let you guess the meaning; later on you might check your guess in a dictionary. Children need to practice this guesswork whenever they can.

Remember how Saul figured out the meaning of *imposter?* (See Chapter 4.) Apply the strategies you examined there.

Suppose your daughter asks you to define a word—for example, *irritated.* You can rely upon her love for games and puzzles to urge her to use clues in sentences to figure out definitions. "I know what that means, Tory. But let's see if *you* can guess what it means when I use it in a sentence. Listen to my hints before you say anything. 'The woman left the party because smoke *irritated* her eyes.' What do you think it means?"

Be aware that this strategy won't always work smoothly. (You saw how I struck out the first time when I tried to give Saul a useful hint about *imposter* that turned out to be not so useful after all!) You may have to try other sentences that have more obvious clues. But once your child gets the meaning, it's one she's put together from your clues *into her own language,* and you have helped her to use vocabulary that is already part of her repertoire.

Go on talking about the same word and suggest other sentences in which to use the word: "Good, Tory! That's right. It means *bothered.* Suppose I said, 'Mother was *irritated* because I forgot to buy eggs for tomorrow's breakfast.' What would that mean?" You might say "What are some things that *irritate* you?" or "What does your brother look like when he's *irritated?*" Finally, if your youngster can write, ask her to set the word down and to construct her own sentence using the word. A picture cut from a magazine or newspaper or an original picture that she draws can illustrate the new word and will provide solid visual reinforcement.

You may want to try some of the following games at home

in your ongoing effort to build a treasury of words that your child can use to identify objects and actions with a high degree of specificity.

The "What's the Best Word?" Game. The purpose in this activity is to pick a word that most *exactly* names a particular object. You can do this with real objects or with pictures in a magazine. For example, you might say, "Okay, Maria, let's play a word game. I'll point to something in your room and say two words. You tell which word names exactly what the thing is. Ready? *Furniture. Desk.*" Ask her to explain the choice, though it might be a while before she can communicate to you the notion of "general" or "specific." Help your child see that a word such as *furniture* can mean many different things and that *desk* is the better word, because it names precisely what the object is. Below are some other groups of words that move from the general to the specific. Expand the group to three as your child advances in skill.

	I	II	III
1.	fruit	apple	
2.	toy	top	
3.	room	kitchen	
4.	cereal	oatmeal	
5.	book	dictionary	
6.	food	vegetable	carrot
7.	liquid	drink	milk
8.	vehicle	automobile	jeep
9.	meat	beef	hamburger
10.	medicine	pill	aspirin

This is not an easy game, but it's worth your efforts. Your child will begin to learn that language should strive for exactness. Ask for a drawn illustration of the most specific item, to reinforce the precision of the word you're stressing. For *food,* there are too many possibilities; for *vegetable* a wide choice, too; only *carrot* gives the specific clue to the listener.

An easier variation of this game is to name some general

objects (such as *furniture, flower, tree, candy, book, drink, jewelry, toy*) and to ask your child to give a specific example or two of each. Show how to do the first one so there's no confusion.

The "Name the Action" Game. Children can learn to name actions with varying degrees of exactness. You want to help your child develop a sensitivity to the way some words capture actions more precisely than others. This is partly a vocabulary-building activity. Children of all ages have at their command language that names action. Words such as *walk* and *move* can be replaced by much clearer ones: *run, hop, hurry, trip* are just a few.

Use your child's innate ability with action language to set up some "Name the Action" games. This one is fun for groups of children at a birthday party. On separate slips of paper write the words for precise actions: *skip, dance, hop, wiggle, jump, drag, crawl, tumble,* and others. Fold the papers and put them in a shoe box or hat. A child chooses a slip from the box and reads (with your help, if necessary) the word silently. The child then moves across the room and tries to perform the action the word suggests. The other children try to guess the word. This game works very well even with older children where the vocabulary is more difficult: *amble, stroll, zip, zigzag, slink, steal.* With this game it's also possible to teach your child that some words mean the same thing on the surface, but have different qualities. For example, *flee, race,* and *hurry* all mean to run in some way, yet each one brings to mind a special quality. *Flee* suggests escape; *race* makes one think of a sport; and *hurry* implies the need to meet a deadline.

The "Build on Image" Game. This game develops your child's skill at expanding a word picture by adding details. It goes a long way in sharpening sensory language, which is especially important for describing and narrating events in writing. (Look back at Chapter 5 if you need a reminder.) Start with simple words that add to the sensory appeal of an object, then move to building sentences of high concrete detail.

Examine one word at a time, helping your child to build images, or word pictures, in several stages, beginning with the name of an object.

1.	2.	3.
Word	Add a Color	Add a Touch Word
sweater	green sweater	green woolen sweater
table	brown table	hard brown table
sink		
rug		
apple		

If necessary, help your child add the words required in 2 and 3. Of course, you can vary the demands for different kinds of sensory details:

Word	Add a Smell or Touch Word	Add a Sound or Color Word
apple	cold apple	cold crunchy apple

These simple image games are muscle builders, ways for parents to help inexperienced language users turn their observations into precise words.

A HUMANE LOOK AT ERROR

Few parents would disagree that how we talk (along with what we say) influences whether or not people understand us and, often, whether or not they take us seriously. How we talk is like what we wear: By our clothing and our speech people make their first judgments about us—our intelligence, our character, our spirits.

Perhaps this is wrong. Certainly men and women are more than their clothing and the manner in which they speak. The true nature of a human being should shine through the relatively insignificant surface levels of appearance. People who dress sloppily do not have sloppy spirits necessarily; people who speak badly are not bad people necessarily. Sensitive human being should probe beyond the superficial layers to find the true spiritual flame burning within.

It's a vision of a lovely, ideal world but none (for better or for worse) that our children will face in their lifetimes. In regard to oral communication, without teaching much of anything about it, elementary school teachers—teachers across the educational spectrum, in fact—insist on "good speech." Employers filling high-level jobs frequently discount even personable, bright, and talented young professionals who speak in a manner deemed unsuitable for the corporate image. Through the century, kids in minority ethnic groups or whose dialects are not considered standard have often watched job opportunities pass them by, in some degree because their speech has branded them as apart from the mainstream.

I do not affirm these conditions as desirable; I merely note them as realities of the modern world. People judge people by how people speak, and whether or not this is just is quite beside the point. You know yourself how irritated you can get at some verbal tic or at some irritating speech pattern or at some annoying syntax. Mayor Edward Koch of New York City raised a fuss a while back about public school teachers who said the word *ax* when they meant *ask*. For Koch, the replacement of a correct consonant blend with an incorrect sound was, simply, illiterate. We all have our bêtes noires: one- or two-word grunts in response to questions; insufficient or unclear explanations; "between you and I" for "between you and me"; "nook-u-lar" for "nuc-le-ar"; "Feb-you-ary" for "Feb-roo-ary." William Safire's column "On Language" in *The New York Times Magazine* is a repository for language mistakes, many amusingly recondite, that are identified by error hunters over the world.

Our children's inappropriate use of language can hurt them. We wouldn't want the man or woman interviewing our youngster for college admission or for a job to recoil at bad pronunciation or usage or sentence structure and to hold it against our child in any way. (Don't rush out to sign up your child for elocution lessons! Read on.) Nobody admits to making serious judgments on a minor matter like a mispronounced word, of course, but very subtle, often unconscious elements contribute to people's judgment of others. Why take chances?

Is there anything mothers and fathers can do to help their children speak appropriately?

Now that I've asked the question, I want you to understand how tough it is to answer. Our first objective in encouraging conversation in the home is to establish the freedom to talk about anything without fear of criticism or ridicule. The sensitive child can easily misinterpret as negative criticisms our well-meaning corrections or comments about how he says what he's saying. Our challenge, then, is to support ongoing discourse at home in order to advance communication and to further the flow of ideas and information. Although our responses to our children's conversations invariably cover many areas from the deeper regions of meaning and logic to the more surface regions such as pronunciation and grammar, our style of responding must remain steadily constructive.

In the household of my youth, my mother, who quit high school in order to work during the late 1920s, was unflinchingly attentive to "proper" speech. Without much education, she never articulated the full range of what she meant by proper speech. She probably couldn't have, even if we had pressed her. But my sister and I knew that it meant a combination of correct pronunciation and word use, slow talking, clear enunciation, and respectful tones of voice. It was everything Mother learned on her first and only job of five years as personal secretary to a leading businessman in Newark, New Jersey. It was also part of her own singular view of appropriate language for well-mannered people. Usually at our moments of most passionate discourse—a tale of injustice, a plea for later bedtime hours, a request for higher allowance—she would insist, "Speak correctly!" her arms folded, hands at her elbows, brow arched, round eyes opened wide. What did she mean? What exactly did she mean?

Calling attention to being correct often diminished the fire of our talk and diverted attention from what we said to how we said it. And although I am thankful that she helped develop our sensitivity toward the relation between language and social convention, I think we may have lost some good conversational possibilities when we focused on the form of our language instead of on its content.

Yet I realized how lucky I was in having no more intense an exposure to being correct. A college friend whose speech was utterly perfect to my ear learned his fastidiousness from his mother, too. A speech teacher or an actress (I can't remember now), she tortured him into accurate enunciation by holding his tongue and putting it on the top of his teeth, on his lips, on his palate, as particular words demanded those placements. She would make him speak "right," by God! Arthur always, and I mean always, sounded like the finest radio announcer— but at what a price.

I mention these anecdotes because I think they reflect many of the concerns parents have. They may help us choose more flexible, less overbearing means to deal with the issue of mistakes in oral language. The painful correction of error after error, especially when accompanied by a parent's impatience, disgust, or anger, can squash the dormant seeds of communication within your son or daughter. You should never make correctness your most important goal in dialogues with children. The central issue for successful home conversation is for you and your youngster to feel comfortable talking together in a stress-free atmosphere. If you see that correctness withers the pods on the vine, do whatever you must to start the plant growing again.

Your good perceptions will tell you how well your child reacts to your suggestions about correct oral language. She may want nothing to do with correctness for a while. Honor her preferences. Please don't turn your talking sessions into a contest of wills. My daughter, Melissa, as a preschooler once illuminated our unenlightened vision. We tried to provide a correct version of a sentence; and she said, simply, "I like it wrong." It is a child's right to cling to her language. The best you can do is to model what you think is right, to call attention to linguistic problems—if you think your youngster is up to facing them—and then to move on to more talk.

That said, I do think that you can develop a collection of

useful strategies that in a relaxed, unthreatening manner will help you call attention to problems and will help your child acknowledge and address them as he communicates.

Let's talk about complete sentences. You may be wondering about the need to have your child speak in full sentences as opposed to sentence fragments, the bits and pieces of conversation we hear around us all the time. We get along pretty well by speaking fragments. Is there any point in encouraging children to speak complete sentences then?

I think there is. In the first place, many people find one- or two-word comments from conversational partners terribly ungratifying. Good teachers regularly demand, "Full sentence responses, please." A sentence can establish a wide range of information. A sentence names a subject. It tells what the subject is doing or what is being done to the subject. It communicates a series of interrelated, interlocking details that expand a basic idea.

In the second place, one of the points I've been making throughout this book is the connection between oral language and the written forms of communication that your child will have to command, either as a reader or a writer. The earlier you can help your youngster establish a "sentence sense," the fewer the problems in written expression later on. One of the major writing errors that start early and persist well into college is the production of incomplete sentences. I want to spend a little time in considering sentence sense, therefore, so that you have a realistic frame of reference as you try to help your child avoid a sticking problem. I don't think kids in school receive enough attention to this area of their language development in preschool, primary-school, or secondary-school classrooms.

Research into language patterns over the last few years indicates (believe it or not) that when people talk, they generally do use complete and complex sentences. This idea challenges old notions that spoken language often lacks grammatical form. A very young child, of course, communicates in words and clusters of words that frequently lack the formal elements of correct sentences. Or, she may string many short sentences together to convey meanings. ("Manda take toy. Take toy in car.") But between the ages of two and four years, she is learning how to use one sentence to convey lots of meaning. She learns how to expand single words into packed phrases, how to use descriptors, and how to elaborate on actions expressed by verbs.

As your child grows more adept with spoken language, you'll be impressed at how well she can form "grammatical" sentences, sentences generally complete and correct in their construction. Don't be overcome by the persistent quirks. My cousin's son did not use subject pronouns correctly until well into his fifth year: It was "Her go away" or "Me want that." At their own pace kids do learn the rules of our language system. The de Villiers remind us that "the progress toward adult grammar is not flawless." Children invent words and patterns; they make systematic mistakes, and these are of great value on the road to language acquisition. One of my colleagues tells her students that they are incredible sentence machines, that they know grammar much better than they think they do.

This knowledge can help you establish an approach to sentences at home. Don't assume that your child cannot construct complete sentences, because all evidence suggests that she can. You are not trying to teach her what she already knows. But you can offer her practice with complete sentences so that your child can improve her skills in and can develop a sixth sense for *written* grammatical language. Despite a child's ability to speak grammatical sentences, writing complete ideas with appropriate punctuation often turns into a game of chance.

Of course, in daily speech both children and adults frequently use incomplete sentences:

"Hi, Margarita!"
"Hi, Beverly. Where's your brother?"
"Sick in bed."
"Why?"
"Oh, nothing terrible. Just a bad cold."
"Too bad."
"Yeah. No football practice."

In the dialogue above, one can argue that there is only one complete sentence: "Where's your brother?" Part of the very nature of spoken communication—its speed, its demand for immediate response, its request for action, its dependency upon questions—insists upon fragmentary utterances. Certainly there's nothing *wrong* with speaking in fragments as part of everyday conversation.

The interesting thing, however, is that not many fragments of children's written work resemble those you might hear in daily speech. The written fragment I most often see is one in which the writer has lopped off an incomplete unit from a complete one. A subordinated element that should be connected to a main sentence is standing off by itself. The child has cut off a dog's tail and is telling everyone that it's a dog, too. Some people contend that a child's writing contains many incomplete ideas because she is used to hearing speech fragments, but I've not seen enough proof of that to convince me.

More to the point, when children begin to read, they will regularly meet incomplete sentences in written language. The signs that surround them—EXIT, NO SMOKING, SALE—though clear enough to convey information, are not complete sentences. In their attempts to catch the eye quickly and to sear an idea or a product into the mind, newspaper and magazine ads scream out "Newest, fastest way to order"; "Value event"; "Right now . . . Super Saver Flights to Florida Only on Airline X." This stylistic use of fragments undoubtedly makes an impression on developing language-users. Certainly newspaper headlines and magazine ad copy read like the kinds of incomplete sentences I have seen in children's writing.

In spite of their abundant use in our spoken and written language, fragments do not earn respect as examples of correct and mature writing. One of the certain ways for your child to earn a red F in English is to write compositions that contain many sentence fragments. Teaching students how and why to avoid sentence fragments and how to correct them are a writing teacher's regular chore in the classroom.

To help avoid problems later on, you should encourage your child to speak whole thoughts in full-sentence responses. When your child's statement does not name a person or an object, when it does not tell what that person or object is doing, ask for more information. Prod your child to speak whole sentences. Ask questions so that he fills in missing pieces. This is not to tell him that he's doing something *wrong,* but to provide him with speech models that he can use later in writing. For this reason, good teachers who know the value of the complete sentence insist on oral responses that express complete thoughts. It is unfortunate that enough teachers do not pursue this goal with much vigor. Also, a good part of their students' lack of attention stems from the teachers' poor questioning techniques. Too often teachers ask questions whose answer can only be *yes* or *no.* When teachers make such questions the mainstay of their repertoire, they prevent children from providing sustained responses.

Now let's look at some other features of your child's oral communication that you might want to call attention to. How will you deal with mispronunciations, annoying word fillers ("You know," "like," "um"), and other inappropriate speaking behaviors?

Do you know about *mirroring?* Some of my colleagues who teach speech have shown me this technique that I find enormously helpful, even for four- and five-year-olds. If you hear an oral behavior that you want to call attention to, "mirror" it, that is, repeat the inappropriate behavior exactly as you heard it. Let's take Mayor Koch's pet peeve and see how to address it if your child mispronounced *ask:*

    Child: Martin axed me to play
    Mother: *Axed?*
    Child: He axed me to come to play outside.
    Mother: *Axed?* He *axed* you?
    Child: He *asked* me to play.

The rising intonation in the parent's voice helps to focus attention on the word. Mother is asking a question about it. The child, hearing the error mirrored, corrects it himself. Critics of this method say that it rudely interrupts the child's train of thought. However, I have not heard children (or adults) who are subjected to mirroring strategies object to it. Most kids see it as a game and enjoy playing.

A slightly different approach has a parent repeating the utterance right up to the problem word or phrase and waiting for the child to supply the right form. Here again, intonation makes the context clear for your child:

> Child: The boy over there axed me to play.
> Mother: *The boy over there . . . ?*
> Child: The boy *ask-ed* me to play.

Notice that in neither case does Mother pronounce the word correctly for her child. She expects her child to do that on his own. In other words, Mother conveys by her actions and speech that she believes her child knows the correct word but simply has not used it. In the first example, Mother has had to repeat the inappropriate form because her child hasn't caught on the first time. The value in the mirroring technique is, first, that it calls attention to the problem immediately after the child creates it. Second, with mirroring we do not establish ourselves as the major generals of language, guardians of pronunciation and sentence structure. We don't provide a "right" answer. Instead, we indicate that we know our children have the abilities to come up with the appropriate words themselves once we identify the problem.

This ear training—listening to inappropriate language forms in order to change them ourselves—is very important in helping young children develop control over their spoken language. Our attitude here is: I know you know how to choose a more acceptable oral behavior. Mirroring works well not only with mispronunciations but also with nonstandard forms ("ain't," "He don't have no coat," for example) or verbal fillers. I've used these strategies with my own children at home and recommend that you try them.

Teachers who use mirroring in the classroom report that they also can monitor what they call "content-related" problems in oral skills. Thus, when a child provides an answer that really does not respond to a question just asked, the teacher mirrors the response:

Teacher: Tell us the story of our trip to the park.
   Child: I hated it.
Teacher: *Hated?*
   Child: We left in the morning and then we . . .

The child provided an evaluation of an experience when the teacher asked for a narrative retelling. Mirroring highlights the problem. A child experienced in these mirroring clues knows how and when to rephrase a statement from the teacher's intonations and body language.

Another similar technique for calling attention to oral behaviors of this kind is to identify the type of response given and then to remind the child of the intent of the original question:

Teacher: Tell us the story of . . .
   Child: I hated it . . .
Teacher: Well, I hear you've had a really strong reaction. But you're giving your opinion. I asked you to tell the story of our trip. What actually happened?

This technique not only signals the problem but also explains it and, hence, may help a child reach for an appropriate solution.

In some cases, of course, especially when your youngster is still building his language register, he may in fact not know the correct form, and you will have to supply it. Do it naturally and without making any judgments about your child's skills or abilities. If you've read any of the works of Chiam Ginott, the great child psychologist, you know how important it is to *describe* behaviors instead of *judging* them. If you must say something, hold a mirror up to behavior. Say what you see or hear. Don't evaluate it.

7

The World as
Conversation Piece

I wrote earlier about the importance of a parent's developing an "eye to the world." I was trying to suggest an attitude toward living with children, a way of reacting with all senses and full mind open and of actively sharing that attitude from the moment your baby slips sweetly into your life. An eye to the world means being able to see even in the most routine events an opportunity for sharing thoughts, feelings, and ideas with young people. And conversation is the means for sharing.

To achieve our goal of elevating conversation to its appropriately central role in the young family's household, we've considered a number of theoretical perspectives on language and language learning as well as some very specific ways of engaging children in conversation. I want to expand those contexts in this chapter, in order to help parents who still feel uncertain of what to talk about with their children. In so doing, I will no doubt repeat some of the issues we looked at earlier. But this is a good place to gather straws. By taking a fresh look at some previous points, I want to establish some ironclad principles for talking with a child at home and for suffusing her language with essential words, concepts, and attitudes. I want you to see the world as conversation piece, everyday activities the atoms and molecules of dynamic interaction between people, and language the crucible for shaping and reshaping experience.

WHAT DO TEACHERS DO
FOR THEIR OWN CHILDREN?

In many ways teachers symbolize the mainstream, educated middle class in America. If we examine how teachers approach language in their homes, I believe, we can identify important steps to take and techniques to use in building skills for everybody else's children. Teachers' kids are not necessarily brighter than other kids, but as a group they do seem to achieve very well in formal educational institutions.

One of the important values teachers hold is an inveterate faith in schools, no matter what their problems, and teachers nurture this attitude in their offspring. Teachers help their children see that by working through formal institutions in our society, we can achieve more and more successful and happy lives. Teachers actively support the notion that literacy and its settings are vital and worthwhile. They believe that although our local communities establish our basic value systems, other cultural networks—the law, religion, government, for example—provide important models for behavior and values. Teachers have high aspirations for their sons and daughters; they set high standards of quality for the care of their children; and they believe in the power of family in shaping a child's future. I'll bet that on any list of educationally socialized kids you can identify now and as your child advances through the grades you'll find teachers' children right at the top.

Why do teachers' kids do so well at school? As I mentioned before, teachers believe in the educational establishment and support its values. In addition, teachers have used their time and energies to learn about child-development theory. Further, and perhaps even more important, they make a conscious effort to apply those theories to their own children. Thus, while many people do know and can learn modern, accepted techniques of building language competency, for example, teachers stand out for their vigilance, their determination, and their systematic efforts to advance their children's skills. In very practical terms, teachers have more time to spend with their families. Child and parent have similar daily schedules—off for work or school at 8:30 or so, home at 3:30 before extracurricular programs begin. Holidays match. Vacations coincide.

I'm not saying that other professional, social, or cultural groups do not have high aims for their children or do not raise their families well. Far from it. Middle-class or, as some sociologists call them, "mainstream," families often share common goals. It's just that the confluence of values, education, and training in a teacher's life make her or him an appropriate subject for examination as we try to generalize about solid conversational practices at home.

In doing research for this book, I spoke to many teachers about how they approach language learning for their own children. I also read quite a bit about teachers and other middle-class parents and the strategies they use for encouraging literacy at home. I want to pass on some of those strategies to you. Many points I make here will sing again the choruses you've heard in earlier chapters. You'll see, for example, some of the points that you saw in the Conversational Inventory from Chapter 1. My purpose here, however, is to develop a kind of master list of pointers that should guide your efforts toward systematic language growth at home.

These pointers emanate from regular home practices by schoolteachers themselves, busy people with time-consuming jobs, family responsibilities, and extensive extracurricular demands on their lives. After school and during July and August they take courses for promotional advancement. Planning for daily classroom activities eats into ostensibly free time. Institutes, in-service training programs, conferences, and workshops erode those attractive hours from 3:00 to 5:00 P.M. and many summer days. Teachers may have lots more space in their regular schedules than the rest of us have, but they cram that space with an incredible amount of activity.

I'm spotlighting teachers' tight schedules so that you'll know that extensive obligations beyond the family do not excuse any of us from finding time to stimulate our youngsters' language and conversational skills. I know that you're busy too; but if busy people like schoolteachers can find time—yes, more than thirty minutes a day!—to talk with their children, so can you.

Ironclad Principles for Home Language Growth

Talk regularly with your child as a bona fide conversational partner. I've stressed all along the two-way nature of conversation. You know, for example, from our look at storytelling that dynamic interchange stimulates and sustains the extended narratives kids need to practice at home. Whether you're asking for a story about a real event or encouraging a make-believe tale, you have to treat your child as a partner in information exchange, not just as a performer or an information giver. The quality of the give-and-take will determine the success of your conversation.

Kids are better than anyone else in spotting a phony situation, and so talking with a child means honest two-way dialogue. By honest I mean real opportunity for mediation, flexible rules that can change after convincing talk, and careful listening that shows you're really paying attention.

Recent research shows that parents who carry on conversations with children *from infancy* influence language growth substantially. Remember Dr. Paula Menyuk's work at Boston University? Simply bombarding your child with a one-way flow of words doesn't help at all. Interaction is the overarching concept. James Britton, former Goldsmiths' Professor of Education at the University of London and an internationally acclaimed expert on language and learning, writes, "Talks in infancy with an older person may make all the difference."

Even for children who have not yet learned to talk, you should engage in dialogues. Make your statement and wait for a response. Ask a question and pause for an answer. The response or answer might be only a quiver in an infant's hand, a slow shift of the eyes to locate your voice, a barely perceptible smile or a wrinkling of the forehead. Before you speak again to answer your own question or to build on your previous remark or merely to soothe your baby with a reassuring cluck or other playful sound, wait for your infant to respond.

With these practices you are training your child in the conventions of dialogue. But more than that, you are initiating your child as a complete partner into one of humanity's fundamental acts, the act of conversation. From his earliest moments you are treating your baby as a special individual endowed with communication skills, as yet inchoate skills, that manifest in oral language. Shirley Brice Heath, the sociologist I keep drawing on for her accurate perceptions of children's language learning, talks of the "negotiation of jointly shared intention in communication" between mother and child. It's a dynamic phrase that should describe one of the primary conversational goals in your household.

In conversing with older kids, preschoolers and beyond, you must be prepared to adjust your thoughts and ideas to suggestions they make in conversations. Thus, if you ask your child's advice about a sweater to wear, a TV program to watch, or a toy to play with, you risk having your own idea challenged. I'm not saying that you must always give in to your child's wishes on every issue, but if you're serious about conversation you have to be aware of its roots in negotiation.

Remember, simply providing experiences unconnected to conversation will not advance your child's language. Only talk will awaken him to literacy. "The way in which parents *talk* to their children about an experience," says the Commission on Reading's important report *Becoming a Nation of Readers,* "influences what knowledge the children will gain from the experience and their later ability to draw on the knowledge when reading. It is talk about experience that extends the child's stock of concepts and associated vocabulary."

Read regularly to your child, especially after he passes the six-month mark. You should be reading to your child as soon as possible. You want even your toddler to take an interest in books. Let him touch the pages and flip through them whenever he wants to. If many of your home books are made of nontoxic cloth or cardboard you won't have to worry when they find their way into your baby's mouth. Show with your words and actions how much you approve of his holding books close and looking at the pictures.

In time, your child will come to acknowledge the special voices you reserve for reading to him aloud. Again your behavior models the conventions of reading and the heart of its process. Meaning resides on those pages that you turn and give voice to. When your child learns to read, that is the crucial skill, the ability to extract meaning from the printed page. I am convinced that many children with problems in reading have not learned that the rows of print on a page create a nexus of meaning. These children see isolated words as information givers and read as if meaning emerges simply by adding together the separate definitions of words. By your voice over a book you connect language, thought, and meaning, the irreducible elements of successful reading.

As part of the process of connecting meaning and print forms, it's critical for your child to watch you reading regularly too. With your own book in hand you are a model. Your son or daughter will see you reclining comfortably in a chair or stretched out in bed or on a living room couch with a book you love. Your face, the intensity in your eyes, the way you purse your lips all will convey the magnificent private joy that print arouses in you. You are one of the few people who can pass on this banner of delight, this notion of books as pleasure givers. Where else, in fact, but at home does a child see people reading for the fun of it? If your fun is watching TV only, don't be surprised or disappointed in five or ten years to see a mirror of yourself before the video screen, and without book in hand.

If you are a regular read-aloud parent, you know the joys of reading to your youngster from some book you've selected carefully, and you know about the importance of using children's books as prime objects for conversation. You also know how to connect situations in books with the situations in your youngster's life.

You should also appreciate the value of having your child nearby when you are reading a book, magazine, or newspaper for your own pleasure. My children would always climb on my lap while I was reading. I'm sure that they were trying primarily to regain attention they felt I diverted unfairly from them. But I think, too, that the natural curiosity I'd tried to stimulate about reading their own books carried over to my books too. Melissa, Joseph, and Saul saw the times I'd chosen for reading as times for conversations. "What are you doing? Why are you reading? Why don't you want to play with me?"

I always tried to use such questions, no matter what their motives, to help teach my children about the eminence of books in our lives. I take the questions as an opportunity to talk about the delights of private reading, about the treasures awaiting people who use others' words and their own imaginations to recreate a writer's world. I compare books with television watching, distinguishing what for me is the most powerful sensory draw of an imagined universe as opposed to one that is carefully reproduced on a video screen. I tell my youngsters how much I like mulling over written words, and after my explanation I do not hesitate to ask my child to sit beside me and read quietly or to do some other quiet activity so that I can read on my own. A silent encounter with a book is no time for conversation.

But on some occasions I like to talk about the book I'm reading. I name the book and author, I tell a little about the plot and characters (if it's a novel) or about the general idea of the book, I read a sentence or two aloud. I try to explain why I'm reading this particular volume now. If it's a magazine or newspaper and I feel ready to give up private reading time for conversation, we look at pictures togeher or discuss the article I'm reading. Kids can share ideas even on adult issues if you summarize them clearly. There's no reason why your son or daughter can't consider some of the issues that appear in the popular press. Taste and tact are the bywords, of course. Much in America's newspapers is scandal, sex, and violence, not appropriate talk points for young boys and girls.

In a 1979 study, teacher-researchers Scollon and Scollon identify a state of what they call "incipient literacy" in their two-year-old daughter, Rachel. With that term they are trying to indicate a kind of *preliteracy,* clearly stimulated by the child's environment. In the way Rachel talked and in the way she reacted to print, she was literate *before* learning to read. That condition of incipient literacy is exactly what you want to nurture in your little boy or girl.

About books and the knowledge gathered from reading, the Scollons indicate six essential attitudes and patterns of conduct that Rachel displayed. Your home program of talking with your child should establish them in your regular household activities. They include:

1. a sense that books are good and that they properly belong in homes
2. an awareness that books are related to *writing,* that the second leads to the first
3. a knowledge that the language we use to read books aloud or to tell about what we have read in books is quite different from the language we use to carry on regular conversation
4. a connection between reading and play. Like play, reading puts off reality; also like play, reading aloud draws upon a variety of cues (some verbal, some prop-based) that make clear how different it is from typical conversation
5. an awareness that when a reading situation involves two people, one is the displayer or questioner (generally the adult) and the other is the observer and respondent (generally the child)
6. a knowledge that in responding to books, one follows a set of conventions or rituals; these include knowing *not* to show everything one knows about text but instead to provide answers focused on the questions asked by the questioner.

You can probably guess why all these are so important. The attitudes and behaviors are exactly what teachers expect children to demonstrate under formal teaching and learning conditions at school. Even the earliest school activities demand an awareness of and ability to use these literacy conventions. Teachers do not reward nonconforming behavior.

For example, if your child is telling a story, it will win approval only by mirroring conventional, literacy-based values. The teacher will expect the kinds of formulaic beginnings and endings we talked about in Chapter 5. She will also expect intonations in your child's voice to mark his utterances as narratives. If your boy or girl does not follow 3, 4, and 6 above, the teacher will probably interrupt the narrative (kids understand this action as rejection) and will ask questions designed to adjust the structure or to draw upon accepted formats.

I keep pointing out that knowing how to read is not important before entering school and that parents should not worry about teaching the skill to their children. I'm sounding that chord again. Do not direct your energies at teaching your child to read. Direct them instead at attitude-building. I assure you that no one else but you will ever be able to establish the literacy credentials your child needs (and her teacher expects) in her first few years. No matter how good the school, it can never create an "incipient literate." Only parents or other close family members can achieve that.

Please don't waste your own valuable time in teaching your child how to read at home! Rather, instill these intangible attitudes that will assure her survival as a learner in the educational establishment. Imagine how quickly and easily she'll be able to figure out how to read if she starts school with all the literacy equipment in place!

Label, label, label. Teachers know the value of naming and, of course, so do you, if you recall the various word games we developed in Chapter 6. I won't belabor the need to point out new words in your ongoing conversations with your children, except to remind you of Secretary of Education William Bennett's assertion that "to succeed at reading, children need a basic vocabulary . . . and the ability to talk about what they know."

You can start as early as you like with your infant, naming bodily parts or features of the room in which she lives or the other rooms of the house. Name and identify toys, family members, furniture, foods—any objects in the child's immediate environment. Use your concern for vocabulary gently to identify words and to tease out their meanings. The mother talking about cherry orchards in the example you'll see later highlights the word subtly and provides a definition to a child who obviously does not know it. You've seen other examples of naming, labeling, and defining throughout this book. Don't take vocabulary for granted.

When you label and define an object you're like Shakespeare's poet; you give the object "a local habitation and a name." You rescue it from anonymity. You ease its passage into your child's unconscious language. The number of schoolchildren who do not know the simple nominal equivalents for everyday items would amaze you. I know that vocabulary is a highly personal entity, reflecting more than an individual's intellectual abilities but also her emotions, needs, and psyche. Still, we must strive for a common core of language if we are to communicate effectively with other humans on the planet. The world won't end, of course, if some of us don't know words or meanings for radishes or laundry detergent, but we're all diminished somehow when everyday extensions of human life vanish into linguistic oblivion even for just a few of us.

In a wide-reaching study, the *British Journal of Sociology of Education* reported in 1981 that the style and content in the language parents used at home with their children could actually predict how well the children would achieve in reading. Enough said.

Establish new contexts for experiences. Labeling is not enough. You have to go beyond the simple naming of objects and features to recontexting. When you establish a new context for an experience, the critical-thinking faculty can grow and flourish. You simply project elements of one event on another, changing a particular feature, adding another, creating a new, imaginative condition. If you and your child are looking at a pine tree and you ask your child, "What would happen if we put lights and decorations on this tree?" you are challenging creative thought by altering features of the existing context.

Recontexting helps your child make sense of diverse phenomena and draw together common or associated elements in our complex and seemingly disparate existence. One of your conversational aims as a parent, then, should be to help your child connect one action or thought with another. You can use a number of strategies to achieve this.

Relate characters in books with real life characters. ("See that little dog? Doesn't he remind you of Harry in the book we read a while back [*Harry the Dirty Dog*]? Why do you think this dog is so dirty? How did Harry get dirty?")

Establish linkages between events in books and similar or sharply different (but related) events in life. ("David [in *Big Boy, Little Boy*] sure had a nice time at his grandma's house. Remember when you slept at Grandma's when Mommy and Daddy had that wedding to go to in Baltimore? What did Grandma watch you do? What did she tell you about the time *you* were a baby?")

Draw parallels between what is happening now and what happened in the past or what might happen in the future. ("Where do you think that robin will go with that piece of string in her mouth? What do you think she'll do with the string?")

Conjoin unique objects or ideas with members of a larger, common group. ("No, I don't have a crayon in my pocketbook, but I do have something else to write with. What do you think it is? What are some other things people use for writing?")

Look at this piece of a parent's side of conversation with a preschooler on a shopping excursion in the supermarket.

> Look at the beautiful cherries, will you? You like cherries, don't you?
>
> Where do cherries grow, do you know? That's right. Cherry trees.
>
> You know that tree on the corner of our block, at Mr. Wilson's house? That's a cherry tree. Why do you think he has a cherry tree in his yard?
>
> It sure does look pretty, doesn't it. Mr. Wilson likes his trees and shrubs. He gets some cherries but not too many. Why not, do you think? I bet you're right. It's the birds and the squirrels.

All those pretty flowers on Mr. Wilson's tree, they become the cherries. Some farmers grow cherries for the rest of us to buy. They grow the cherries in large orchards. Do you know what an orchard is?

Orchards are places where farmers grow fruit trees. When the cherries are ripe how do you think they get down? Yes, some fall, but then they're all bruised and we wouldn't want to buy them. You've got it! People pick them. How do you think they pick them?

It would be hard climbing up a tree and staying up there for a long enough time to pick many cherries, don't you think? No, I think people use ladders and buckets. Do you remember when Daddy almost fell off the ladder? He was painting the house and he moved too quickly. Lucky I was there to steady it. Ladders can be dangerous, yes. How do you think people who pick cherries keep from falling off ladders? We should check it in the library.

You think they use the cherry-picker trucks? Maybe. No. I think those big cranes are used for buildings and telephone repairs. I don't think they use them for picking cherries. It's just a nickname. You know cherries are high up on trees and those cranes go high up so workers can do repairs.

How do you think the cherries get to supermarkets? Remember your truck book? That's right. I bet they use those large refrigerator trucks. They can carry fruits and vegetables. Trains? That's a thought. Maybe they use trains if they're going long distances. That's another thing to check out with Mrs. Coleman, the librarian.

What would happen if I took those cherries and cooked them? What could we make with the cherries? You like cherry pies, don't you?

Let's focus for a moment on the mother's language here. I've started with this simple one-way exchange both to highlight the parent's role as conversational initiator and the value of even the simplest of environments in stimulating dialogue. We're examining talk in a supermarket, easily viewed as a routine and insipid activity in our lives. Yet, as you see, for a parent who is awake to her surroundings, even the least spectacular setting can be a rich source of language learning for a child. Using a combination of narrative, comments, questions, and reactions (you can pretty much fill in the child's responses on your own here), the parent is like a mild electric current, stimulating the child's mind to thought and analysis.

I want especially to emphasize the new contexts Mother keeps trying to establish. A fruit bin in the supermarket is at first just an occasion to talk about the cherries lined up like small red lights before mother and child. But notice how almost immediately we are beyond the supermarket walls and considering a tree that the child knows in his familiar neighborhood environment. Again, we see a mini-science lesson, a handful of details that are no doubt fascinating to the child, details about the relation between the scented white flowers he knows and the fruits he's examining now. Note the natural way in which Mother provides the label *orchard* and then a definition for it.

When Mother moves into uncertain territory, she identifies the library as a resource for information that she does not have at her fingertips. The reference to books here as a repository of wisdom is part of the mother's ingrained values and attitudes toward literacy. Children who hear about the library, who visit libraries often, not only to find good stories to read but also to find answers to problems or questions, are children who learn to esteem books.

Mother again connects the experience in the supermarket with a past experience her child has witnessed. By linking ladders for picking cherries with a more familiar ladder, Mother manipulates the scene for her youngster. The two of them carry names and concepts from one context to another, related one. To the teacher at school the ability to span contexts will act as one of the key markers of your child's literacy.

A few other points are important here. Mother links the world of books to the flesh-and-blood moment. The reference to the truck book revives for the child a previous experience with print. Here, he must unite his surroundings with the words and illustrations on a page he saw a while ago. Conversation at this moment makes physical reality and representational images coalesce.

You have already seen the importance of connecting a picture of an object with its real-life counterpart when you read books to your child. Thus, if you're reading a story about cherry trees, you might want to hook them up with what's in the supermarket or in your refrigerator. What I'm trying to indicate here, though, is that you don't want to miss the obverse. As this mother has, you want to use a real event to recall a print experience. The cherries in the market provide an occasion for mother and child to consider what they read in a book. Whenever you can, then, help your child see both that existence infuses books and that books infuse existence.

Next, note the effort at the end of the conversation to alter an observable feature in the context. By cooking the cherries, we transform them into something else—a pie, a sauce, jam. But the child has to reason to that point. Mother's question challenges him to maneuver objects at hand, to whisk them into some future condition while the present condition remains nonetheless unchanged. Cooking cherries makes them special. Yet they do not stop being cherries when we cook them. The child must predict the outcome by manipulating information in his mind without losing the existing context. Shaping and re-shaping experience, changing one or two features in an available scene to project new consequences, connecting books and life— parents have an important responsibility in exposing their children to these challenges.

You also want to note the quality and variety of questions Mother asks here as a way of reminding yourself of the questioning strategies we explored at great length in Chapter 3. We do see some simple yes-no questions here that act as markers for shared experience. These are not demanding questions— "You like cherries, don't you?" "You know that tree on the corner of our block at Mr. Wilson's house?" They are merely surface perception checkers. Mother simply draws her child into conversation with those questions.

But notice how other questions probe deep thinking. The report of the Commission on Reading says that the kinds of questions parents ask influence what children learn from the events in their lives. Your questions can move your child merely to put his experience in his own words, a kind of low-level cognitive skill. Or, you can ask questions that go deeper like the *why* and *how* questions we see here—"Why do you think he has a cherry tree in his garden?" "Why not, do you think?" "When the cherries are ripe, how do you think they get down?" "How do people pick the cherries?" These questions provoke thought. "Thought-provoking questions," the Commission asserts, "stimulate the intellectual growth needed for success in reading."

Finally, in this brief record note all the critical thought skills the mother engenders with her questions, comments, and narrative. I've already mentioned how she challenges her child to predict the outcome of an event as the two of them consider cooking the cherries. But other points in the conversation require the child to practice that important skill. When she asks how the cherries get down from the trees and how they get to the fruit stall at the supermarket, Mother is asking her child to project actions into the future.

Also, the child must compare and contrast—cherries in the supermarket, cherries on Mr. Wilson's lawn; ladders for picking cherries, Daddy's ladder for painting. The child must consider causes and outcomes, even if they are not fully resolved at the moment and must await a later date. How do the cherries get down from the tree? How do people who pick the cherries keep from falling off the ladders?

Building new contexts and integrating related experiences stimulate the same mental operations demanded by our educational institutions. Without those skills your child's readiness for school will be sharply limited. Shirley Brice Heath shows very clearly how much academic success depends on this ability to shift contexts. She uses the example of a battle in the American Revolution under a particular military leader. How does a student show that she understands the success of that battle? She certainly has to know more than the names of key army personnel and the details of the equipment, numbers of soldiers, and so on.

Her understanding depends on establishing a large frame in which this particular event belongs and on realizing that even a small change in battle conditions might force a completely different outcome. A successful student, then, is a "contextualist" who knows how to "predict and maneuver the scenes and situations" and who understands "the relatedness of parts to the outcome or the identity of the whole."

Your earliest efforts at connecting events and concepts will help you prepare your child for the demands of school.

Eat at least one meal together. In our house, and in the houses of many teachers I know, we make an extra effort to have dinner together. When I have to travel, I try telephoning right before or right after dinner so I can stay up-to-date on the daily news. Even a hasty meal with rapid-fire conversation perks everybody up.

At dinner, conversation flies, a mixture of random chitchat and pointed questions about activities. With three kids, someone's always having to wait a turn, but everybody talks sooner or later. Language at the dining-room table helps us blow off the steam heat of the day. We talk of grievances, accomplishments, funny moments, special surprises, casual meetings, failed opportunities—anything, really. Dinner conversation is the day's activities in high-speed automatic replay.

Think about the rigorous mental exercise your child performs when she speaks about the day's events from her perspective. If you ask a question like, "What was best about your day, Emily?" your child must recall and then sort through all her day's experiences. She must evaluate them and then exercise her judgment as she shares her unique experience with the rest of the family. This is an important moment. She's tapping her memory to relate an event that you probably have not experienced. Maybe it's a moment next door, a moment in nursery school, a moment in her bedroom. But it is her perceptions and her language and her mental operations that give locus to the event. She has to recall details; she has to follow a coherent sequence; she has to eliminate minor details; she has to reflect her knowledge of the narrative format. Hence, she is a true conversationalist.

At dinner, you can review the day's events through conversation. But the evening meal is not sacrosanct as the only acceptable family eating and talking time. Many of us come from households where dinner had almost ritualistic importance, and we often feel guilty if we're not sitting together with our mate and children from six to seven o'clock or so each night. But life-styles have changed; fathers and mothers work erratic hours, which often extend into the evenings. As kids grow older, their after-school activities often prevent their regular attendance at a prescribed meal hour late in the day. If you can manage dinner together as a family unit, fine, but don't feel guilty about not being able to bring it off regularly.

I vote for breakfast as the all-together meal. We all start off from the same place in the morning. True, some of us have to get going earlier than others, but the range of time difference between one person's schedule and another's is usually not as wide in the morning as it is in the evening. It seems to me that breakfast is the easiest meal of the day to arrange so that everyone eats at the same time.

Talking at breakfast is usually a powerful occasion for language in action. In the morning over a meal, you plan the day's events: who's going where, what's happening, who's playing with whom, who's driving whom, what chores need doing. Breakfast talk lets us learn family members' schedules and, if possible, to adjust our own activities to suit those of others.

The point I'm trying to make here is that a meal with your children is a wonderful occasion to initiate and sustain conversation. Which meal it is doesn't matter. I look back wistfully on at my own elementary- and junior-high-school days when I was able to walk home for lunch, and I still remember how much I enjoyed talking with my mother and sister halfway through the day. Breakfast, lunch, snack, dinner, supper, leisurely meals or meals on the run, dress-up restaurant or cafeteria or fast-food meals, picnics, barbecues—the combination of food and family and conversation creates magical moments for communication. Seize the opportunity to talk with your child in the relaxed setting of a meal with the family.

In *Ways with Words* Heath describes the special nature of family activities in her "townspeople" group, the mainstream families whose children achieved so much better in school than either of the other two groups she studied. (Incidentally, the mainstream families with preschoolers on which Heath bases many of her conclusions about children and adult interactions all had a mother teaching in a Carolina public school during the research project.) I want to end this section with a statement from Heath because she crystalizes all the advice I've been trying to provide in this chapter. And she also helps me challenge once again the idea that simply more talk at home will improve your child's language.

Parents of children who achieve early successes at school *invent* social activities for their youngsters and just as important, *call attention* to those activities so that the child both participates in an event and reflects on it with thought and language. "It is as though in the drama of life," Heath says with remarkable insight (and, here again, the emphasis is mine), "townspeople parents freeze scenes and parts of scenes at certain points along the way. Within the single frame of a scene, they focus the child's attention on objects or events in the frame, sort out referents for the child to name, give the child ordered turns for sharing talk about this referent, and then narrate a description of the scene. *Through their focused language adults make the potential stimuli in the child's environment stand still for a cooperative examination and narration between parent and child.*" Be a focusing, scene-freezing, narrating, cooperative examiner at home and you'll have a key to the kingdom of language socialization.

WHAT SHALL WE TALK ABOUT?

What follows here are possibilities for talking with your child. I see these as springboards, of course, for your own ideas that will grow naturally as you initiate and develop conversations with the young people in your families. I expect that you will put into play many of the strategies we've examined here and in earlier chapters and that you'll do whatever scaffolding is necessary, that you'll raise questions that sustain dialogue, and that you'll be pressing toward critical thought skills like classifying, comparing and contrasting, showing causes and effects, exploring sequences, predicting outcomes, altering certain features in a context, breaking down larger concepts into smaller ones and shaping smaller concepts into larger wholes, and others, certainly, that we've looked at together. I also expect that you'll be trying to connect these conversations, wherever possible, with some of the stories you read and talk about with your child. Here, Chapter 9, "Fifty Talk-About Books for Young Children," will come in handy.

Surely I've left out many of the talk points that keep conversation flowing in your house, but I'm hoping that this free-ranging list will add to your repertoire. If I've left out any really good ideas that you'd add, I hope you'll let me know.

Remember, there are no right answers to expect from these suggested questions of your child, and there are no recommended trains of thought her mind should follow. Your aim throughout in prompting conversation is to dig deep into your child's perceptions and to initiate a flow of language that brings them to the world. Listen. Praise. Beg for more.

Conversation at Home

Talk about the various rooms in the house, the different pieces of furniture, where they came from, who uses them, how they could be rearranged, what colors could be changed, how your child would redecorate, how many rooms you have, what other rooms you might want and how you'd use them, what's your child's favorite room and why. Compare and contrast features of rooms—neat versus disorderly, noisy and silent, bright and dark—and talk about how they got that way and how they could be changed. Using furniture or other familiar objects at home, talk about shapes and name them—triangles, squares, rectangles, circles. Talk about any pets at home and how to care for them and where they live in natural habitat, about why people keep pets, about what it would be like to change places with a pet for a day: What kind of day does your child think he'd have? Make a book of child-drawn pictures of various rooms in the house with a sentence you write from your child's dictation for each room; then read and talk about the book.

In the bathroom talk about body parts, about the scale and what it's used for, about where water goes when it goes down the drain and when it's flushed, about baths and showers and why we take them, about bottles in the medicine cabinet (especially those with the skull-and-crossbones labels) and about what some of the medicines do for us, and about why we keep them in a separate place in the bathroom. Talk about how (and why) we might organize them in some order on the shelves, about what we do when we hurt our finger and it's bleeding, about what your child would want to say to a child who was hurt and whom your child was helping. Talk about soap and why we use it, about personal hygiene in general, about bathroom privacy, about old-style bathrooms and plumbing, about the dangers of hot water, about toothbrushes and hairbrushes and the various creams and lotions you use, about makeup and nail polish, and why people buy and use them.

In the kitchen talk about appliances (refrigerators, stoves, toasters, and so on) and what they do and how they work, about the dangers of hot surfaces and safety measures we take to avoid being hurt, about mealtime planning ("It's Mama's birthday tomorrow and I want to make a special dinner for her. Help me set the meal. What should we make? What do you think she'd like best? Why? What do you think she might say when she sees our surprise?"). Talk about cooking ("Make your own egg this morning. What happens when we put butter in the pan? What does the egg look like when it comes out of the shell? What happens to the egg when we cook it? Suppose we mixed up the egg instead of breaking it directly onto the pan. What would happen? What's your favorite kind of egg? Daddy's? Where do eggs come from?" "Help me make cookies? What kind shall we make? How shall we make them? What shall we put in the bowl first? Next? What if we put raisins and nuts in instead of chocolate chips—what would happen to these cookies if we prepared them that way?"). Talk about table etiquette: What are the rules? Why are there rules? Who made the rules? What rules does your child dislike? Why?

Talk about names and uses for items in the cupboard and the refrigerator, about possible ways for grouping the items logically—that is, all cans of fruits on one shelf, vegetables on another, snacks on a third, *or* all cans on one shelf, boxes on another, bags on a third, *or* large items here, small items there, middle-sized items there, *or* breakfast things here, lunch things there, *or* finding items on the cupboard shelves that start with the letter *a, b,* and so on. Talk about reasons why particular groupings are useful, about where the items come from and how they are produced, about which are your child's favorites and why. Read and talk about box tops, box side-panels, backs and fronts of boxes, cans, packages, ingredients lists, recipes, cookbooks, menus, pictures and drawings and post-it notes on the refrigerator. Talk about measurements and utensils, pots, pans, griddles, cups, teaspoons and tablespoons. Talk about telphones and what to say when we answer a call, about talking clearly and listening carefully, about taking messages and relaying them accurately to the right people, about "crank" calls and about the kind of information not to give away to someone you don't know, about emergency use of the telephone.

In your child's bedroom, talk about the various toys, about which are favored and why, about who brought the toys, about toys your child might want to invent, about putting toys and other objects around the room in their reserved place when playtime is over, about establishing some logical system of arranging toys and games or clothing in drawers or in closets. Talk about clothing, favorite shirts or trousers or skirts or dresses or bathing suits or hats: Why does your child like what he likes? Change features of the clothing: "What would happen if I put bells on your shoelaces?" "Suppose we put your baseball cap on your teddy bear?" Let your child play dress-up with her or your old clothes; ask her for a narrative to accompany the outfits: Who are you? Why? What are you doing? Compare toys, dolls, games. Set imaginative conditions: "Suppose Teddy could talk. What would he say?" "Suppose your Raggedy Ann could talk and walk and go to nursery school with you? to the supermarket with us? What would her day be like?" Set a hypothetical problem or situation and ask for outcomes: "Remember that snowstorm last winter? Suppose we had left your bedroom window open. What might have happened? What would we have to do?"

Plan a system for cleaning the room: What do we do first, second, third, and so on? Why that order? What other order might we use? Separate one task from the rest—making the bed, for example. How do we do it? What are the steps? Talk about sleep at night, about dark bedrooms, about fears, nightmares, good dreams. (Many books explored in Chapter 9 deal with the theme of fears children experience at night. Use them to link your child's reactions to those that book characters experience.) Talk about decorating the bedroom. What would your child put on the walls, the ceiling, the various corners of the room? Talk about books, books, books! Read books and magazines to your child. Ask your child to read them to you. Even if he can't read words, you'll delight in the way he invents stories from the pictures or in the way he recalls the story as you read it to him earlier.

Looking out the window from your child's bedroom, talk about the changing scene below, about the face of the various seasons on your street. Talk about what you see out the window at the moment; then change conditions: "It's February now: What will the oak tree look like in the spring? What else would you see out the window in the spring? What people do you see regularly from the window? What are they doing? What do you think they'll do after they pass from your view?" Talk about day and night, dawn, dusk, twilight. Talk about the stars, the moon, constellations, animals that sleep by day and hunt for food by night. Talk about where animals sleep, especially the local animals and birds that your child knows. What would it be like if we slept for a night in the various homes animals set up for themselves?

In the living room or family room talk about family space, about accommodating many different ideas of rest and relaxation in a single room, about appropriate behavior in such a room. Talk about any untouchables (Grandma's fragile hurricane lamp, a wispy seashell that you cherish for sentimental reasons) and why they are untouchable. What objects does your child own that he doesn't want anyone to touch? Talk about sitting on living room furniture. Find out what your child likes and dislikes in the living room and why. What changes would he make? Talk about television watching, television schedules for children, appropriate programs for kids, television etiquette.

(See Chapter 8 for more on television watching and home conversation.) Talk about programs before your child watches them; talk about programs after your child watches them. If you've viewed together, talk about possible changes in plot and action. Compare one character or show with related ones.

In the Neighborhood and Community

Follow the advice for talking about scenes outside your windows, only expand the tapestry of action. Talk about the houses on your street, their familiar tenants, the cars parked on the street or in driveways. Talk about street safety, about crossing at corners and not between cars, about not chasing balls that bounce off the curb, about looking carefully in both directions when your child crosses with permission. Talk about the trees and bushes and flowers that mark your neighborhood and compare and group the different plants. ("Let's look at all the different kinds of trees here. What is ours like? Mr. Wilson's down the street? How are they alike? different?") Talk about other children on the block and what your child imagines that they're doing at a given moment. As men and women go off to work in the mornings, ask your child to describe what she sees. What are the people doing now? Why? What are they wearing? Project activities that await these people during the day. Talk about weather changes on the street and their subsequent effect on our senses: How does the air smell after snow? What do we hear in the rain?

Talk about community visitors and workers, people who show up on your streets from time to time—letter carriers, truck drivers and deliverers, telphone repairers, police officers, salespeople, sanitation workers, street cleaners, gardeners. What are they doing? Why are they doing it? What would it be like if your child could do their job for a day? What would be fun? What would be hard work? Discuss the various shapes of objects on the street—trucks, letterboxes, garbage cans, garden plots, roofs, windows. Trace the route of a letter you mail with your child.

Talk about your visits to community places—before you reach your destination, while you're there, and after you return home. Talk about the supermarket, pharmacy, Laundromat, hardware store, delicatessen, post office, department store, dry cleaners, gasoline station and auto repair shop, pet shop—the list is vast. Each of these is a potential treasury of conversational interchange, both about the specific events occurring on your visit and the impact of work at the place on the community and beyond. What is the purpose of the store? What are the people doing there? Note the various sensory details of the places, the sounds, smells, actions, colors, and touch sensations. Ask your child to recall these sensations days after the visit and to describe what he recalls seeing there. At the doctor's office look at magazines and books and talk about surrounding details. Talk about what doctors and dentists do and why they do it and how people get to be health-service professionals.

Talk about clothing people wear to do their jobs or to face the weather. Why white outfits for nurses and health-care people? Why uniforms for police and postal workers? What are the various features of the uniforms? Why do we wear heavy clothing in the winter? Suppose it were summer now: What might we be wearing? What would our street look like in summer?

Talk about holidays unique to the months of the year and how the holidays affect the appearance of the street. Talk about what the holidays mean. If it's Thanksgiving, talk about the familiar symbols—turkey, cranberries, pilgrims, Indians—and what they stand for and why we use them to commemorate the occasion. During one holiday ask about another soon to arrive. How would the shops look? What do we do on that holiday? How does one holiday compare with another? How many holidays can your child think of? Which does he like best and why? How do we make a particular holiday treat—Christmas cookies, Thanksgiving pudding, barbecue burgers for the Fourth of July.

Talk about famous people's birthdays that we celebrate—Lincoln, Washington, Martin Luther King. Talk about other famous people and events throughout history—Knights of the

Round Table, the dinosaur age, prehistoric men and women, to name just a few among thousands.

Go to your community library regularly to investigate these and other matters and talk about what's there. What do librarians do? How do they help us? Walk alongside the shelves or bins, examining books, showing their covers, asking your child to talk about them. What do you think this book will be about? What other book does it remind you of? What real-life event does it remind you of? Flip through the pages and talk more. Don't confine your talk to here-and-now books that focus exclusively on the immediate world of the contemporary child. Your child will not learn much about history, geography, or civics in school for quite a while, unfortunately, so you want to stimulate interest in topics such as foreign lands or places long ago—children in pilgrim days, brave men and women who served their countries, Vikings and other outstanding explorers, keen scientists, political leaders, athletes, inventors, many others.

Even for the youngest child, point out the card (or automated) catalogue. What is it for? How does it help us? How are books arranged? Examine the magazines and talk about the pictures. Look at the videotape and the record and audiotape collection. Which does your child recognize? Which would she like to take out of the library for home use? Why? Note people reading and working in the library. What kind of behavior does the library require? Why?

Beyond the Community

Talk about upcoming trips, vacations, excursions to places beyond your community—museums, beaches, picnic sites, relatives' homes in neighboring communities or cities far off. How will we get there? What will we see along the way? What will it be like when we get there? What can we expect to see in communities other than our own? Depending on where we live, of course, most of our home communities are fairly insulated from people different from us. When we go beyond our neighborhoods, we see the full, rich identity of our cities, states, and country. Talk with your child about people he may not have noted near your home—old people, handicapped people, people of varied ethnic heritage. How are these people similar to us? different from us? Talk about prejudice and fair treatment. How should we judge whether people are good or bad, kind or unkind, thoughtful or thoughtless?

In the automobile, talk about the scenes out the window. Play word games. Identify all objects that are red, round, tiny, slow-moving—you or your child sets the category and the two of you name objects to fit it. Name items that you see that begin with a particular letter (*t:* trees, tires, telephone poles; *a:* automobiles, apples, arms). Look for license plates from states other than yours. What are those states like? Talk about the people in the cars. Where do you think they are going? What can you tell about them from their faces? After a special trip, take turns in naming your favorie part of the journey; then take turns naming what you didn't like about it. Talk about what awaits you at home, about all the activities your child wants to take part in during the week. Compare the place you've just been to with your own home, street, or city. Reflect on the events you've seen and witnessed; change one or two conditions of the scene and ask your child to imagine what it would be like with those changes. What would your child have done if he'd exchanged places with one of the people you visited or met on your trip?

For travel by train or plane or bus do much of the above and more. Consider the special nature of the mode of transport: Kids have an incredible fascination with vehicles. Terminals where you await transport are fascinating places about which to talk with your child, so alive are they with people coming to travel and workers who maintain the system. Ask about the people you see. What are the workers doing on the tracks? What does the pilot do in the cockpit? Who collects the money and gives out the tickets? At the zoo talk about the animals, where they live when they're not in cages, how you think they feel in their current setting. What advantages do zoo animals have? disadvantages? What happens to sick animals? Who takes care of them? Where do we get the animals we see in the zoo? Watch feedings and talk about them. What do particular animals eat? Who feeds them? (After your visit ask your child to explain the process; listen for the sequence and help out where necessary.) Talk about animal babies, how animal families care for their offspring. If a particular animal—a lion, an elephant, a monkey—could talk right now as we're looking at him, what do you think he'd say? Compare animals; group them. How are tigers and lions alike? different? Which are the mammals? Which are the "cat" animals? the birds? the ape family? Talk about appropriate behavior at the zoo, the differences between enjoying the animals and bothering them.

At museums relate past events with present events. How did ancient peoples meet their daily needs? How do their utensils, weapons, vases, containers, compare with ours today? Why are these objects in the museum? Where did they come from? Who found them? Talk about paintings; ask your child to describe what he sees. Take leaps in imagination: What would it be like to live in times past? How would your child spend his days? What would it be like to be a child in ancient Egypt? among Vikings? in pre-Christian Chinese dynasties? among Plains Indians? If you're looking at a portrait, how would your child like to meet the person if she could? Why or why not? If you're looking at a landscape, how would your child like to visit the scene? Why or why not? Talk about your favorite parts of the painting, the best colors or shapes. After you've seen a few paintings or drawings or sculptings, ask your child to name her favorite and say why she likes it.

At the beach or riverbank, note flora and fauna and talk about what you see. Where does the water originate? What's on the other side? Talk about water safety and avoiding risks. Talk about workers at or on the water—lifeguards, concessionaires, sailors, clammers, fishers. Talk about recreational sports—waterskiing, sailing, swimming, diving, snorkeling. Talk about the fish and animals who live on or in the sea. What would it be like to be a whale? a gull? a shark? a trout? Look at the sky and cloud formations and ask your child to say what the clouds look like to him and to make up a narrative about them. Talk about people you see on the sand or in the water. What are they doing? Why?

These are only suggestions. But you can see why I say that the world you can inhabit with your child is a conversation piece.

8

Conversation in the Electronic Age

As a parent, you no doubt feel profoundly guilt-ridden about the prominent role television plays in your child's life. Educators and child-development professionals are singing the same familiar tune: Many of the nation's literacy problems emanate from the talking picture box at the center of your living room or den.

The voices echo Newton Minow, who called television the "vast wasteland." They echo the sentiments of the explosive *The Plug-In Drug* by Marie Winn, who indicted television as both mindless and addictive. They echo sociological and psychological studies that connect, with varying degrees of success, what or how much we watch with how we act, what and how we think, and how we look and feel. We're reading constantly about this experiment or that showing the interrelations between violence on the screen and violence in real life, demonstrating the manipulation of children's tastes through sophisticated advertising campaigns, connecting children's lack of achievement as readers with the increasing amounts of time spent riveted to the video screen.

In some homes kids are watching five or six hours of TV each day, more on weekends. In the age group from two to twelve, on the average, children see more than twenty-five hours of television a week. By the time they graduate from high school they will have sat before a television screen for four thousand hours more than they have sat in classrooms—fifteen thousand hours of TV, eleven thousand hours of school. About half of all fifth-graders in America watch much more than two hours of television each day. These same youngsters spend about four minutes a day reading at home. That's right. Four minutes.

A 1979–80 study by the California State Education Department connected children's poor school performance, including IQ measures, with the amount of television the children watched. The New England Medical Center links obesity and television viewing for kids six to seventeen: The more TV they watch, the greater their chances for being overweight adolescents.

Programs that show aggression apparently stimulate aggressive behavior in children, even for kids who are not normally predisposed to violence. In an experiment several years ago, researchers divided ninety-six normal preschool boys and girls into four groups. The first group watched models perform live aggressive acts. The second group watched films of these models. The third group watched an aggressive cartoon figure on film. The fourth group, the control, watched no models at all. Then the researchers brought all the children to a play area and deliberately frustrated them somewhat. Afterward the children were exposed to both aggressive and nonaggressive toys. Children in the three groups that viewed the aggressive behavior themselves performed much more hostile acts than the children who saw no aggression.

The figures will astound you. Almost 80 percent of the kids who watched the cartoon character and almost 90 percent who watched the filmed or real-life actors copied in some way the hostile behavior they had just seen. Kids who watched the actors on film seemed affected most.

Even when the bad guy or gal gets punished for doing wrong, kids remember much more vividly the violent acts performed by the characters than any of the punishments imposed on them. Kids who watch favorite television figures use violence to achieve ends tend to accept violence, break rules easily, avoid cooperation to solve problems and differences, grow inured to aggression in everyday life.

If the news were all bad, of course, we could deal with it easily. Banish the television monster from our homes forever and be done with it.

I know how attractive you sometimes must feel this proposal is. Meals start late because a favorite TV show preempts them or, worse, meals are taken amid flickering lights, voices, and shadows, and the constant "Sh!" of family viewers. Homework is postponed or undone because some team of adventurers awaits new dangers on Monday night prime time. Early-morning cartoons turn the house into a circus of noise and action even before you've had a chance to wake up fully.

It may be tempting to wish television away like a bad dream. But banishing the TV is no solution. (You'd rather have a video arcade in your living room? A home-computer game station? Who's to say that what we have now is any worse than what we could get?) Remember David Niven, the frustrated television kicker in the film *Happy Anniversary?* ("My inspiration!" I hear my wife cry in moments of intense anguish while our kids' voices blast another off-key television commercial at dinner.) But the guy who kicks his console to bits is only booting the messenger.

Yes, there's truth in Marshal McLuhan's point that the medium is the message (and the massage). And many thoughtful parents actively try to influence the quality of television programming for youngsters by forming watchdog groups, writing to network executives, and speaking regularly with advertisers. But financial realities, public tastes, and network philosophy make the effort to affect quality entertainment a Sisyphean enterprise. From the bottom of a rugged mountain you push the rock up a bit, but it always slides back.

I am convinced that for parents today who themselves have grown up with the TV screen as childhood companion, the truth is that the message is not so much the medium but *how the medium is used in the home.* What we do with television finally establishes the foundation on which to build an intelligent response to the omnipresent entertainment machine that gives us parents so much pleasure—and so much guilt. When the adolescent hero of Ed Minus's delightful 1986 novel *Kite* gives in to onanistic pleasure, he twinges. "Satisfied again," he says. "Sorry again." Isn't that our axiom, crystalizing the modern parent's dilemma about television?

CHILDREN AND TELEVISION: ON THE BRIGHT SIDE

You've heard all these familiar instructions about children's television viewing, and they've been ringing in your ears for years now.

Watch television together, parents and children before the same screen at the same time.

Encourage programs with positive values.

Avoid violent programs.

Limit viewing sessions.

Don't use television as an electronic baby-sitter.

Preview programs your child intends to watch.

Don't let the screen control your child's life.

Eat meals far from the television room.

Avoid the mindless flop-down, flip-on habit and the back-and-forth channel-changing race.

Most of this advice is well-intentioned but, in total, it hardly reflects the reality in our own and our kids' lives.

It's hard to find time to eat together, nonetheless watch TV together. Even if you could regularly view programs with your kids, would you want to? Would you choose for yourself what your children choose to see? Do they want to see what you want to see? All I have to do is recommend a program to my youngsters and their eyes glaze over. I register their brainwaves: "If Daddy wants us to watch it, it has to be boring."

The point about not making TV your baby-sitter is a good one too, but pretty tough to enforce, especially when you're not always home but the TV is. Home care givers, live (not electronic) baby-sitters, even nursery-school teachers find compelling reasons to rely on the video screen. And when kids burst into their homes alone, they fly to the television like moths to light. They're calling up the only available companion at the moment. Voices and actions on the airwaves fill the void of an empty room. Next time you're ready to throw a fit about television-watching rules, remember your child's needs. Sure, if you were home all the time, maybe you'd be able to assure adherence to a strict viewing code. But you're not home all the time, and you have to make adjustments for your own family scene.

What I'm saying here is that not following sensible guidelines from psychiatrists, teachers, and pediatricians does not make us bad parents.

My wife and I view ourselves as pretty vigilant overseers of TV time in our house, but we've learned that we must sometimes give in to programs we don't always like. Television viewing is an important ingredient in a child's social acceptability. You've heard children share stories with their friends about favorite TV programs—lots of what we'd call junk among them. When *The Incredible Hulk* was popular a few years back, it was not a program we thought suitable for our eight-year-old, and certainly not for our five-year-old. We banned the program from our household, only to remove the ban soon after. We realized that our kids saw themselves as outcasts among their friends, who compared notes regularly about the Hulk's adventures. We swallowed hard and turned away and tried to use other strategies than banishment to deal with the issues we objected to.

There's a larger issue here. When Steven Spielberg accepted the Irving Thalberg Producer's Award in 1987 from the Academy of Motion Picture Arts and Sciences, many critics praised his eloquence in asking that we reclaim a legacy of print, a legacy of reading books and plays. But another point he made then was equally important. "Movies have been the literature of my life," he said. He was talking essentially about today's filmmakers who were weaned on the media, but his point resonates for all the children of our day. The literature of the video age is our children's literature, and I think they are lucky to have an expanded base from which to draw on characters, themes, and story lines. I grew up on the imagined worlds of books (they weren't all good and they weren't all about good, non-violent characters), and my kids are growing up on those imagined worlds too, but also on the imagined worlds of movies and television. They get Babar the Elephant, Mother Goose, and the Ugly Duckling; but they also get Captain Kangaroo, Bert and Ernie, and Darth Vader.

And no one can deny the positive influences television can have on a child's growth and development. *Sesame Street, Electric Company, Mr. Wizard, Square One, 3-2-1-Contact, Romper Room,* and *Mister Rogers' Neighborhood* are wonderful teachers. So are the excellent travelogues and other programs about faraway places and times that we see on public broadcasting and network television. New words and concepts, new ideas, new cultures— these are as much the legacy of the video age as our worries about children's viewing habits.

In fact, early investigations of television's effect on children in modern industrial countries like England, the United States, and Israel were very encouraging. Classic studies in the '50s underscore the favorable effects of television on learning. If children watch worthwhile programs, talk in school and at home about what they watch, and think critically about video experiences, television can be a potent teaching force.

You might be interested in a 1983 report made by Gavriel Solomon to the American Psychological Association. He and one of his colleagues discovered that they could improve reading-comprehension test scores of sixth-grade children by teaching the children to ask probing questions about the programs they watched and, hence, to become more active television viewers. This and other studies suggest that even though youngsters tend to see television viewing as passive and nontaxing, when they are asked to look at a program more deeply and to think about it more seriously, children can learn significantly from it. It's the same point we make to children about reading: If you learn how to engage the sentences and paragraphs on a page, to think about them critically, you become a much more adept reader.

Working with "noneducational" television programs in England, Michael Scarborough writes for the Independent Broadcasting Authority that conceptual skills for ten-year-olds showed much greater depth and sophistication than if the youngsters had used print materials of equal content and difficulty. Even four- and five-year-olds can learn to exercise critical judgment about what they see on television. In an effort to enhance television literacy for young children, Aimee Dorr and her associates have developed a television-viewing curriculum that helps children raise serious questions about the level of reality they see on the TV screen.

In her excellent book *Mind and Media: The Effects of Television, Video Games, and Computers,* Patricia Marks Greenfield, professor of psychology at UCLA, contends that the moving visual images on the screen can help children learn certain kinds of information, particularly information about space and about action and transformation. Visual motion suits the mental abilities of many young children, she points out, and heightens the potential for learning through television. One of her most remarkable conclusions, though, as far as I'm concerned, is that "children learn to assimilate information about action, process and physical transformation through their exposure *to all sorts of television and film.* These are . . . effects on thinking that are produced by the technology and the forms, *rather than by any particular content.*" (The italics are mine.)

Greenfield cautions us not to use this conclusion as a rationale for allowing children to watch too many hours of entertainment television, but the point is clear and sharp. Television is a powerful teacher, and content does not necessarily inhibit learning of key skills. Surely it's better to have kids learn from a balanced viewing schedule that includes intellectually challenging programs. But it's important to note that redeeming qualities may exist even for programming you'd rather have your children avoid. (Please don't read this as an endorsement for violence, nudity, and rough language as recipes for children's viewing diets!)

Considering the positives and negatives, then, I do not intend here to vilify television, to exacerbate your guilt, or to scrape raw an already irritated sense of helplessness in facing our most intimate and familiar invader from high tech. It's not that I disagree with the advice we've been hearing for two or three generations now. I believe in the essential merit of limits and standards for television watching, and I'm going on record as supporting controls on children's viewing in the home.

But we might be missing a golden opportunity for conversation in our constant anxiety about television's overtaking family life. Kate Moody, whose 1980 book *Growing Up on Television* is intensely critical of network programming, points out over and over again how important it is to discuss with children all the issues bound to flicker across the screen.

So you want to remember that the box that talks is also a box to talk about. You want to acknowledge television as another conversational prod to stimulate important thinking skills in your children and to help move them further down the road to language competence. If we see television as a means for using and advancing our children's language, we may be able to address some of the concerns that plague us about television in their lives.

Listen again to Patricia Greenfield: "The damaging effects the electronic media can have on children are not intrinsic to the media but grow out of the ways the media are used. . . . And television watching *can* become a passive, deadening activity if adults do not guide their children's viewing and teach children to watch critically and to learn from what they watch."

TELEVISION TALK

Although I have tried to touch upon social and moral issues about television, my main concern is how to use the medium as an occasion for talking with your children. Guiding their viewing and teaching them to watch critically and to learn from what they watch are goals you can achieve by means of conversation, as opposed to strict rules and regulations. If all else fails, you can lay down the law; but first, you want to try observation, discussion, and negotiation. Let's put some of the familiar do's and don't's about children's television watching in the context of spoken exchange between parent and child.

1. *Find out what and how much your children are watching.* What is your child's television day like? Even if you spend most of the day with your youngster, don't take for granted that you know the full story of the video parade marching through her or his life. Older brothers and sisters, a spouse returning from work, a neighbor's child visiting as the two mothers sip coffee in the kitchen: These are potential television turn-ons. When you leave your child with the television on as you go to answer the telephone or the doorbell, images you cannot see are fleeting across the screen. In nursery schools and day-care centers television watching may be a regular activity, and you should know what the children are viewing.

Where do you begin? Start with talking. "What programs did you see on television today? What did you like best? What silly thing did Lucy or Big Bird do?" Jane Brody, the personal health columnist for *The New York Times,* recommends keeping a log of what and how much your children watch. (See below for a sample I've developed.) Make the log-keeping a joint enterprise; keep an oversized chart on the refrigerator or on a wall near the television set and for a week or so work together to write in the names of the programs and the time your youngster sits before the screen. If your child can write letters or numbers, invite her to write; if you have to make adjustments because there's too much television watching in your house, the task will be easier if the records appear indisputably in your child's own hand. You'll be surprised at how the hours add up.

TV Viewing Log

	DAY	PROGRAM	TIME SPENT
1.	_____	_____	_____
2.	_____	_____	_____
3.	_____	_____	_____

4. _____   _____   _____

5. _____   _____   _____

But before you leap to judgment and slash viewing time, observe your child watching the screen. When my daughter, Melissa, watched TV as a preschooler, except for the occasional program that held her complete attention like the wonderful *Mister Rogers' Neighborhood,* television programs were simply background music for her other activities. Even as she watched programs she had requested, she frequently played with a toy, riffled through a book, drew a picture. In these cases she focused her attention on the other activity and not on the television set. She heard everything that went on, certainly at an unconscious level, but was able to tune herself in and out of the program whenever she wanted. I learned a great deal from watching her watch television.

Although such activity is alien from my own habits, I can understand how older children like Melissa, who is now sixteen, can read and study from time to time with the television blasting. I need utter silence, no distractions, when I'm reading or writing. But for many people, the murmur of a television or radio is a way of obliterating distractions. The constant hum makes its own kind of silence and eases concentration.

My son Joseph, on the other hand, was a very intense viewer as a young child and still is. By that I mean that the screen riveted him and prevented attention to anything else. He would grope for a drink or a snack without ever taking his eyes off the set. For such a child you might want to consider a more abbreviated viewing schedule so that he could give his attention to other activities during the day.

2. Establish reasonable time guidelines for viewing.

With the log at hand, talk with your child about acceptable viewing time in connection with other planned or spontaneous activities. How much does your child think is enough time for watching television? How much do you think is enough? Listen as your youngster talks; expect her to listen as you talk. Make sure that she understands why you want her to watch only a limited amount of television each day. A three- or four-year-old may not have a finely developed sense of time. Hours and minutes may not have any real meaning, and you might want to talk about long programs versus short programs and the need for limiting what we watch so that we can do other things, like go to the library or the zoo, visit a neighbor, play in the backyard or out front.

Draw from your own experience. Which viewing session do you give up because you want to—must?—do something else? Why is the "something else" important? Once you agree on what's a reasonable amount of time for television each day, don't expect your child to adhere to it loyally. The temptation to flick the set on regularly is hard to suppress, and you should prepare to suggest alternate activities when a small hand reaches out instinctively for the television knob. Also, your child will view the arrangement as tentative, no doubt, and subject to daily (or, perhaps, hourly) renegotiation. It's all right to give in occasionally and to allow more viewing than normal—these are not rules scratched into stone—but the changed plan should always be connected to conversation. "Why is it important for you to watch another half hour of TV today? Which show could you give up in order to keep within the time limits we agreed on?"

Video recorders in many of today's homes cancel the desperate "I have to watch this show *now!*" arguments that plagued parents in years past. If a program is worth watching and your child has to miss it for some reason, record the show and set it aside for later viewing within schedule limits. But be careful! VCRs can escalate viewing time. Your child will want to see both regularly scheduled shows and the tapes of missed programs or of favorites viewed many times before. Add to these opportunities the innumerable tapes of films, cartoons, and special programs, all for rent at your local video shop, and you have unending hours of visual and auditory stimulation emanating exclusively from the television screen. VCRs make more vital than ever the need for television viewing schedules that families adhere to faithfully.

When kids get older, your guidelines may have to be even tougher than those you develop with preschoolers. If, for example, your child doesn't do homework regularly or puts it off to the last minute in the day and does a hurry-up job with it, you should insist that homework precede television watching, and you should give solid reasons for this ruling. Let your youngster explain his point of view. Together, perhaps, you can set up a trial period to test a new viewing plan.

If homework habits improve, open discussion again and loosen up the rules a bit. Even if your child interprets your initial actions as heavy-handed or unilateral, you'll know that you aired them, substantiated them, and opened them for review. Wherever possible, conduct these negotiations with an eye to options, which should be spelled out in advance so that your child can weigh them carefully. A program viewed at six or seven in the evening means that a favorite at nine o'clock must fall by the wayside for other obligations. Which does your child choose? Press for a decision; see that it's adhered to; praise the enterprise. We want to seize every opportunity we can to encourage informed and reasoned choices and to help youngsters feel good about making decisions, which sometimes may be difficult or unpleasant. Open conversation offers a testing ground for the kind of problem resolution that faces us as adults and, because we've been poorly guided ourselves, that often confounds us. We're giving our children a better break than many of *us* had!

3. *Encourage advanced planning for program selection and play an active role in the choice of shows your child watches.* With the arrival of the Sunday papers or the weekly television magazine guide, spend a few minutes going through the television section and helping your child match her interests and preferences with the amount of time you've agreed to set aside each day for viewing. Again, the key word here is conversation. You don't make the choices. You help guide them by means of discussion. Let your child tell you which shows she likes to watch and why.

Wanting to balance educational programs and entertainment, you indicate specials that you think would be of interest. Keep a list and oversee the selection.

Checking the television guide in your local newspaper or magazine well in advance of viewing is an efficient and painless way of learning about the content of shows your youngster watches. Video guides often provide critical commentary that flags particularly good or bad shows, especially movies and specials, throughout the day. What I like most about going through a television guide with youngsters is getting them to talk about their expectations for the show from the brief program description and then checking their expectations after the program airs. A discussion like this helps a child practice critical thought skills like predicting outcomes, making comparisons, and analyzing ideas.

Even a one-line description can mushroom into a delightful discussion. A short while ago *The New York Times* printed this blurb on "What a Nightmare, Charlie Brown!": "A rebroadcast of the half-hour animated special about Snoopy's bad dream." Saul had never seen this Charlie Brown special. We talked about the written description, about why Snoopy might be having a nightmare and about what he might be dreaming about.

Saul thought for a moment and then delivered a three-minute monologue on Snoopy maybe doing something bad (like biting one of Charlie Brown's friends) and having Charlie Brown yell at him and then Snoopy going into his doghouse and dreaming that Charlie Brown kicked him out and that Snoopy needed to find another place to live, but maybe Charlie Brown would worry about Snoopy and go out looking for him. We talked about nightmares in general, what they represent, and how they are only dreams and not real.

Although I encouraged it, Saul wouldn't talk of his own nightmares, which he has from time to time. When he awakens full of terror, there's little I can do but hold him and try to soothe him. Now, as he was free of the immediate fear of a bad dream, we faced the issue with some distance and rationality. It didn't matter that Saul wouldn't or couldn't recount his own nightmares; I could tell from the powerful hug he gave me before he ran off that this was an important conversation for him. (We'll leave to the psychologists an analysis of the universal childhood fears of displeasing the authority figure and of subsequent rejection and abandonment that Saul projected on Snoopy.) I know when Saul sees this show that he'll think of his own nightmares and of our conversation, and that they may make him less fearful. I know, too, that we'll have some fun comparing what Saul thought would happen with what actually appeared on the screen.

Even a discussion about the brief title of an upcoming episode or a film will stimulate your child to think of television as more than just a passive exercise. It will also help you to stimulate language in a pleasurable context. On the same page of the blurb on "What a Nightmare, Charlie Brown!" we noted a PBS *Wild America* program called "Animal Oddities." Saul and I talked about the word *oddities,* and then he volunteered the strange animals he knew about—the furry platypus who has a duck's bill and duck's feet; the opossum who sleeps hanging upside down by his tail; the cheetah whose coat is covered with spots.

Talking with your child about upcoming programs is clearly another means for sustained conversation at home. Good teachers always engage children in talk about books in advance of reading. Once again, you're providing useful practice for a coming classroom activity.

4. *Whenever possible, monitor programs and watch and talk about them with your child as you view.* You have several possibilities in trying to achieve this noble but elusive goal.

First, and most obvious, is to check out in advance the programs you want to let your child see. That is, watch the shows before your child watches them. In this way you'll know what Punky Brewster is like or how violent Dangermouse really is. You'll certainly be able to make informed judgments about what your child should watch, and you can influence his or her choices based on real information. But few parents have the time to do advanced screening and, despite the good it can do,

I don't recommend it unless you have lots of time on your hands.

Another possibility is to sit beside your child and watch television together. You'll see everything he sees and will have a mental record of all the sounds and images that work on your child. You'll be able to lead conversation about what you're watching—an unusual character, an extraordinary piece of action, an item of language that needs discussion and clarification.

Yet, as I said before, the life of busy parents and busier children often preclude relaxed joint viewing with no distractions. Kids watch television beyond our supervision. And in the few moments of spare leisure time we ourselves can afford to give to television, we're not always inclined to concentrate on the antics of Bert and Ernie, King Friday, or Fred Flintstone.

Still another, and perhaps the most realistic, approach is to take your work to the viewing room. Or, if you have more than one television, let your son or daughter watch TV where your own activities take you. Portable sets travel from room to room. Move the television to the place that you have to do your work. Then, go about your business, just keeping half an ear and eye to the screen. With this approach, you won't feel that you're cheating yourself or your child.

As you would if you were sitting and watching with concentration, make occasional comments about characters and actions that you see when you look up from your work. Ask questions. Encourage your child to offer comments and judgments about the antics she's watching. Your goal is to help clear up any puzzling behavior on the screen, to provide commentary that reflects the social values you believe in, to talk about unfamiliar language, to invite observations from your child about what she sees, and, simply, to be available for any questions.

Although families often do look at television together, research suggests that parents rarely engage children in conversation that heightens awareness of what's on the screen. Yet some researchers, pointing to the fact that people do many different things as they watch television, insist that television is essentially a social activity. Discussion and social interaction occur regularly as people watch together. In *Television and Human*

Behavior, George Comstock and his colleagues say that about 25 percent of the secondary activity associated with viewing is given over to conversation; about half of the conversation focuses on what's being viewed; and about a fifth occurs after viewing, some of which takes place while people are watching *more* television. Kenneth Bruffee, who sees the social nature of television viewing as the essential hope for its teaching possibilities (he calls it "collaborative learning television"), reminds us of social interaction and electronic media *in extremis.* Remember the *Rocky Horror Picture Show* cultists who dressed up weirdly, like characters in the film, and performed with each other while the movie was being shown? There, social interaction among the audience is more important to the viewers than the events on the screen.

You have to acknowledge a paradox when you consider all this information carefully. On the one hand, social intercourse, verbal exchange, is neither alien to television watching nor essentially distracting for viewers. Structures already exist in our viewing habits to allow interaction and conversation, and thus viewing television together is a potentially powerful stimulus for informal teaching and learning at home. On the other hand, though we apparently are comfortable about talking with each other as we look at television, we don't seem to be directing our conversation usefully to children in order to help them process what they are watching.

You should try to use the intrinsically social nature of television watching to talk with your child about what she's viewing. Studies show that discussions of programs can help children weigh the social attitudes displayed on the screen, attitudes that might otherwise go unquestioned.

The *Journal of Communication* reports on an experiment with two groups of four- and five-year-olds. With the same adult (a teacher in this case), each group watched an *Adam-12* episode about kids who play hooky from school and get into trouble. With the first group, the adult made only neutral comments, like suggesting that the children sit together and watch a TV show. With the second group the teacher provided running commentary about the values reflected in the episode. She said, for example, "Oh, no! That boy is in trouble" and "He was playing hooky and that is bad." With this second group, even a week after the show, children knew more exact information about truancy and reflected the teacher's favorable attitudes and judgments. Not so the other group.

In viewing an *All in the Family* episode that set characters in nontraditional sex roles (a husband who cooked, a wife who repaired home appliances), a group of children—five-year-olds among them—decreased their stereotyping of sex roles. This result was particularly pronounced when an adult made positive comments, during natural pauses in the action, about the characters' untraditional, "gender-reversed" activities. Patricia Greenfield cites a group of elementary-school children who viewed violent *Batman* episodes. Adult interpretations of the show made the children much more critical of the violence they saw on the screen.

Parents' interpretations and explanations are shown to be very important in the television-viewing experience. They help shape the values children take away from the electronic screen.

5. *Talk with your child about television programs he or she has seen.* Of all the suggestions I've made, this seems to me the most practical and the most essential. You've got to talk with your child about the television shows and movies she watches during the day. If you're a working parent whose hours at home are subject to tight schedules, you won't find it easy to watch TV regularly with your children. Preschoolers, even kindergartners and first- and second-graders, are ready for bed when you finally find time to look at television. And your choice of shows is not always one that matches what your child wants to—or should—watch. But you certainly can talk about the day's television experiences while you're both doing something else. As part of your repertoire of conversational touch-points with your child, television viewing should have a prominent place.

Television and films are very important parts of our children's lives, whether we like it or not, and we need to show interest in their interests in the media. When you talk together about a program your child has seen but you have not, you're helping to put your child center stage. He becomes a teacher essentially. He must practice critical thinking skills. He must recall and summarize the action, or plot, of the episode; he must provide details of the characters' appearances, actions, and behaviors; he must answer questions you raise in order to understand the program better. Here is another opportunity for storytelling and for your role as a conversational stimulus. Encourage your child to expand ideas and to explain concepts. If you draw on the kinds of questions I've presented in Chapter 3, you can involve your child in dynamic thinking and learning from the electronic media.

Greenfield says that "by discussing shows with children, parents or other adults can increase the benefits and decrease the negative effects of watching commercial television programs." If you can't be there during television time, don't miss the opportunity to talk about what your son or daughter has watched in your absence.

When your child tells you about the narrative line of a program he's watched, listen carefully to the sequencing of events. Ask questions about chronology. Which event came first? which second? It's not easy for a youngster to recall the activities he wants to talk about in perfect order, so don't be surprised to hear about the climax before you learn about the events leading up to it.

Also, I've discovered that young children especially need help in distilling the occurrences in a half-hour or an hour show into a manageable unit for conversation, one that adults (and other children) can listen to without losing interest. As they can with storytelling of any kind, kids can get stuck in details. Use some of the strategies that we explored in Chapter 5. You'll probably hear an endless stream of "and then . . . and then . . . and then." You should focus your child's talk by saying, "Now what were the most important parts of this story?"

It's also tough for kids to provide an appropriate response to an adult's question, "What was the show about?" We usually expect someone to give us a few sentences that capture the gist of the production and we don't expect to hear all the details along the way. For children, however, the details are the program. The sensory stimuli bombarding a child's consciousness from TV are recorded in the mind and body as discrete occasions, and they easily can lose their temporal and logical coherence as time and memory fade. Certainly, the details *appeared* in an ordered fashion as your youngster watched. Certainly they should add up to a total impression about the television show. But your child probably has not formulated that impression in language.

It may be useful in this connection to think of many bits of iron filings randomly ordered on a sheet of paper. Some touch each other, others lie alone in their own desultory space. Bring a magnet close and hold it under the paper; in a sudden leap the filings cohere and cluster together in the force of the magnetic field.

The events of a television show are, after your child views it, those random bits of iron in your child's mind. When you press her to say what she thinks the main point of a show was (it's the "What was the show about?" question), you create the opportunity for a magnetic field. You're asking for a controlling force to hold the pieces together.

When you ask, "What was that TV show about?" you are asking for a powerful convergence of thought and language that create a *generalization*. Generalizing is a critical skill that your child needs in order to read and perform well in school. One of the standard items on reading proficiency and aptitude tests is the "main idea" question, which almost always requires generalization. When a teacher asks a youngster to state the main idea of a paragraph or of a story, she's asking the child to generalize. Tell me, the "main idea" question asks, tell me what your mind comes up with after you've added together all the details. I realize that *add* is probably not the best word here—there's little arithmetic about the process. To generalize when we read, we try to find a thread through the details, some element that connects the essential information and makes most of the details cohere. Up and down the educational spectrum teachers emphasize this skill at generalizing, and the language of reading instruction is filled with words and phrases that high-light it: *main point, thesis, main idea, key idea, major point, con-trolling idea, proposition, proposal, major premise.*

I hope that you're coming to see the point I'm making here. Like other storytelling sessions I've encouraged you to establish at home, when you talk with your preschooler or elementary-school child about a television program, you can furrow a field for future planting. Practice with generalizing at home in an unthreatening setting on a topic the child loves (a television program she's chosen to watch and to share with you) and you will assure a successful crop at school later on.

Don't expect miraculous growth of skills here. You know yourself how tough it is to generalize, to develop a short, co-herent statement that sums up the essence of a complex ex-perience. In response to your "What was the show about" question, your youngster may only name a character or two on the show. You'll have to keep asking questions to draw out the main point. Don't lose patience. Be prepared for responses that are way off target. You no doubt will have to ask follow-up questions, to offer your own "main ideas" for shows you've watched together, or to abandon the question for the moment if it doesn't get the results you expect after some probing. But keep coming back to it as you talk of other programs. Asking your child regularly, "What was the show about?" helps provide practice in that important skill of generalizing.

Talking about television provides a range of home topics for discussion and clarification, including issues related to content, language, and social awareness. At dinner one day, Saul was recounting with great delight a movie he had seen in which one character described another as "not playing with a full deck." Saul kept saying the phrase over and over again, obviously quite amused. On a hunch I asked him what the words meant. He didn't have the slightest idea. So, first we looked at the word *deck:* Saul had figured out from the language context that the speaker meant a deck of cards. "But nobody was playing any cards," he said, perhaps seeing humor in the fact that people talked about doing something they really were not doing. Who at the dinner table knew what "not playing with a full deck" meant? Joseph said it meant that someone didn't have all his marbles.

We were rather quickly then into the metaphorical nature of language—not that I ever used those terms—and that we're always making comparisons between things. Why? To make ideas clearer, to add spice to spoken and written language. The words "not playing with a full deck" had come to be a way of describing someone whose thinking abilities were being questioned. Imagine how silly it would be to play a card game if some of the cards were missing. And, with pieces missing, you didn't have a whole working unit. A brain with pieces missing wouldn't work right either.

We saw that the expression was used offhandedly and humorously, but we also saw that nobody would like to be described in that way. The talk about language led to a conversation about values, about how words can wound, and how important it is to be careful when we talk about other people so we don't hurt their feelings. It was good to air these ideas as we had other times in the past. The old "sticks and stones" rhyme is a lie: names do hurt young children. A simple and eloquently captured moment to support this point is Countee Cullen's poem "Incident":

> Once riding in old Baltimore
>   Heart-filled, head filled with glee,
> I saw a Baltimorean
>   Keep looking straight at me.
>
> Now I was eight and very small,
>   And he was no whit bigger,
> And so I smiled, but he poked out
>   His tongue, and called me "Nigger."
>
> I saw the whole of Baltimore
>   From May until December;
> Of all the things that happened there
>   That's all that I remember.

You know about television and social reality in some of the studies I cited earlier from Patricia Greenfield's work. Kids easily develop misconceptions of the world from what they see on the screen, and parents must be the connection to reality. At every opportunity, place the social values your youngster comes away from the set with in a broader, real-life perspective. This is especially true for commercials, those powerful, attention-grabbing bullets that rip into our living rooms more than ten minutes out of every hour of television time.

When you look at television shows and commercials, watch especially for stereotypes of race, sex, religion, politics, economic status, color, and geography. The world of television, writes Dr. Victor C. Strasburger, member of the American Academy of Pediatrics' Task Force on Children and Television, is essentially a world in which blue-collar families barely exist, white people disproportionately outnumber minorities, blacks and other minorities are generally portrayed as bad guys, men outnumber women three to one, women work in the home and have minor positions, elderly people are oddballs, and "sick, retarded, handicapped, and fat people play small roles."

None of us wants our children to have a warped view of the world, but unless we pay attention to the peculiar social vision fostered in television land, we risk raising children disconnected from reality. Make sure you expose your children to various minorities and ethnic groups. Help them see that character is related to thought and action and has nothing to do with race, color, or religion. Help them see that gender does not limit women and men to certain jobs, skills, and attitudes.

And the only way to achieve these goals is to talk, talk, talk about the electronic visitor in our living rooms.

Fifty Talk-About Books
for Young Children

DENNIS THE MENACE

"I LOVE A GOOD STORY. I EVEN LIKE A BAD STORY."

What follows here is a highly personal treasury of favorite books for young children. Unlike other bibliographies you may have examined for youngsters, this one has as its main purpose the opening of doorways to conversation between you and your young child. These are books that I like and that I've used with preschoolers—my own children, neighborhood kids, nursery-school boys and girls I've visited in more structured settings—so I know how the texts and illustrations work with little people.

As you can imagine, in preparing this collection I had a tough time deciding what to include and what to pass over. I've mixed classics with less familiar selections, oldies with new releases, general-interest books with "issues" or "problem" stories, fantastic tales with realistic ones.

But I've had to omit more than I care to think about. I have often left out titles from the supermarket shelf, books like the Little Golden Books that you can pick up for a dollar or so at your local grocers. I've left out picture dictionaries, poetry collections, well-known fairy tales, and myths and fables. I've also left out any books I've discussed in previous sections of *Talk with Your Child*, as well as books in the same series as a book I've mentioned there. For example, in Chapter 4, we considered *The Berenstain Bears' New Baby*, but I'm not including any other references to books by Stan and Jan Berenstain. I hope you'll use these classics whenever you can. Almost every page, through words and pictures, catapults you into lively dialogue with your child.

You'll find several common features in the presentations below. For every story, I provide a summary, perhaps in more detail than you're used to. I wanted to give you enough information about each book in case you're too busy to examine it before reading with your son or daughter. These summaries will save you time; you can simply skim the books just prior to story time.

I've been disappointed myself in the recent spate of parents' texts that boast descriptions of books to read to kids. The descriptions usually fall short of telling me enough so that I know whether or not to choose the books. A description like this from Nancy Larrick's otherwise informative *A Parent's Guide to Children's Reading* is not very useful if I don't know the book and want to judge its appropriateness for my child:

Do You Want to Be My Friend? by Eric Carle. Crowell, 1971. The seven words of the title lead through an intriguing series of brilliant full-color pictures which tell a dramatic, even touching story.

I don't have enough information from this blurb to help me choose. What is the book about?

So, you'll read relatively comprehensive summaries here. And, although we are limited by space, I've also tried to give you a flavor of the book beyond a discussion of its content. I reproduce an illustration now and then. I love some of the drawings so much that I couldn't resist showing them to you, especially when they help frame a good discussion point or question. Here again, it's idiosyncratic author's license that motivates me. I hope you'll like the illustrations as much as I do and will find them a useful adjunct when you're ready to pick a book to share with your youngster.

Just as important as the summaries and illustrations in this selective listing are the conversational touchstones you'll find for each book.

I've tried to indicate some really interesting ideas to talk about with your child. For each story you'll find many questions that you can use before, during, and after the reading. The questions address both words and pictures. Of course, you should use these only as guidelines—question models, if you will, not model questions. I hope that you'll make up your own questions based on what the book is about and about what you feel your child—your unique, special child—will find interesting in it. I also hope that my question models will help you construct conversations about children's books you've chosen on your own, ones you do not find on my list.

I've almost always left out questions about content, expecting that you'll use the question-asking skills you considered in Chapter 3 to talk briefly about story line and sequence of events. Though you'll want to check on whether your child understands what she's read, my interests here are in shaping that basic understanding, in stretching the plastic of your youngster's thought into critical and creative speculation.

I also have tried to direct your attention, where necessary, to vocabulary worth exploring as you read. No dictionaries, please! We're interested only in knowing whether or not your child has some sense of a key word or concept upon which important details of the story may hang. For example, unless you talk about the word *sissy* as you read the delightful *Oliver Burton Is a Sissy*, your child may miss the significance of the title. I like talking about one or two key words in advance of any reading I do with children.

And for the wordless moments, the suddenly uncommunicative grunts, or the reluctant dialogues you'll face now and then, remember to respect your child's wishes for silence. We all have sessions we'd rather savor in silence than infuse with forced conversation. Good books often command silence. They evoke moods we don't always want to share, strike deep feelings we cannot always identify, stimulate inner concentration that detaches us from the world here and now. These conditions may impel your child to privacy. If he won't talk during or after you read, cherish the intimate moment of a good read together. You'll read that book again, and next time is soon enough for conversation.

I'm interested in hearing about "talk-about" books you've tried on your own. Please let me know which you've used and how you've chatted about them with your son or daughter. We want to keep alive a network of stories that stimulate households over time and distance to the delights of shared book talk and enlightened conversation between adults and children.

Alexander, Martha. *Move Over, Twerp*. New York: The Dial Press, 1981

Youngsters love to handle small books, and this is one about a little boy with a large problem. Children will appreciate the dilemma posed here as well as the solution the main character invents.

Jeffrey is so excited when his mother tells him he is old enough to ride the school bus alone. His excitement quickly turns to disappointment when he learns that the big kids control the back of the bus. Although they don't pick on Jeffrey, neither do they allow him to sit in the seat he has chosen. "Move over, Twerp," they tell him. His family gives him lots of advice, everything from taking a new seat to fighting physically for the right to remain where he is. But none of those solutions is right for Jeffrey. Then one day after school he goes to his room, consults some books, and works out his *own* plan.

The next day on the school bus he again takes his favorite seat. When the big boys call him Twerp and tell him to move he retorts, "I'm not moving and my name isn't Twerp." Then he opens his jacket and reveals a T-shirt with a picture he has drawn of Supertwerp. His humorous boast is, "It's SUPER-TWERP." Jeffrey's solution wins the admiration of the big kids and allows him to remain in his favorite seat.

School-age children have all experienced or witnessed situations in which older kids have imposed their will on others. Many have been involved in similar incidents and will understand Jeffrey's plight. Talk to your child about Jeffrey's first day on the bus alone. How did he feel when he boarded the bus? Why do you think he was so excited? Why wasn't he afraid? Why was it so important for Jeffrey to sit in the seat he had chosen? What other possible solutions might he have tried? Would any have worked as well? What would you have done if you were Jeffrey? How would you have felt when the big boys said to move? Why do big kids sometimes pick on little ones?

You may want to spend some time talking about name-calling. What words do you use when you're angry with someone? How do you think those names make people feel?

Whom do you go to for advice when you have a problem? What do you think was the best idea that Jeffrey's family had? Why didn't any of the suggestions work? Why is Jeffrey a special kind of kid? Why was Jeffrey's own idea such a good one? Why did all the kids laugh *with* him? What is the difference between laughing *at* someone and laughing *with* someone? What would you have done if you were Jeffrey?

Martha Alexander gives young children a hero who is a regular kid and a solution that is within his reach. We often forget that humor sometimes moves mountains and that levity carries a bright candle to a dark room.

Barrett, Judi. *Benjamin's 365 Birthdays*. New York: Atheneum, 1974.

Children love birthday parties (who doesn't?), and the excitement and joy of inviting friends to a party is a wonderful treat. Today is Benjamin's ninth birthday. His friends arrive at noon with gifts, and it is his special day for tearing off the wrappings and finding out what is inside. Benjamin is so excited; he loves his bird and birdcage, his marvelous yellow velvet trousers, his roller skates, jigsaw puzzle, and model airplane. But after the party is over Benjamin grows sad. He realizes that he must wait a whole year for this joy again. He closes his eyes and tries to imagine the excitement he felt while opening his presents. Suddenly he realizes that he can relive this excitement by rewrapping a present and reopening it the next morning. What fun! Days later when Benjamin has run out of new presents to rewrap, he looks around his house and begins to see gift possibilities in ordinary things—his pillow, his bathtub, a flower, the refrigerator. Every day for the rest of the year Benjamin surprises himself with another gift.

In 366 days it is again Benjamin's birthday. His friends arrive at noon and find him on his roof. They are invited to climb up and join him there for a party. His friends are confused and do not understand why Benjamin has wrapped up his house. But Benjamin knows why. He has given himself the greatest present. He has learned that everything around him is a gift and always will be. He has learned to appreciate the unheralded things in life.

Judi Barrett's book has lessons for us all. Before you begin to read, a look at the ribbons, wrapping paper, and gift on the cover will certainly initiate good conversation. As you begin the story, encourage your child to notice the different shapes of the presents and ask what might be inside each of those boxes. Which would your child like to receive? Why?

More questions: What would you serve at your birthday party? How do you think Benjamin feels when he is opening his presents? How do you feel at your birthday parties? Help your child identify other feelings besides excitement. Remember, birthdays are laden with emotion and often difficult for young children. Let him know that all his feelings are appropriate—including anxiety over the presence of many guests as well as the demands for "good" behavior.

Other questions to ask: Why does Benjamin wrap up all those objects later on? What are some of the special things that you might wrap up? Why do you think Benjamin is having his party on the roof? Why has he put wrapping paper on his house? What would make you as happy as Benjamin?

This is a book to read over and over. Your youngster will find something new in Ron Barrett's illustrations with each rereading. Let him take the lead when he is ready. Although the Barretts are writing about birthdays, a child may become interested in something unintended, such as the fact that all the characters are dogs, and that there are no parents in the story. You will learn a great deal about your child by listening to his questions, and by building your conversations out of his concerns.

Berger, Barbara. *Grandfather Twilight*. New York: Philomel Books, 1984.

Do not miss sharing this magnificent book with all your children. Its beautiful, dreamy illustrations and its soft, lyrical story will inspire wonderful conversations. Each child who reads this book will bring something different to it. Grandfather Twilight lives in the forest. Nightly he removes a pearl from an endless strand in a special chest and saunters through the trees. As he moves, the pearl grows larger and larger in his hand until he reaches the sea where he delivers it into the sky and then silently returns home, having again completed his evening task.

Barbara Berger has given us a poetic explanation of how the moon appears each evening. Let your child react to the whimsical logic and to the sentient peace created by the artist. I would suggest snuggling up and reading this story at a quiet time. Don't stop to talk until you are done. Then say, "How does this story make you feel?" "What did you like about it?"

For some children you will need to stop then, possibly to reread and savor. Here are some questions to start conversations:

1. How do *you* think the moon got into the sky? Who is Grandfather Twilight? What was really in his chest?
2. Look carefully at the illustrations for additional information not in the story. I love the picture on page 3 of the gentle man sitting and reading with his animal friends hovering around him. How do the birds and animals feel when they are around Grandfather Twilight?

What would you do if you could meet him? Would your Grandfather Twilight have a beard? What would he look like?

Brett, Jan. *Annie and the Wild Animals.* Boston: Houghton Mifflin Co., 1985.

A lovely surprise awaits you when you share this book with your child. Using an unusual format, the author-illustrator has framed each of her pictures with a wide border, which tells just as much of a story as the words or the main pictures.

Try something different and say to your child, "Let's see what's going on in these borders." (You might want to explain what a border is.) On the first page the border shows a girl, a cat, snow, birds, and an assortment of winter clothes.

Here I would ask, "What do you think the story is going to be about?" "Why do you think the girl and her cat spend lots of time together?" Go through the book and examine the borders first, and encourage your child to tell her own story. "How does all that snow make you feel?" "How would you like to live out on the edge of the forest?" "What feelings would you have in the winter?" "What different feelings would you have in the spring?"

The story itself is a simple one. Annie's cat has been acting peculiarly for days, and now it is gone. Because she lives in the woods and is so lonely, Annie places corn cakes at the edge of the woods to try to attract another small, furry pet to be her friend. Instead, a series of wild animals appears and none of them is an appropriate friend. The illustrations throughout allow us to see winter passing in the forest. The reader knows before Annie does that her cat, Taffy, is safe and has had three kittens. Annie's loneliness is very real, but your child will know that Annie will soon have a whole family of pets to care for.

Your child may mention the absence of adults in the story. Annie lives all alone in the forest, yet she is well dressed and has a beautiful cottage. Talk about the real elements in the story, and those that couldn't happen. The book also brings up some emotional issues, and you will want to decide if your child is ready to discuss them. Some questions that come to mind are: How do you feel when you are alone? When do you like

It had been snowing for days.
Winter was lasting too long.

being alone? When do you like to have people around? When have you ever felt really lonely? What would you do if your pet ran away? How would you go about finding him?

Brown, Marc. *Arthur's Nose.* Boston: Little, Brown & Co., 1976.
    Arthur is an aardvark who is unhappy with his nose. It is so big that the other children complain that it bothers them. Arthur has trouble playing hide and seek, and his nose gets terribly

red and runny when he has a cold. So he goes to see Dr. Louise, the rhinologist (who of course is a rhinoceros) to see if he can get a new nose. She suggests that Arthur try on different noses so that he can decide which one he likes best. As his friends wait outside wondering what the new Arthur will be like, he tries on everything from a tiny chicken's beak to a long elephant's trunk. Finally Arthur emerges and he hasn't changed his nose at all. "I'm just not me without my nose!" he exclaims happily.

This is the first in a series of Arthur books. Marc Brown takes a humorous approach, yet it and his comical illustrations bring up important issues of self-image. Why did Arthur want to change his nose? How did it feel being different from his friends? Do you have any features that you are unhappy with? What part of you would you like to change? Why? At the end of the story Arthur's friends express concern that Arthur may be different if he changes his nose. Ask your child why Arthur's friends were worried that he would change. How would you be different if you had freckles or blond hair instead of brown hair? What feelings must Arthur have had to make him consider changing his appearance? What do you think Arthur learned in Dr. Louise's office?

The use of boldly outlined, deeply colored illustrations and a simple text help to draw attention to the normal feelings all children and adults have as they question their appearance and learn to accept and like themselves. You will want to discuss some of the more difficult vocabulary: *aardvark, nuisance, decision, rhinologist.*

Browne, Anthony. *Piggybook.* New York: Alfred A. Knopf, 1986.

Anthony Browne has created an intellectually challenging picture book. It may make you chuckle with recognition and sneer with disgust as you ponder the situation and study the piggy illustrations. In the end it might make you and your family appreciate each other a little bit more.

The book is called *Piggybook* partly because it is about a family named Piggott, but the illustration on the cover implies a deeper meaning. Mrs. Piggott, the mother, is carrying the rest of the family on her back. A good opening question to talk about with your child would be: Why is the entire family on the mother's back? Ask it before and then again after you have read the story. As you read, pay careful attention to the illustrations, especially noting the details and how they change. Browne foreshadows the changes of his characters into pigs by initially transforming the background illustrations. Help your child notice the wallpaper design, the doorknobs, and the mantel decorations. See how many other references (some more subtle than others) you can find.

Initially, the story is about a typical family, a father, a mother, and two sons. The father goes off to his very important job, and the sons go off to their very important school. That is, after their mother serves them their breakfast. They sit and order while she does all the cooking and cleaning; then she goes off to her job. Notice the illustrations again. The pictures of the demanding males in the family are big and bold, while the pictures of Mrs. Piggott are small and in sepia tones. Ask your child why we don't see Mrs. Piggott's face? What do you think she is thinking?

One day the boys come home and Mrs. Piggott is gone. She has left a note on the mantel. "You are pigs." Now the changes are less subtle, the physical features of the characters actually change, and Mr. Piggott and his boys act more and more like animals. Talk with your child about these changes. Just as we see the Piggotts on the ground, snorting and looking for scraps, Mrs. Piggott walks back in. They beg her to stay. They have learned their lesson and from then on everyone helps with the housework. Return to the title of the book. Would *Piggyback* be as good a title as *Piggybook?* Why or why not?

One message is clear—if you start acting like an animal you grow more and more like one! Yet make sure that your child knows that people do not *really* turn into animals. Remind your child of Pinocchio and how his actions changed him into a donkey. Use your imagination. What kind of behavior would make you think a person was acting like a dog or a horse or a turtle? Talk about other animal characteristics and how humans

sometimes display them. Remind your youngster of some of these familiar statements: I worked like a horse; you dirty dog; bug off; birdbrain; you're a chicken; a sitting duck. What do they mean?

Take time to discuss families and how they must cooperate. Ask your child what she could do to help the rest of the family. In what ways is each of the members of your family "piggish"? What would your child have done if she were the Mommy in

Piggybook? How do you think Mrs. Piggott felt when she left home? Why did she come back? What did the Piggotts learn when they were on their own?

This tale has a little of everything: truth, fantasy, humor and sadness. It will stir up feelings in both the children and the adults who read it.

Caines, Jeannette. *Abby*. New York (City): Harper & Row, 1973.

Abby is an adopted child, brought into a family of a mother, a father, and an older brother, Kevin, when she was almost a year old. She loves looking through her baby book. Kevin finds her a pest because she's a girl; they have a little spat; but all ends well as Kevin asks Ma if he can take his sister to school for show-and-tell.

There's more to this wonderful little book than the important social theme of adoption, which gets a subtle, upbeat treatment here. Abby is special, a lively, indestructible child for whom adoption is just another condition that makes people different from each other. When she learns that Kevin was not adopted, she asks mother if they can adopt a boy for him.

The energetic illustrations by Steven Kellog bring the urban family household to life, and, along with the story itself—simple dialogue exchange between Abby and her mother and brother— are brimming over with potential subjects for conversation with your child. My favorite picture is the one coming right after Kevin answers, "No, no, no!" to Abby's question about whether he likes girls. Abby is looking at herself forlornly in the mirror. About this page I'd ask, What does Abby see in the mirror? How does she feel? Why does she feel that way? Why did Kevin say that he doesn't like girls? Other questions to explore about the story: (1) Why does Abby like looking at her baby book? What do you think she finds there? What is in your baby book? (2) What does it mean to be adopted? Which adopted children do you know? (3) How can you tell when Abby gets angry at Kevin? What do you do when you get angry at your brother or sister?

Illustrations on almost every page invite you and your little boy or girl to explore activities sure to be familiar in your child's life. Ask what Abby's mother does when she returns from the market and how Abby helps her. Ask about what Kevin does when he arrives home. The author makes no reference to those actions, but the illustrations will stimulate conversation.

Caple, Kathy. *The Purse.* Boston: Houghton Mifflin Co., 1986.

Growing up isn't always easy, for with each change there is also a loss of the old and familiar. Katie, the determined little star of this book, is influenced by her big sister, and decides it is time to replace her money-holding Band-Aid box with a purse. They shop together and purchase the perfect purse. But, alas, there is nothing now to put in it, no money to make that familiar *clinkity, clinkity, clinkity* sound. So Katie sets out to earn some new money. Soon she has $2.30. When she puts it into her new purse, it makes only a disappointing *clunkity, clunkity, clunkity.* Without wavering, Katie looks for a solution and asks her dad to take her shopping. With her newly earned money Katie purchases a new Band-Aid box, and her understanding dad buys the Band-Aids from her. Now Katie has a purse and inside it is her Band-Aid box with her money and the wonderful *clinkity, clinkity, clinkity* sound she loves so much.

This charming story depicts a warm, loving family in which a child is encouraged to think for herself and find solutions. The illustrations, like the text, pay attention to little details. Pictures vary in size, and some pages have several that carefully follow the chain of events in the story. I love the expressions on Katie's face, especially on pages 10–11.

Of these I would ask: What is Katie doing here? What is she expecting to happen? What emotion does her expression tell you she is feeling? Look at Katie's face in these pictures. What do you think she is thinking in each one? Why is she pouring everything out of the purse? What would you do if you were Katie? When can you think of a time when your excitement turned to disappointment?

You will want to talk about Katie's determination. Think of

all the times Katie's plans did not work out. What do you think made her continue trying? Discuss the different jobs that Katie did to earn new money. What could you do to help in your house if you wanted to earn money?

And talk about growing up, how exciting it is and how scary too. How did it feel packing away the crib and setting up the new bed? Remember the first day of nursery school? Let your child know that change is sometimes just as hard for a grown-up as it is for a child.

Carle, Eric. *Do You Want to Be My Friend?* New York: Thomas Y. Crowell, 1971.

This delightfully illustrated book by Carle has only ten words.

Two of the ten are *the end!* It's a perfect book to help you build reading and thinking skills with young children. A pink-eared mouse asks the question that's the title of the book to many different animals: a horse, an alligator, a hippopotamus, a seal, many others. The blurb says "every child will spontaneously create his own story based on Eric Carle's striking and imaginative pictures." Don't buy the word *spontaneously,* however; this is a book that parents should actively help a child understand by discussing the various pictures.

You will note on the first page, for example, that the mouse is talking to an animal's tail, an animal revealed only when you turn the page. Help your child build critical thinking skills by encouraging him or her to predict the animal from the tail. (First time around may be tough; second, third, and subsequent readings produce great delight as children know which animal is waiting.) The body of a snake stretches at the bottom of every page until the next to the last where we finally see what animal this is. The mouse does not find a friend until the end of the story when he meets another mouse. Good questions to ask for lively conversations:

1. Why did the mouse want a friend?
2. Why don't the other animals want to become his friend?
3. What friends do you have? What is a friend? Why do we all like having friends?

Carlstrom, Nancy. *The Moon Came Too.* New York: Macmillan Publishing Co., 1987.

Written in verse, this delightful picture book will certainly appeal to toddlers and preschoolers. I always find that books that rhyme are extremely readable and have the additional advantage of allowing a child to participate in the reading by filling in the word at the end of the sentence.

A young child is going on a trip to Grandma's. With obvious delight she prepares for the visit, choosing only her most necessary possessions. Certainly the child needs her favorite stuffed animals and toys, a horn and flashlight, clothes, and of course three hats, her fishing equipment, and a wagon to carry it all.

Mother, daughter, and cat enjoy the ride and arrive just in time to share all the treasures with a very pleased Grandma, and to look up and notice that the "moon came too."

The detailed drawings by Stella Ormai complement the simple text well, supply supplementary information, and will form the basis for much of your conversation. Ask: What kinds of things does the little girl like to play with? What does her room look like? What else do you know about her by looking at the pictures? Why would you like a friend like her? What do you think her name should be? Ask what special toys your child would pack if she were going on a trip. Why did you choose the ones you did? What clothes would you take? What clothes would you take if Grandma lived in Florida?

The story shows a little girl and her mother, but doesn't make mention of a father. You might want to talk about where the father could be, and possibly about different types of family units. Another obvious topic would be vacations. Talk about going away from home, the good parts and the difficult parts of traveling. Find out what your child misses when she is not at home. How does it help to take familiar things along? If you were able to take only one special thing, what would it be?

Cooney, Nancy. *The Blanket That Had to Go.* New York: Putnam, 1981.

Suzi has a blanket that she carries everywhere. It is her special friend, and she loves to feel it when she is sick, tired, or sleepy. One day Suzi's mother tells her that kindergarten will soon be starting and that children do not take blankets to school. Suzi knows she cannot go to school without her special blanket-friend, and so she tries to figure out an acceptable way to take her "lovey" with her. Nothing seems appropriate, and Suzi grows more disillusioned until one day she has an idea. She cuts the blanket in half. Although it is still too big, by the time school begins a few days later, she has unraveled her blanket fragment to a size just right for her pocket.

This is a story that will appeal to young children because it so realistically portrays a hero they can identify with. Talk about

Suzi's attachment to her blanket, and relate it to your child's favorite stuffed animal, toy, or blanket. What is special about your "lovey"? How does it feel, smell? How does it make you feel? Why did Suzi *need* her blanket in school? Why don't all children carry their blankets to kindergarten? Ask your child if he might feel better having something from home in his pocket? Will Suzi always need a piece of her blanket? Why or why not? What might happen if the children or teacher saw Suzi with her blanket? How would she feel then?

Crews, Donald. *Freight Train.* New York: Greenwillow Books, 1978.

With vivid color illustrations and a simple text, Donald Crews tells the story of a freight train. After swiftly describing each car, he takes us through tunnels, past cities, in darkness and in light as the train is "going, going, gone!"

Donald Crews is a master illustrator, and children love this story as it moves quickly past them the way a freight train would, leaving them somehow transformed for having watched it pass. On one level *Freight Train* can help you explore colors as well as the names of all the different cars on a train. Some children will learn the story by heart and will be able to read it to you because of the simple, memorable text. But this book is so much more than the sum of its individual parts, and you can heighten your child's experience by talking about it.

Some good questions for your discussion:

1. Talk about the word *freight.* What does it mean? Where do you think the train is going? When will it get there? How long has it been traveling? What things would you see if you were riding on this train?
2. What do you think each car is carrying? Who needs those things? Where do they come from?
3. Where would you like to travel on a train? What would you like to see? What sounds does a train make? Who uses trains?

DePaola, Tomie. *Oliver Button Is a Sissy.* New York: Harcourt Brace Jovanovich, 1979.

Oliver Button doesn't like to play ball with the other boys. Oliver Button likes to dress up and dance. He likes to pretend he is in a show. After much discussion, his parents enroll him in a dance class. When the boys in school learn about it they make fun of Oliver, and someone writes on the wall "Oliver Button is a sissy." Even this does not deter him. But when Oliver enters a talent show and does not win, he is sure the boys will be even more cruel and he refuses to go back to school. His mother encourages him, but Oliver hangs back in the school yard, waiting for everyone to go in. Then on the wall, he sees "Oliver Button is a Star."

DePaola is celebrating the unconventional child here, and he lays the groundwork subtly for debunking sexual stereotyping. The very first page tells us that Oliver didn't do things that "boys are supposed to do." After you get your child to discuss the narrative events, you'll want to talk with him about the things people are "supposed" to do. What are some of the things Oliver's father expects from his son? What other things are boys supposed to do? What things are girls supposed to do? Is a girl allowed to do boys' things and vice versa? If your child is a boy, find out if he likes doing any "girl" things and vice versa here too. You want to lead your child to see that people can choose to do what they like and that their actions don't make them less a boy or a girl. Also, many men and boys build lives and careers around some of the unboyish things Oliver likes to do. Talk about the men dancers and actors who give pleasure to millions of people.

There are many raw feelings to explore here. Use the illustrations to talk about how Oliver felt when he saw the message on the school wall. Who do you think wrote that message? Why? What does the message on the last page of the story mean? Who do you think wrote it? Why does Oliver feel sad when he doesn't win the talent show? Why doesn't Oliver want to go to school? DePaola's technique here is frequently to provide several illustrations for a single page, and you'll want to call attention to them for their sheer delight.

Some words you might want to highlight as you read: *sissy, routine, talent show, master of ceremonies, baton-twirling.*

Fitzhugh, Louise. *I Am Five.* New York: Delacorte, 1978.

This simple book captures the whimsy and fun of a five-year-old's mind. The hero, a delightfully drawn imp of a girl, shares responses to the question she poses herself at the beginning of the book: "Want to hear all about me?" She says that she talks a lot, that she knows how to be nice enough to get a hug, and that sometimes she feels like kicking everybody. She shares her fears, her likes and dislikes, and her new bathing suit. She ends the book as she began, with questions to the reader: "How old are you?" And "What are you like?"

You'll have fun answering those general questions at the end of your reading, but there are many other conversation prods in this book. I like starting with some basic sensory responses. All drawings here are in black ink; alternate pages are white and yellow-orange. None of the illustrations has color. Fitzhugh manages to convey all the indomitable exuberance of her hero in black and white; nevertheless, your child will enjoy talking about what color she thinks the little girl's hair and eyes are, and what color and texture her dress, socks and shoes, and bathing suit are. Also, what would your child call the girl? The girl's dog? (Neither has a name in the book.)

You'll also want to talk about motivations and feelings. Why does the girl sometimes feel like kicking everybody? Why is she scared of the dark? Does your child know anyone else who's scared of the dark? The little girl says she hates, in this order, teeth, bedtime, and all those starving people. (The last, somewhat subtle for five years old, must be connected to the illustration; the little girl is sitting at a table with a full plate of food she obviously doesn't want to eat. Someone must have said to her regularly, "You have to eat all your food because of all those starving people!" You may have to explain this point to your youngster.) Find out why your child thinks the little girl hates teeth, bedtime, and starving people. Then ask about your son or daughter's dislikes. The girl says that sometimes she feels like a fat silly and other times she feels so good it positively amazes her. Talk about why she might feel that way.

This book honors the ups and downs of the preschooler's feelings, thoughts, and attitudes. You want to validate the idea that people's feelings do not always stay the same and that we all have ups and downs.

Gackenbach, Dick. *Harry and the Terrible Whatzit.* New York: Clarion Books, 1977.

The imaginative Dick Gackenbach tackles fear, here of dark, damp places, with a humorous tale of a young boy who bravely faces his fear head-on.

Harry is afraid to go down to the cellar. He warns his mother not to go either. She doesn't listen to him, and when she doesn't

return quickly, he arms himself with a broom and goes to look for her. His fears are confirmed when he meets the "double-headed, three-clawed, six-toed, long-horned Whatzit." He confronts his outrageous monster and demands to know where his mother is. Moment by moment his courage builds, and as he controls his fear, the horrible monster shrinks before his eyes. Harry then continues his search and finds Mother outside picking flowers. He explains how he chased the Whatzit away with a broom. Although at first he doesn't think she believes him, she later tells him she will always feel safe knowing Harry is around.

Many preschoolers suffer with fears, and this story of a boy who masters fear by confronting it and banishing it will interest your child. It will also help him or her talk about frightening things. The illustrations give us information that the text does not include about Harry's thoughts. Take note of Harry's expressions throughout the story, and ask, "What do you think Harry is really thinking?" "How come he doesn't always say what he feels?" "When have you ever been afraid to say what you are thinking?"

Of course you will want to relate Harry's fears and his method of overcoming them to your child's. Find out what frightens your child. Share some of your own childhood fears. Look at the illustration of Harry meeting his monster for the first time. "Why is the Whatzit hiding behind the furnace?" "What might the monster be afraid of?" Gackenbach also brings up a more subtle problem of childhood, the belief that parents are not really listening and don't believe the things that children say. This is clearly an important message to parents, and you should be aware of it and may want to find out if your child ever feels this way.

Goodall, John. *Paddy's New Hat.* New York: Atheneum, 1980.

This delightful British entry is one of a series of Paddy stories. The format, with small pages and overlapping half pages, will appeal to youngsters and at the same time will provide an excellent vehicle for developing thinking skills.

The story begins with Paddy, a pig, purchasing a new hat. When a gust of wind blows it into a police recruiting office,

Paddy finds himself enlisted, given a uniform and an assignment. The first adventure begins with Paddy being dragged, hand-cuffed to an escaping prisoner, and landing headfirst in a barrel of water. His next assignments do not end any better. Finally he makes a real mess of the traffic outside the Royal Palace and runs away in disgrace. While running, he discovers a thief stealing the queen's jewels. This time Paddy bravely captures the burglar and becomes a true hero. He retires from the police force with honors from the king and queen and goes off happily in the new hat he has repurchased.

You will want to help your child notice the details of each illustration, which provide clues for the story's development. What do you think Paddy is thinking on each page?

You will need to explain the meaning of the word *recruiting* and to help your child understand what has happened to Paddy. How do you think Paddy feels being recruited? As the story progresses ask lots of "What will happen next?" and "Why do you think so?" questions. This book offers excellent opportunities to stretch your child's ability to make inferences and draw conclusions. How do you think Paddy felt when he saw the burglar going into the Palace? What does it mean to be a hero? How do you imagine you might become a hero? Who do you know that is a hero to you? Where do you think Paddy is going at the end of the story?

Hoban, Russell. *Bedtime for Frances.* New York: Harper & Brothers, 1960.

It is time for bed and in this classic by Russell Hoban, Frances, a very verbal little badger, is stalling for time in all the familiar ways that human children use. She asks for milk, kisses, and stuffed animals until finally the lights are turned out and the last good-night is said. Frances cannot sleep, so she sings an alphabet song. When she gets to the letter *T* she thinks of a tiger and becomes frightened. She tells Mother and Father about her fears; they encourage her back to bed. After that Frances sees monsters, imagines scary things coming into her room through cracks in the ceiling, and worries about what lurks outside her window. Mother and Father have shown patience up to this point, but when Frances wakes them to ask if she can sleep in their bed, they tell her that she will get a spanking if she does not go to sleep immediately. When she hears the next scary noise at the window, she starts to go for help but then, remembering the promised consequence, forces herself to take a careful look at the source of the noise. She sees that it is only a moth, and she settles down to sleep at last.

There are many good books that deal with bedtime and fear of the dark, but I especially like this one because of the patient, understanding way Frances's parents deal with her problem. When they threaten a consequence, you know they've exhausted all possibilities! (I wish, however, that the consequence were not a spanking.) Because Frances is so verbal she will help your youngster to talk about any similar fears that he may have.

You will want to ask lots of questions. Why do you think Frances is taking such a long time to go to sleep? How does it feel to lie in bed and not be able to sleep? What keeps you up? What else might Frances have done to help her fall asleep? What do you like to do to help yourself get to sleep? Do you think that Frances's parents' threats to spank her were unfair? Why? How do you think Frances felt when she was told about the spanking? What things frighten you at night? What would you like your parents to do if you kept coming out of bed to say you were scared?

If bedtime is an issue in your home, this book will be useful in dealing with your child's fears. Those children who are not afraid of nighttime noises will also enjoy Frances's shenanigans.

Holabird, Katharine. *Angelina and the Princess.* New York: Clarkson N. Potter, Inc. 1984.

Angelina is a sweet, likable little mouse, and the series in which she appears will appeal to many young children, especially those taking ballet lessons. Before you begin you will want to introduce some ballet terms: *pliés* and *pirouettes,* and the words *determined, memorized,* and *congratulated.*

Angelina is a dedicated ballerina who aspires to stardom. She has a chance to audition for a very important role to be danced before the Princess of Mouseland, but alas she wakes up with a fever on the important morning. Not willing to miss her opportunity, Angelina sneaks out of the house anyway. Because she is ill, she performs poorly and is not chosen for the important role. Although she claims she will never return to ballet school again, her mother convinces her that she must go back and do her best, even in a small role. The day of the Royal Performance arrives, and minutes before the curtain, the star sprains her ankle. Luckily Angelina has memorized the leading role and gets to dance before the Princess. Not only does she fulfill her dream but she also saves the day.

Talk about Angelina's determination. What made her go to the audition even though she was sick? Do you think it was smart for her to leave the house when she had a fever? When have you wanted to do something so badly but thought you'd be prevented from doing it? When have you ever missed an important event because you were sick? How did that make you feel?

If your child has ever been in dancing school or in a school play, you can discuss how it feels to try out for a special part. When have you wanted something and not gotten it? How does it feel when your best friend gets the part you want?

This book has a fairy tale quality to it, and I think that should be something you will want to talk about with your child. What happens at the end of the story to make Angelina so happy? How would the story have ended without the accident? Which way do you think is more like real life?

Howard, Jane R. *When I'm Sleepy*. New York: E. P. Dutton, 1985.

Taking a simple idea—how it would feel to sleep where different animals sleep—Jane Howard creates a soothing, nighttime story. A young girl being tucked into bed imagines how it would feel to sleep in a basket, a nest, a cave, a swamp, standing up, hanging upside down, or under water. The illustrations flesh out the individual environments with lots of detail, and provide lively, visual information for your preschooler. Your youngster will especially love the drawing of the child snuggled up in the bird's nest. The words on that page say "or fall asleep in a downy nest." You may have to explain the meaning of *downy,* and then ask: How would it feel to curl up in a nest of feathers? How would it feel if the nest were made only of straw and weeds? How would it be different if you were alone in the nest? Would you like sleeping way up high in a tree? What would you like to eat in your nest? Or ask how your child thinks a bird would feel sleeping in a bed? How would a fish feel? a hippopotamus?

Howe, James. *The Day the Teacher Went Bananas.* New York: E. P. Dutton, 1984.

In this wonderfully silly story a gorilla accidentally gets sent to school to be a teacher. He shows the children how to count on their toes and how to paint with their whole bodies. He eats sixteen bananas for a snack. He gives the children a grand time. Unfortunately, the mistake is discovered and the real teacher, Mr. Quackerbottom, comes to replace the gorilla, who is sent back to the zoo. When Mr. Quackerbottom comments that the children behaved as if they belonged in a zoo, they happily oblige and go the next day to visit their favorite teacher during lunch!

You and your child will enjoy a good laugh when you read this lighthearted story, enhanced by Lillian Hoban's delightful drawings of schoolchildren. Use the story as a springboard for imagining other implausible situations, and how they would turn out. What would happen in school if an elephant were the teacher? A mouse? A pig? What would it be like for a human teacher teaching a class of animals? What would happen then? You might want to draw attention to the title and the play on the word *bananas.* An opportunity to be silly and creative at the same time will really stretch your child's ability to think and use language.

Hughes, Shirley. *Alfie Gets In First.* New York: Lothrop, Lee & Shepard, 1981.

This is the first in a wonderful series of books for preschoolers. Shirley Hughes creates a cozy, loving environment for her characters. She depicts the familiar everyday events of a young child's life. Alfie and his sister, Annie Rose, are the stars of these books, and your child will enjoy watching the children grow and change as your child himself grows and changes at the same time.

Alfie and his mom and sister are returning home from shopping. Alfie is all excited and races to be the first in. His mom opens the front door and puts the groceries inside and returns to get Annie Rose. Suddenly Alfie slams the front door hard. Now he is inside with the keys, and Mom and Annie Rose are locked out. It is then that Alfie realizes what he has done, and he starts to cry. Mom makes suggestions for him to reach the lock but he is too upset. Several neighbors and neighborhood workers come to help, and just when the window cleaner is about to slip through the bathroom window, Alfie surprises everyone and opens the door all by himself.

The illustrations for the text are full of details and can stand on their own merits. See how much of the story your child can tell without your reading it to him. Guide him with some questions like: Where are Alfie and Mother in the beginning of the story? What do you think they are buying? Why is Alfie running? What can you tell by looking at his expressions?

Look particularly at the scene where Alfie slams the door. What do you think he was thinking when he pushed the door closed? What *hadn't* he thought about? When have you done something without thinking about how it would turn out? What would you do if you were locked inside the house and all alone? How would you feel? How do you think Alfie felt when he opened the door all by himself and saw all those people standing there? Find out if your child thinks Alfie did a bad thing by slamming the door. Talk about how people often do things without thinking first.

Hughes, Shirley. *David and Dog.* Englewood Cliffs, NJ: Prentice-Hall, 1978.

Author and illustrator Shirley Hughes has produced a beautiful picture book. *David and Dog* concerns a boy named David and his stuffed animal, Dog, whom he takes everywhere. One day, rushing to the ice cream truck near his big sister's school,

David unknowingly drops Dog. That night when David realizes that Dog is missing, his family searches everywhere, but to no avail—Dog is not to be found. Big sister Bella offers David one of her teddies, but of course it is not the same as his favorite, and David has difficulty sleeping without his beloved pet.

The following day, a very sad David goes with his family to the school fair. The day does not go well for David until suddenly he spots Dog on the table at the toy stall. Unfortunately, while David is trying to locate his parents, a little girl purchases Dog. David is beside himself, and although Bella tries to explain the situation to the little girl, she will not give Dog back. Just then, the girl notices the huge yellow teddy Bella had won earlier. Bella does a very wonderful thing: She offers to trade her new prize for David's Dog. David has never been happier and hugs both Bella and Dog very hard.

This charming story realistically portrays a relaxed and happy family. Note with your child the details of family life, the easygoing personality of the mother, the homey clutter, the care in the parents' search for David's Dog. Talk about David's attachment to Dog. What makes one toy so special? Ask your child to tell you about her favorite toy. Has she ever lost or misplaced it? How did your child feel without it? Why is that toy so special? What feelings did David have that night as he searched for Dog? How do you think the rest of the family felt? Why couldn't David sleep with Bella's teddy?

You will also want to focus on David's relationship with Bella. Why was Bella so kind to David? How does having all those teddies of her own help her understand David's loss? Do you think most sisters would give away a giant teddy they have just won? Why?

In this book Shirley Hughes demonstrates the power of love, and we realize that when we are treated caringly, we learn to care for others. It is a potent lesson for us all.

Joyce, William. *George Shrinks*. New York: Harper & Row, 1985.

George wakes up to find he has shrunk to the size of a mouse!

Next to him he finds a note from his parents telling him to make his bed, brush his teeth, have a good breakfast, take out the garbage, and watch his little brother until they come home. As the story ends his parents are entering his room and the reality is that the whole thing has been a dream.

Joyce has created a winning combination. He supports a simple text with very humorous illustrations. Young children understand well how it feels to be small, but to imagine oneself being the size of a tiny animal is very amusing. Talk with your preschooler about some of the illustrations. I particularly like the one of George brushing his teeth. Notice the expressions on George's face throughout. Good questions to talk about with your child:

How did George react when he found he had shrunk? How would you feel to find yourself only inches high?

What things could you do that you cannot do now? What things would be too difficult? What might be dangerous?

How might the story have been different if George had turned into a giant? If you could choose, would you rather be very tall or very small? Why?

Keats, Ezra Jack. *Peter's Chair.* New York (City): Harper & Row, 1967.

The remarkable Ezra Jack Keats illustrates this bittersweet tale of little Peter, who is feeling jealous and neglected because of a new baby sister. His play tower of blocks crashes to the floor; Mother says, "Shhhh! . . . we have a new baby in the house." They've painted both his cradle and his crib pink; Father tries to enlist Peter's help in painting Peter's high chair pink, too. He snatches his own little chair and with his dog, Willie, a toy crocodile, a bag of goodies (doughnuts and dog biscuits), a baby picture of himself, and the chair, he runs away.

Not far, happily. He stops in front of the house and arranges his things, but when he tries to sit in the chair, he discovers that it is too small. From the window Mother asks Peter to come back to the family—there's something special for lunch— but he pretends not to hear. Then he gets an idea and plays a trick on Mother. He leaves his shoes sticking out from under the curtain, and unsuspecting Mother thinks he's hiding there. Surprise! He pops out from behind the dresser. (Only the visual illustrations explain the trick, so be prepared to talk about why mother thinks Peter is behind the curtain!) Sitting in a grown-up chair, Peter suggests to Daddy that they paint his chair pink.

You'll come up with dozens of questions for this one, I know. Among some that you might use to talk with your child about this book are: (1) Why have they painted Peter's crib and cradle pink? How do you think Peter feels about it? (2) Why does Peter take his little chair up to his room? (3) Why does Peter decide to run away? What other reasons might children have for wanting to run away? (4) Why does Peter take his baby picture with him? (5) What trick does Peter play on Mother? Why does he play a trick on her? What tricks have you played to fool me? (6) Why do you think that Peter decided to come back? (7) Why does he want to paint his chair pink? (8) Why is the book called *Peter's Chair* and not *Peter's Trick,* say, or *Peter Runs Away?*

McPhail, David. *Pig Pig Grows Up.* New York: Dutton, 1980.

Pig Pig just doesn't want to grow up. He squeezes himself into his crib, his high chair, and his stroller with hilarious results. He just refuses to give up his babyish behavior. Pig Pig's mother has stopped fighting with her son and is allowing him to remain a baby. One day as she pushes a very heavy Pig Pig in his stroller, she reaches the top of a hill and collapses. The stroller remains perched at the top for a moment and then starts rolling out of control down the hill right toward a baby carriage. Pig Pig realizes that he must act immediately and manages to bring his stroller to a full stop before it hits the baby. Pig Pig saves the baby and acknowledges that he will never be a baby again.

With humorous exaggeration, McPhail has dramatized the very real struggle many children have with growing up and relinquishing their babyhood. What did Pig Pig like about being a baby? Why was Pig Pig afraid to grow up? Why wasn't his mother more insistent that he act like a big boy? What would have happened if she refused to treat him like a baby?

Find out what your child liked (or likes) about being a baby. Make comparisons: What was nice about that period of his life? What does he like about being a big person now? Share with your child the knowledge that there is a little baby left inside us all, and that being cuddled and held feels good even when you are big. (What a great time for a hug!)

You will also want to discuss the ending and how proud Pig Pig was when he acted like an adult for the first time. Why wouldn't Pig Pig climb back into the stroller and allow himself to be babied again? Find out when your child felt proud of himself for acting like a grown-up.

Murphy, Jill. *Peace at Last.* New York: The Dial Press, 1980.

Here is a bedtime story with an unusual twist. Mr. Bear is tired and wants to sleep, but all the noises he hears keep him awake. First, Mrs. Bear's snoring keeps him up. Then he moves to Baby Bear's room, but Baby Bear is making airplane noises.

Mr. Bear moves again and again, only to be disturbed by a ticking clock, a dripping faucet, and an assortment of nighttime animals. As the sun finally rises, he climbs exhaustedly into bed, thinking, "Peace at last." Finally he falls asleep, awakened soon after by the ringing alarm clock and cheery "good morning" greetings from a rested Mrs. Bear and Baby Bear.

You will want to discuss the meaning of the title *Peace at Last*. What does peace mean to a grown-up? When has someone told you that he or she needs some peace and quiet? Why can Mrs. Bear sleep and why is Baby Bear happy playing instead of sleeping? Why do you think Mr. Bear wants to go to sleep so badly?

Talk about nighttime with its silence and noises. What sounds kept Mr. Bear up? What noises do you hear in your house at night? When have you ever had trouble sleeping? What noises make you feel safe? (Many children will say that they like to hear the television playing or their parents talking.) What noises are scary noises? What noises are annoying noises?

This charming story is also a visual treat. The illustrations are a combination of full-page paintings done in rich, warm colors, and small black-and-white sketches. Some of the backgrounds are black, others are white. Talk about the colors and how they make you feel. Help your youngster understand the passing of the hours by the artist's use of different colors. Be sure to examine the illustrations carefully because they too are full of the nighttime noises. And please be sure to catch all the delightful expressions on Mr. Bear's face. I especially love the look of loving annoyance as he leaves a snoring Mrs. Bear.

Rice, Eve. *Benny Bakes a Cake*. New York: Greenwillow Books, 1981.

In the simplest of language, with complementary illustrations, Eve Rice suggests to the young reader the combination of emotions felt by a young boy on his birthday.

Benny's special day begins with a big wet kiss from his dog, Ralph, and a hug from his mother. Then Benny helps Mama bake his birthday cake. We move slowly through the stages of mixing, stirring, and sifting, enjoying each step just as a toddler would. Throughout the process we notice that Ralph is always near the cake, sniffing and licking his lips, and of course the stage is being set for what we as adults know is inevitable. After the cake is iced and decorated, Mama suggests a walk. "But where is Ralph!?" Oh, no, Ralph is happily enjoying Benny's birthday cake! Benny is inconsolable. Nothing helps—he just cries and cries. Suddenly, there is a knock at the door and there is Papa with a new birthday cake. The day is saved for Benny.

Eve Rice has written a birthday story with a slow, lyrical quality that appeals to a preschooler. Notice how she pays special attention to the little details of a job, just the way a child would.

Talk about birthdays, talk about the pleasures and the disappointments. Relate Benny's experience to your child's. Ask her what she expects a birthday to be like. How does it feel when things go wrong on a special day? Assure her that her feelings are very natural and appropriate. Talk about pets. Find out what she thinks about Ralph's behavior. Why did Ralph eat the cake? What do you think Mama should do to Ralph? How do you know that Ralph is upset? If your child has a pet, relate his experience to Benny's. Has your pet ever ruined anything of yours? What could Benny's mom have done to have avoided the accident?

Rice, Eve. *New Blue Shoes*. New York: Macmillan Publishing Co., 1975.

Author and illustrator Eve Rice has a magical way of taking an everyday event and transforming it into a sensitive story rich in meaning. Her understanding of a young child's inner life shines in the small, old-fashioned drawings, quiet, yet strong. This book is enhanced by a text that is perfectly matched in mood to the pictures.

In *New Blue Shoes,* Mama takes Rebecca shopping. Rebecca is very definite about what she likes and what she wants, and although Mama suggests brown, Rebecca knows that she wants blue shoes. She finally finds the perfect pair, and Rebecca is very happy with her choice. But as she and Mama stroll home, Rebecca doubts herself. She fears that she will look silly in blue shoes. Luckily for Rebecca, she has a very supportive mother who helps her overcome her insecurity.

Here are some ideas for initiating conversation:

1. Talk about a special shopping day and the events associated with it. What do you like about a shopping trip? Where do you like to shop? What special treats usually go with such a day?
2. How do you know that Rebecca likes to go shopping with her mother? What do you think they talk about while they walk to the stores?
3. Rebecca tells the man exactly what color shoes she wants. What is your favorite color for shoes? How do your shoes compare with Rebecca's? What happens when you and your mother disagree about what you should buy? Why did Rebecca's mother let her have her own way?
4. What happened to Rebecca as she was walking home? Why did she start to doubt her purchase? Why is Rebecca afraid that she will look silly? When have you ever been afraid that someone would laugh at you or make fun of you? Explore this area with your child and talk about how Mama helped Rebecca feel good about herself.

Rockwell, Harlow. *My Nursery School.* New York: Greenwillow Books, 1976.

The large, detailed illustrations here and the very simple sentences provide many occasions for talk both with children already attending nursery school and those not yet in a preschool program. Rockwell shows many of the everyday experiences that await children, from the two teachers (here one is male, I'm pleased to note) and the ten children to the various objects and activities available for a child's observation and play. We see and read about "six guppies in a tank and a furry hamster in a cage." We see seeds children are growing and the clay, scissors and paste, blocks, paints, and puzzles they play with. We watch the children in the playground; we join the juice and cracker recess; we see the basket of dress-ups.

Yet the simple sentences at page bottom belie the wide range of activity suggested in the illustrations. On the first page, we read, "I go to nursery school." The picture shows a child kissing her father at the door. He is carrying a lunch pail as the mother looks on. Talk about that page with your preschooler. Where is the father going? Why? Why does he carry a lunch pail? What kind of work do you think he is going off to do?

The next two facing pages show a very busy nursery-school room, and you'll have fun exploring it with your child. What are the children doing? What are the teachers doing? Which of the activities would you like to do? Subsequent pages, as I've said, highlight the individual activities first represented in the aggregate here, so that talking about them now will build pleasant recognitions as you turn pages together later. I especially like talking about the simple lump of clay that Rockwell shows us as we learn that the child will "punch it and poke it and squeeze it and roll it flat." What do you think the child will make with the clay? What have you made with clay?

Whether your child already attends nursery school or will do so in the near future, be sensitive to feelings about the experience. Talk about the little girl in the story. Does she like nursery school? Why or why not? (Listen carefully; your youngster may be talking about herself and not about the book character.) Develop those higher-order thinking skills by asking your child to compare the nursery school in Rockwell's story to the one your son or daughter goes to: How many teachers are there? What are they like? Do the children play with clay and paints— what do they make? For a child not yet in a preschool program ask her to imagine what her nursery-school class might be like or to compare it to a nursery-school setting she might have visited (perhaps to deliver or pick up an older sibling) or might have seen on television. What's important here is encouraging your child to see likenesses and differences, even to make generalizations.

Russo, Marisabina. *The Line Up Book.* New York: Greenwillow Books, 1986.

A determined child and a mother impatient to serve lunch set the simple frame of this story whose details any child, with some good interchange, can recognize as familiar and relevant. Sam is laying a long line of blocks from his bedroom door; his goal is to make the line longer and longer. Mother's calls from the kitchen do not deter him. When he runs out of blocks, he uses toys from the bathtub, shoes and boots, and his toy trucks to extend that line. Mother's patience thins: She's already counting to three, while Sam tries to figure out how to lengthen the line to the kitchen. With his hands over his head he lies down. Success! Mother praises his ingenuity, but she tells him to come when she calls next time.

Talk about Sam's lineup. Why does he want to build a long line? Have you ever built such a line of blocks? What things other than blocks could you use once you ran out of them?

Talk about Sam's determination. Why is Mother annoyed? Why does Sam disregard her calls? Why didn't he stop his lineup, go in for lunch, and then come back to play? Should he have stopped his game? Why couldn't his mother have said, "Why don't you come in whenever you're finished, Sam?" You'll also want to talk about the illustrations here, down-to-earth paintings with lots of little, familiar details.

Rylant, Cynthia. *Night in the Country*. New York: Bradbury Press, 1986.

Night in the Country is a book you'll want to savor. You'll find a sensory experience of rich, dark illustrations and clear text shining like the evening sky on each page.

The story is simple. The setting is nighttime, and people in their houses are either sleeping or listening to the sounds of the country animals—the owls, rabbits, frogs, and raccoons. Listening closely, one even can hear an apple fall from a tree. As morning lights the sky, we learn that the night animals will either sleep or spend the day listening to us.

Night in the Country is a mood setter. Find a quiet place and snuggle up close because you will find that conversation will flow easily after you share this melodious book with your youngster. What to talk about? Say to your child, Let's close our eyes and imagine we are in the country. What are you doing in the country? Whom are you visiting? What sounds do you hear? How does your body feel when it slides into bed at night? Encourage your child to create her own story. Build important thinking skills by asking your child to compare the sounds of the country night with the sounds of a city night, or with the sounds right outside her bedroom. You know how important recontexting is, and here's a simple and convenient place to achieve it. When your child connects the text experience with her own—nighttime in the book, nighttime in her life—she learns that books are mirrors of human life and are inexhaustible sources of enlightenment about the human condition.

Take time to discuss the illustrations in this book. Their lushness affects young readers deeply. Talk about the way colors impress your youngster. What colors make you feel warm? Cold? Happy? Frightened? Sad? The possibilities for conversation with this book are as varied and as wide as your child's imagination.

Schwartz, Amy. *Bea and Mr. Jones.* Scarsdale, NY: Bradbury Press, 1982.   Bea is bored with kindergarten; she is ready for a challenge. Mr. Jones is tired of the pressure of the advertising world; he needs to relax. And so they decide to trade places for the day, with very interesting results. Bea dons her father's suit and boards the 7:45 for New York. She fits in well at Smith & Smith Advertising, laughing easily at the boss's jokes, and coming up with imaginative advertising jingles. Mr. Jones does wonderfully in kindergarten; he knows all the answers and serves the snacks without spilling a drop. Everyone is happy, so happy they decide to make the trade permanently. Bea continues at the office and Mr. Jones remains the star of kindergarten.

I would use the situation itself as my conversation starter. After discussing the story line and introducing some of the more difficult vocabulary (*memo, genius, teacher's pet, promotion, challenge*) I would ask: When have you needed a change? Whom would you like to trade places with? What funny things might happen? How would you look different? How would being a child make the job difficult? How would it add to the adult job? Can you imagine your mom or dad or grandma or grandpa trading places with you? What funny things might happen then?

Be sure to discuss the ending of the story. How might you have expected the story to end? Why were you surprised? How would you feel if you traded places with someone forever? Who might you like to trade with for a little while?

Sendak, Maurice. *Where the Wild Things Are.* New York: Harper & Row, 1963.

No list of children's favorites should exclude the master storyteller, Maurice Sendak. Although *Where the Wild Things Are* won the Caldicott Award in 1963, many librarians believed the monster drawings would frighten young children. Yet I've never read this book to a child who did not find Sendak's monsters friendly and reassuring. Sendak is well known in literary circles for his ability to understand the child's mind; Sendak was one of the first to address childhood fears imaginatively.

In this fantasy, a young boy named Max is sent to his room without any supper because he was being such a "Wild Thing." There he falls asleep and dreams that his room becomes a forest from which he is transported into the land of the wild things. As terrible as they are, Max tames the wild things with his special trick and they proclaim him king. Several beautiful pages follow in which Max leads the monsters gaily through their wild antics, wordlessly illustrated by Sendak in a way that is so captivating that the monsters appear to be dancing to music. Finally, Max stops the "rumpus" and sends the wild things off to bed without their dinner. Realizing that he misses his family, he sadly says good-bye and sails off for home, finding his hot supper still waiting for him.

You might want to read this book through without pressing for talk. Let your child initiate discussions; you follow his lead wherever it takes you.

When your youngster wants to interact, talk about Max. What do you think caused his parents to call him wild? What do you do that's wild? I hope that you have a chance to deal with labeling. One of Sendak's subtle messages is that we can become the labels people bestow on us. What does it mean to be called a "wild thing"? Why do Max's parents use the label for him? What names do people call you? How do you feel when you are labeled? Do you agree that "Sticks and Stones may break my bones but names will never harm me"? (Point out that names do hurt.)

Other questions: Why does Max send the monsters to bed without dinner? How would you like to be among Max's monsters for a while? What would you do with them?

Small, David. *Imogene's Antlers*. New York: Crown Publishers, 1985. David Small has created a humorous book that will

enthrall young readers. The magic of this story is all in the hilarious illustrations.

Imogene has awakened to find that she has grown antlers. She dresses and comes down to breakfast with some difficulty, but apparently enjoying her plight. Unfortunately, her family does not see the humor in her situation, and her mother faints at each new turn of events. The cook and the kitchen maid are much better humored and make use of Imogene's antlers to dry towels and feed the birds doughnuts. After a very full day, Imogene retires, happily remembering the wonderful events. When she awakens the following day her antlers are gone. Her family is overjoyed to have her back to normal until, on the final page, she walks into the breakfast room, and we see she has grown a full set of peacock feathers!

You will love the fantasy here and will have fun reading this book with your preschooler. Your older children will enjoy it as well. You probably will need to discuss some vocabulary that may be unfamiliar to your child: *antlers, fainted, miniature,* and *milliner.* The illustrations will be helpful in explaining the meaning of these words. Please pay special attention to the drawings and notice the look of sheer delight on Imogene's face.

Imogene clearly is enjoying herself. Allow your child time to take in the details of each picture and the silliness of the whole idea. Some questions you might want to talk about: How would you like to be Imogene? What part of her day do you think would be the most fun? What part would be the most difficult? How would you use the antlers if you were Imogene? What might your family say if you came to breakfast with antlers one morning? How would your father react, your sister, your brother?

What other animal features would it be fun to borrow? How would it be easy or difficult or helpful to have these animal attributes? (Encourage your child to imagine having the neck of a giraffe, the stripes of a zebra, the shell of a turtle.)

Spier, Peter. *Oh, Were They Ever Happy.* New York: Doubleday & Co., 1978.

The Noonan children decide to give their parents a big surprise. While Mom and Dad are out for the day, the youngsters paint the whole house! It all started when the babysitter didn't show up and then one of them had this great idea. Out came the paints, the brushes, and the ladders. The kids may not have been neat but were they creative! And so happy with their results!

The acclaimed illustrator Peter Spier has written a light-hearted story with lovely drawings, page after page, of children painting their vision of a beautiful house. The two-page spread of the bathroom during the cleaning of the paintbrushes is my favorite. What a mess! What fun!

As you examine the illustrations with your child, ask what the children are doing in each case. What do you think their parents will say when they get home? Do you think that the children are behaving badly? What do you think they are saying to each other? How would you have liked it if they had asked you to help?

Some other points to talk about with your child are:

1. How does it feel to do something different from everyone else? When can this feel good? When has this made you uncomfortable?
2. When have you given your parents a surprise that you thought would make them happy, but that they just didn't like? Why don't parents and children sometimes think the same way?
3. Talk about the word *mischievous*. What kinds of things that children do can be called dangerous? What activities can you think of that parents might not like but are just playful?

Stanovich, Betty Jo. *Big Boy, Little Boy.* New York: Lothrop, Lee & Shepard, 1984.

The illustrations here by Virginia Wright Frierson are just magnificent: soft, delicate brush water colors on fine quality paper. The drawings look real enough to be photographs. Keep your eye on these drawings for good conversation; the text does

not always refer to all aspects of the visual experience on each page.

In this story, David spends time with his grandma. She is busy with her own work, and says so very gently as David invites her to build blocks, to hammer, and to draw. She says that she'll watch David make a train from blocks and that she'll watch him hammer. She asks him to draw a picture for her. Later, when they sit together and talk, Grandma, much to David's pleasure, says how big he's grown, and she points to all the things he did that day as evidence. Grandma reminisces about when David was much younger, when he couldn't even write his name, and when Grandma made up stories for him and held him on her lap and sang to him. A yawning David says he doesn't remember too well what it was like to be little, and Grandma offers to tell

"Clean the brushes."

him a story and to sing to him. The last page brings the story gently to an end.

You'll want to have your son or daughter explain what Grandma is busy with each time she says she can't play with David. (She's talking on the phone, potting a flower, setting out a wild bird feeder.) Change a feature of the context: If Grandma had time, what would she play with David? Some other questions to raise: Why does David say he can't remember being little? What do you remember about yourself when you were little? (Here, share some of your recollections about your child when he was two or three.) If your child has grandparents, make connections. What stories does your grandma tell you? What songs does she sing to you? What pictures have you made for her? Spend some time with the last page of the book. What does it mean that in his dreams David remembered about being little? What do you remember in *your* dreams about being little? Also, talk about getting bigger and how we tell when a child is a big boy, not a little boy. One of the messages here is that even big boys like the luxury of being little again—David enjoys having his grandmother hold him and sing to him. Be sure to approve of that point. Find out what your child likes to do now that he also liked doing at a younger age.

Stevenson, James. *The Worst Person in the World.* New York: Greenwillow Books, 1978.

This story tells about the worst person in the world and his encounter with the ugliest creature. But Stevenson really is writing about friendship, loneliness, desire, and capacity for change.

Mr. Worst is one of the grouchiest characters in children's literature. He eats lemons and finds them too sweet! One day he meets the ugliest creature, who tells him it's not looks but personality that counts. Ugly goes home with Mr. Worst and decides a party is just the thing he needs. Ugly cleans and decorates and invites all the guests, only to be thrown out after all his efforts. Mr. Worst tries to return to his old ways, but something has changed inside him. He puts on a party hat and finds Ugly and the children and invites them back before all the ice cream melts.

How did Ugly change Mr. Worst's life? What kind of person is Ugly? How do you think he felt being so ugly? What did he do about it? What did Ugly mean when he said a pleasing personality is all that counts?

Talk about Mr. Worst and the way he lived. Why do you think he chose to live that way? The book doesn't say anything about his past. Where do you think his family might be? How did he get to be so grouchy? When have you ever felt grouchy? How would it feel to be alone all the time? Stevenson writes a lighthearted, comical story with supportive drawings, small, sketchy pictures with soft watercolors that complement the text and characters very well.

Of course this book is the perfect conversation-opener for

a discussion about unusual friendships and how different people attract and help each other.

Stock, Catherine. *Sophie's Bucket*. New York: Lothrop, Lee & Shepard, 1985.

Catherine Stock tells the story of a child's first day at the seashore and how it turns into an unforgettable event. Sophie awakens to find two packages on her bed—a bucket and a bathing suit. She learns that next week her family will be traveling to the seashore, a place she has never been. So much of this story unfurls in the magnificent, soft watercolor paintings that you'll want to pay special attention to them.

Ask your child what she thinks might be in the packages? How does she think Sophie feels finding them there? Point out their different shapes. Guide your child to understand the concept of anticipation. Ask: How does it feel to look forward to something? Why is it sometimes hard to wait for something? Help her remember a time when she anticipated an event (possibly a birthday, holiday, or family outing) and how it became more exciting as the day neared.

Don't be fooled by the apparent simplicity of this book. It is crammed with wonderful ideas to talk about. Throughout the story the author makes comparisons—shapes, sizes, textures, temperatures, colors. Watch for them as you read.

Saturday finally arrives and Sophie's family gets into the car for the trip. The next day Sophie wakes up in a different house. Help your child understand what the author omits. What happened in between? Say to your child: What happened between these two points? How did Sophie get to the new place? Why doesn't she remember it?

The rest of the story takes place at the seashore. All the delights of the ocean, the sand, and the sun are Sophie's. She collects her treasures (a good word to highlight) and packs them up to carry home in her bucket.

I mentioned contrasts and comparisons. Be sure to draw your child's attention to the hot sun and the cold water, the sinking sun and the rising moon, arriving early and leaving late, the stars on the bucket and the stripes on the bathing suit. See how

many more comparisons you can find—both the text and the illustrations have many more.

Another wonderful conversation-starter: After Sophie arrives at the beach and takes in the enormity of the ocean and the sky, we are told "Sophie felt so small." You'll want to discuss this feeling because it is a very common feeling of childhood. When do you feel small? What makes you feel this way? What things are you bigger than?

Don't overlook the opportunity to talk about the sensory dimensions of this book. What different textures do you think Sophie felt at the beach? What smells do you associate with the seashore? What colors and sights will Sophie remember? What sounds do you hear at the beach?

Turkle, Brinton. *Deep in the Forest*. New York: E.P. Dutton, 1976.

Wordlessly, Brinton Turkle tells the story of a little bear who strays from his family and wanders into a log cabin in the forest. There he tries out the porridge, the chairs, and the beds of the human family who live there. When Papa, Mama, and Baby return they discover a terrible mess—and a bear cub asleep in Baby's bed! The bear moves fast. He escapes and finds his family, as he silently tells himself never to wander away again.

Sound familiar? *Deep in the Forest* is *Goldilocks and the Three Bears* in reverse. Although the book is a delight on its own, conversational opportunities will be greatest if you read and talk about it after your youngster is familiar with the Goldilocks story.

Guide your child through the pictures and then help him to understand what the author-illustrator has done. You now have a perfect opportunity to improve your child's ability to compare and contrast. How are the stories alike? How are they different? Which story do you think really could happen? Who was frightened in this story? What are the differences between a bear wandering into a cabin and a girl entering a stranger's house? Younger children may not be able to grasp the subtle humor inherent in this reverse situation, but when your child is old enough you will really have fun.

Vincent, Gabrielle. *Ernest and Celestine*. New York: Greenwillow Books, 1982.

Using just a few words and offering softly colored sketches, Gabrielle Vincent conveys a full range of emotion in this simple story about friendship. Ernest is a bear—large, warm, and paternal. His friend, Celestine, is a mouse—small and childlike.

They live together and care about each other. One day as they walk in the snow, Celestine loses her favorite stuffed animal, Gideon. Ernest tells her it is too late to go back and look, but after she blames him, he puts her to bed and goes out in the night himself. He finds the toy irretrievably frozen in the snow and goes to a store to purchase several new stuffed animals. None of them can replace Gideon, and Celestine is miserable until Ernest comes up with a plan—he will make a new Gideon from the pictures Celestine draws.

This simple story for your preschooler is about true friendship, and it delivers its message powerfully.

You will probably want to read the book straight through and let it create its mood. When you are finished, review the process of Celestine's loss. What are the steps leading up to it? What are the consequences of Gideon's absence? Then, talk with your child about friendship. How can a bear and a mouse be such good friends? What does each have to offer the other? What special traits do you like in a friend? How can you be a good friend to someone? Why does Celestine blame Ernest when she loses the toy? How must Celestine feel? Why doesn't Ernest argue with her? Although your child may be young and inexperienced with friendship, point out how Celestine and Ernest suggest a model, and how the characters take turns giving to and caring for each other.

Viorst, Judith. *Alexander and the Terrible, Horrible, No Good, Very Bad Day*. New York: Atheneum, 1972.

Everyone, young and old, will identify with Alexander as he suffers through a day when nothing goes right. From the minute he awakens with gum stuck in his hair, Alexander is off on the wrong foot. He is "smushed" in his car pool, his teacher doesn't appreciate his artwork, he is excluded by his friends, the dentist finds a cavity in his tooth, the shoe store is sold out of sneakers in his size, his bath is too hot, and he gets soap in his eye! These seemingly minor indignities cause Alexander to exclaim again and again, "It has been a terrible, horrible, no good, very bad day," and then to conclude, "I think I'll move to Australia." As his awful day comes to an end, Mother finally tucks Alexander into bed and tells him, "Some days are like that. Even in Australia."

Judith Viorst understands perfectly how the small problems in life may overwhelm a child. Her artful use of the refrain adds the insult of one incident to another and will allow your youngster to see humor in Alexander's humorless day.

I suggest that you share this book with the whole family, allowing them to enjoy Ray Cruz's terrific illustrations that so perfectly show Alexander's frustration. After you have read the story, you will have to ask only, "When have you ever had a day like Alexander's?" to start a rousing conversation. Have your child tell you about his terrible, horrible, no good, very bad day. You tell about yours. What a wonderful way for your youngster to realize that everyone has difficult days, and that things do improve.

In additional readings you will want to use the different incidents in the book to stretch your youngster's ability to solve problems. What could Alexander have done when he realized his mother had forgotten his snack? What would you do if your friends didn't include you when they played? How can you get a grown-up's attention when you really have a problem? How did your bad day compare with Alexander's? Review the sequence. Which frustrating events came first? Which came next? Which came last? What can Alexander do to help him get through his next ugly day when it comes?

There are not many books that stimulate conversation as easily as this. You will probably want to own your own copy so that you can quickly pull it out when your youngster is having an "Alexander day" and then just let him talk.

Waber, Bernard. *Ira Sleeps Over*. Boston: Houghton Mifflin Co., 1972.

When Ira is invited to sleep at Reggie's house he has a big decision to make. Should he take his teddy along or not? His parents say yes, but his older sister tells him Reggie will laugh at him if he brings Tah Tah along. Even the bear's name will make Reggie laugh, she says. Ira agrees. The boys play, wrestle, and romp until it is time to turn out the light. When Reggie takes his teddy out, Ira goes home, much to the surprise of his family, and returns to Reggie's house with his teddy.

Ira tells his sister that he'll feel fine without his teddy bear, that he'll love sleeping at Reggie's without it. What is he really feeling? Why, then, does he say what he says? What are some of Reggie's "big plans" for the sleep-over? Which games, you should ask your son or daughter, would you have liked to play if you had slept at Reggie's house? How do you think Ira feels when Reggie says they'll tell ghost stories and that his house gets very dark at night? Why does Ira keep asking his friend what Reggie thinks about teddy bears? Why does Ira decide to take Tah Tah, and why does he change his mind again? When Ira sleeps over, why does he take his own teddy bear out of the drawer? How do you think Ira feels when Reggie tells him the name of Reggie's bear, Foo Foo? Why does Ira go next door to get Tah Tah after that?

Of course you'll want to connect Ira's experience with your child's. If your child has slept at a friend's, talk about the things they do on sleep-over night. If your child has a pet toy or stuffed animal or blanket or diaper that he snuggles with at bedtime, ask if he'd leave the object at home for a sleep-away. Find out why or why not. Would anybody laugh? Suppose a friend or a friend's brother or sister did laugh: How would your child respond?

Bernard Waber's drawings are loaded with information beyond the text, so be sure to talk about the pictures. Look for subtle expressions on people's faces. I especially love the smug smile on Ira's sister's face, just after she raises the teddy bear issue.

Wells, Rosemary. *Morris's Disappearing Bag.* New York: The Dial Press, 1975.

Here is a Christmas story that you will enjoy reading all year round. Morris, the youngest child in his family, is delighted to receive a teddy bear for Christmas, but he soon learns that his older siblings have no interest in trading their presents for a chance with his bear. As they all take turns with the hockey equipment, the chemistry set, and the makeup kit, Morris feels

increasingly dejected. Sitting alone under the tree, he discovers
an unopened present—a Disappearing Bag. With this magic
bag, not only can he disappear at will, but he also achieves
instant popularity. Now Morris's brother and sisters are very
willing to let him play with their toys, which only this morning
were too dangerous for their younger brother. Morris holds no
grudges however, and happily tries all their new games as his
siblings rush to take their turn with his Disappearing Bag.

Rosemary Wells weaves two very different elements into this
simple story. The first is the element of fantasy, the second the
element of family relations. Your preschooler will love the
magic of this incredible bag. You can ask: Where did this disappearing bag come from? Why didn't anyone see this present
before? When would you use Morris's bag? How do you think
it would feel to be invisible? What would you do if you could
be invisible?

Although the element of magic is fascinating to many youngsters, other children will express their interest in Morris and
his position as youngest in the family. Talk about this issue.
Ask your child: Why would you like to be the oldest (youngest)
child in the family? If you were the oldest (youngest), what
would you enjoy doing? When have you felt left out? Morris
had a magical solution to his problem. What kind of solution
can you suggest?

Wells, Rosemary. *Noisy Nora.* New York: The Dial Press, 1973.

Nora wants attention. Father is busy with big sister Kate and
Mother is taking care of little brother Jack. Nora has to wait—
and wait and wait and wait! So Nora slams doors and knocks
over chairs and lamps, but alas none of these noisy distractions
gets her the loving attention she desires. Finally in anger Nora
screams, "I'm leaving. And I'm never coming back." A sad
silence falls upon the house, and Nora's parents stop everything
to search for her. The sadness doesn't last for long, because in
her own unique style Nora cries, "I'm back!" and crashes out
of the closet.

Noisy Nora is fun to read. The lines are simple and short and
have punch because they are written in verse. The softly colored

pen-and-ink drawings suit the story and provide many humorous details. Allow your child the time to enjoy them.

Talk first about Nora. What is she trying to do? Why do you think she makes all that noise? How does she ask for attention? Why is everyone ignoring her? When will it be her turn for attention? What could Nora have done while she was waiting? How could she have gotten attention if she really needed it? Now relate the story to your child's own family and ask, how do you feel when Mom and Dad are busy with your sister or brother and cannot play with you? When do you feel left out? What do you do when you are alone and cannot have attention? Why is waiting for attention so hard? This is a good time to talk about appropriate behavior and also to discuss why running away is not a good solution, just a funny part of Nora's story.

Whitney, Alma Marshak. *Just Awful.* Reading, MA: Addison-Wesley, 1971.

This is a story about the fear that accompanies being hurt and having to go to the school nurse. It is simply written, and young children will enjoy and identify with it.

James hurt his finger at lunchtime and tells his teacher, who sends him to the nurse. There he sits between a "stomach ache" and a "sore toe" and waits fearfully for his turn. Finally he is called in and the friendly nurse tells him about the three-part treatment: the washing, the bandaging, and . . . and . . . the big HUG! Now James feels terrific. He has faced the unknown and has overcome his fear, with the help of an understanding adult.

The expressions on James's face tell the whole story, so spend some time examining the illustrations. His own blood on his finger and the fear of being all alone make him feel just awful. Every child will understand perfectly how nervous James feels. Some ideas to explore:

1. Why is James so nervous? Why is he afraid of the nurse? Who do you think he wishes was with him?
2. What does it mean to feel lonely? When have you felt lonely? How did you make yourself feel better?

3. What is the worst part of going somewhere new? How did you feel before visiting the dentist for the first time? What made you feel better?

4. Why did the nurse tell James everything that she was going to do? Why do you think that helped James? How do you feel when an adult says, "Oh, that doesn't hurt" when it really does? Why might it make you upset?

Whitney, Alma Marshak. *Leave Herbert Alone.* Reading, MA: Addison-Wesley, 1972.

Everyone is always telling Jennifer to "leave Herbert alone." Herbert is the cat next door, and Jennifer is a three- or four-year-old. Whenever Jennifer goes near the cat, he runs for his life, but Jennifer does not understand why. She is so excited each time she sees him that she screams with joy, or grabs him too hard, and of course Herbert wants no part of her. One day, Jennifer is sitting on the porch eating a tuna-fish sandwich when Herbert walks by. She knows that if she calls out to him, someone will tell her to leave him alone. Very quietly she whispers, "Herbert," and to her delight he responds. As he comes closer she holds out some tuna. Very slowly Herbert sidles up and licks it off her hand. Then she reaches out and pets him ever so softly. Herbert sits down next to her and begins to purr. Now no one tells Jennifer to leave Herbert alone anymore.

This has always been one of my favorites because it reads aloud so well. You can hold your child in suspense as the ending approaches and Jennifer cements her relationship with the neighbor's cat. As drawn by the talented David McPhail, Herbert is a winning character, and his expressions are priceless.

For example, note Herbert smiling at the sweet thought of the bird he is about to savor, only to be interrupted by the crash of Jennifer's drum. When you talk about the expressions on his face, you'll want to ask, What was Herbert thinking? How did he feel when he heard the noise and saw Jennifer? What does seeing Jennifer always mean to Herbert? You will want to help your child understand that Jennifer has a reputation, and that sometimes she might even be blamed for something she hasn't done. Why does Jennifer get blamed?

Please guide your youngster to understand that although Jennifer was always told what *not* to do, no one told her what she *should* do. You could ask: What do you think Jennifer did to Herbert? What should her mother or father or brother have told her? What ways do you know for making friends with an animal? How do you think Jennifer felt about herself every time Herbert ran away? When have you felt that you are always making mistakes?

Change contexts. Suppose Herbert were a dog. How does your child think the animal would have reacted?

How did Jennifer feel about herself after she won Herbert over? What do you think she learned? How do you think she will behave next time she wants to make friends with an animal? How do you feel when you figure something out for yourself?

Wildsmith, Brian. *Python's Party.* New York: Franklin Watts, 1975.

The talented Brian Wildsmith populates this brilliantly illustrated book with talking jungle animals. Hungry python, the antihero, suffering hunger despite his daily hunts, devises a plan to win over the hiding animals. He offers to give a party. Hesitantly, the animals, still nervous of course, approach as he talks. "I promise to behave myself," he calls out to assure safety to everyone. The party has a theme: The animals will compete to see who can do the cleverest tricks. Parrot, who volunteers to be Master of Ceremonies, announces all the acts.

As you look at the various tricks announced by Parrot, check the illustrations carefully. Wildsmith's prose does not always explain the drawings. You'll want to ask your child to explain the various tricks from the clever illustrations. For example, Parrot cries out about the opening act, "The first trick is to be given by Gnu and Jungle Fowl, with a little help from Chameleon." And that's it. Talk with your youngster about the tricks. On the gnu's right horn the chameleon is catching flies with a graceful green tongue. Two speckled jungle fowl on the gnu's back stand on their beaks with their feet in the air. Everyone applauds.

Hyena walks for twenty yards propped on two melons; four

monkeys ride Leopard's back on their heads. Lion is the comedian; he splatters himself with mud and asks everyone to guess who he is. Here you have a good chance to play with the notion of predicting outcomes. Whom does your child think the lion is disguising himself as? The other animals offer guesses, but no one supplies the right answer. Fox, Genet, and Hyena all perform marvellous feats. Ask your youngster what trick your domestic animal—your dog, cat, canary, goldfish—might perform if he were at Python's party. What trick would your child perform as a guest?

Then comes Pelican's turn, and the animals are awed. Five or six friends leap into his wide mouth and he carries them about.

Not so great, says Python, stretching. I can get more of you than that in my mouth! Excitement replaces caution, and one by one the animals climb in. What will happen? Ask your child before you go on. The animals who don't like the darkness eagerly declare Python winner of the contest and beg to come out. Nothing doing. Python is hungry and won't release anyone.

The animals banging inside, Python takes a snooze. Elephant comes by to save the day. He stamps on Python's tail; Python cries out in pain, and the animals rapidly tumble out of his mouth. Elephant ties a knot in Python's tail to remind him not to play mean tricks again. And to the animals he says, "Let it remind you, too, never to play with Python, even at his own party."

Many questions will surface as you talk about this tale of scheming and duped innocents. Why do the animals go to Python's party? They know he is dangerous. Would you go to Python's party? Depending on your child's level of maturity, discuss some of the implications of Elephant's caution, "Never play with Python, even at his own party." Children need to recognize that not all apparently friendly people, especially strangers, are friendly in fact, and it's a good idea to recall Python's party when temptation defeats caution in the presence of overly friendly people.

If you pay attention to the language here, you'll find some good opportunities to develop definitions of unknown words by means of the visual clues. For example, Wildsmith says that Pelican's mouth is *capacious,* a five-dollar word, you might think, for a preschooler. But from the widely opened beak I'll bet that your youngster will be able to guess at the meaning. Also, some of the more exotic animals may be strange to your child—gnu, jungle fowl, chameleon, genet, pelican, hyena. Ask for descriptions of these animals from the illustrations. On your next visit to the zoo, point out the animals and connect them to Wildsmith's story. Other words to talk about: *cunning, slither, master of ceremonies, agile,* many others. I love Wildsmith for his boldness with language. He is not afraid to use words that kids might not know. However, his prose and drawings invariably provide ample clues to meaning.

Wood, Audrey. *The Napping House.* San Diego: Harcourt Brace Jovanovich, 1984.

Occasionally we find books that do not lend themselves to the usual methods of reading and questioning I have been advocating here. But this one is so wonderful I urge you not to miss it. *The Napping House* is a humorous, wonderfully enjoyable tale in which the language, the illustrations, and the events are all intertwined, build at the same time to a crescendo, and then descend together.

The story is about a house with a sleeping granny and on top of her a child, a dog, a cat, a mouse and then—a flea. The flea of course starts the chain reaction, and one by one each awakens until everyone is up.

There are many possibilities here for language enrichment and growth in critical thinking. This is a cumulative tale, that is, the author builds the story by adding one detail at a time and repeating all the others with each retelling. (Remember the song "There Was an Old Lady Who Swallowed a Fly?" Wood uses the same technique here.) What a wonderful way for you to build sequencing skills and to enhance your child's ability to recall details. Help her to remember the order starting with the bed and building up to the flea and then down again to the empty bed.

The vocabulary in this story is rich and playful. The author uses the words *napping, snoring, dreaming, dozing, snoozing,* and *slumbering* to describe the sleeping people and animals. See how many of these words your youngster can find. What other words describe sleeping people—Mommy, Daddy, a pet? You will also want to pay attention to the lively words used after the flea wakes the dog.

Just as the story and language build, so do the marvelous illustrations. Look first for the change in colors. By a masterful use of shading Don Woods demonstrates the passing of time with minimal language. The soft blue on the page slowly lightens, and as the sun rises, the blue turns greenish and then bright yellow. Help your child understand the passing of time as morning approaches. How does the sky look outside your kitchen window at sunrise?

Look closely at the details in the illustrations. Notice the movement on each page as each character turns peacefully in his sleep. I especially love the way the bed sags with each addition and the look of contentment on each of the faces. Watch closely for clues and regularly ask: What do you think is going to happen next?

Zion, Gene. *Harry the Dirty Dog.* New York: Harper & Row, 1956.

Created more than thirty years ago, Harry remains a favorite with today's children. His story touches on many themes that easily stimulate good conversation. The illustrations lend themselves to many "What do you think will happen next?" questions.

Harry is a clever little dog who hates baths so much that he buries his scrub brush in the backyard and runs away to have a little fun. As the day progresses he gets dirtier and dirtier at the railroad, near the coal chute (you'll have to explain this), and at the playground with the other dogs. But by day's end he is lonely and goes home to his family where, unfortunately, no one recognizes him. Doing his tricks does not help, so in desperation he digs up his scrub brush and jumps into the bathtub. As the children bathe him and the dirt washes off, they again recognize Harry and shower him with love. He falls asleep dreaming of all the fun he had getting dirty.

You'll find it easy to talk about pets, bath time, and getting dirty after reading this book. Here are some questions you might want to ask.

Why does Harry like to get dirty? At what places does he find dirt? Why is it fun to get dirty? What are some ways children get dirty? How does it feel to play in the mud? How do parents feel about children being dirty? What animals besides Harry like being dirty?

Why did Harry hate taking baths? Why did he hide his scrub brush? How do you feel about bath time? When do you hate taking a bath? What makes you enjoy it? dislike it?

Talk about Harry. Why would Harry be a good pet to have? What does Harry do that shows he is a smart dog? Talk about your child's pet or the kind of pet he would like to have. What tricks would your child teach a pet? What would a book called *Harry the Dirty Cat* be about?

Zolotow, Charlotte. *William's Doll.* New York: Harper & Row, 1972.

William wants a doll to cuddle and feed and to hold and take care of. His brother calls him a "creep"; the boy next door says he's a "sissy." His father says that boys don't play with dolls and buys him a basketball instead. William gets very good at basketball, but he still wants a doll. One day his grandmother comes to visit and William tells her that he wants a doll more than anything in the world. "Wonderful," she says, and takes him to buy his special doll. Grandmother understands that boys need dolls to learn to do all the things they will do one day when they are fathers.

Although this book was written in 1972, it appeals to today's boys and girls. Today, many boys do play with dolls and girls build with blocks, yet sexual stereotypes still persist. And while enlightened parents give little boys dolls at one and two years old, when a seven- or eight-year-old carries a doll people still turn around and stare.

William's Doll is a book with an important message. Tenderly, with understanding, Charlotte Zolotow tells children and parents that it is normal and healthy for boys to want to nurture;

that nurturing can help them develop into warm, caring, competent fathers; and that we as parents should encourage our children without falling prey to unfortunate stereotyping.

Find out how your own child feels about William's wanting to take care of a doll. What does William's father think is wrong with caring for a doll? Why do some people think it all right for a girl to cuddle a doll, but not for a boy? What are some other things that some people consider not all right for a boy to do? What are some things that girls are not supposed to do or like? Your male child may have always had a doll and may not understand what the fuss is all about. Help him to understand that the world is more understanding now than it used to be.

You'll also want to talk about Grandmother. How does she know what is best for William? What does she do when she talks to him? Talk about your child's grandparents and how they are special to your child. Why do grandparents sometimes know exactly what is best for their grandchild? What is special about your grandmother? How does she understand you?

Lastly, talk about the feelings that the book explores. How do you think William felt when his brother called him a "creep" and the neighbor called him a "sissy"? Talk about these words and the connotations they have. How do you think William felt when his father bought him everything except what he asked for? Why do you think William confided in his grandmother? Notice the absence of the mother in the story. Where do you think William's mother was? What do you think she thought about William having a doll? Try to relate the story to *Oliver Button is a Sissy* as well as to any experiences your own child may have had with choosing unconventional toys, games, books, activities, or friends.

Index